UNTIL DAWN

Also by Kingston Medland

THE EDGE
SHADOW OF THE SOUL

UNTIL DAWN

Kingston Medland

HEADLINE
FEATURE

First published in 1996 by
HEADLINE BOOK PUBLISHING

A HEADLINE FEATURE hardback

10 9 8 7 6 5 4 3 2 1

British Library Cataloguing in Publication Data
Medland, Kingston
Until Dawn
I. Title
823 [F]
ISBN 0–7472–1631–2

Phototypeset by Intype, London
Printed and bound in Great Britain by
Mackays of Chatham PLC, Chatham, Kent

HEADLINE BOOK PUBLISHING
A division of Hodder Headline PLC
338 Euston Road
London NW1 3BH

To my parents, with love.
And Joan Deitch – without whom the dream might not
be a reality.

Thanks always to Catherine, my love.

Andi and everybody at Headline; Dr R. Stoddart of
Manchester University for answering questions about
dead people; Barry James; Northwich Police
Constabulary for their help; Ralph for information
about modems. And you, the reader, for sharing this
vision.
Now, picture this . . .

Prologue

The fire-coloured hatchback drew up outside the gates of the deconsecrated church, where rusted iron spikes reached up to touch the pale sliver of moon.

The driver climbed out and removed a pair of bolt-cutters from the passenger seat. He quickly defeated the padlock by snapping its thick chain, which rattled noisily to the ground in the dead night. Then he pushed open one of the wide gates. It creaked, like a prop in a low-budget horror film.

The man returned to his car and drove slowly into the abandoned burial ground. He followed the weed-filled road, careful not to steer into ruts or on to sacred soil. Approaching the large church, he circled it, remembering the many Sundays he had spent here as a boy. It had been a bustling place then, with women in flower-patterned dresses, sober-suited men . . . obedient children trying not to fall asleep during the long summer sermons, the chill bite of winter ensuring their attention later in the year.

Now the church was derelict. The stained windows glowed no more; they were dirty, smashed or boarded up. The tower clock had stopped, and litter blew about the lych-path. He thought the sight inside would be something similar. A ruin.

He could not imagine anyone coming to pray here now. There was none of the respect he remembered from his childhood. No faith . . .

Steering at a low speed, down one of the narrow lanes, he eventually arrived at the spot he was searching for.

Leaving the headlights on, he got out of the car and flipped up the hatchback to remove a spade and crowbar. He waded into the untended grass until he found a particular headstone. In the glare of the lights, he saw it was chipped. He placed the crowbar on the ground and began to dig . . .

Several feet down, the spade struck something hard. Excited, his body coated by a sheen of sweat and dirt, the man began to scoop earth away with his bare hands and eventually found the rim of a coffin.

He paused, smiling, contemplating the happy reunion that lay ahead. After this, there was just the other coffin to uncover, in this double grave.

He reached up and placed the heavy spade on the grass beside the hole, and felt for the crowbar, with which he would lever open the coffin.

He stood still and let a handful of soil trickle through his fingers; it felt dry and chalky. The bodies in their boxes could well still be whole: not just tattered rags of flesh hanging off rotten bones. Conditions suggested mummification – the skin would be slightly discoloured, leathery to his touch, and heavily stitched from the incisions of autopsies that had taken place over a quarter of a century ago.

Each corpse would be dressed only in a cotton shroud, tied in a twist above its head. Once he had completed his digging, the man decided, he would take them safely home. He had been disappointed on arriving back at Bradbury to find that his old family residence was occupied by strangers, but his parents could move into his new place with him. Oh, how tenderly he would care for them. He was overflowing with love.

And there will be others to love, he thought, and began to prise open the first lid . . .

PART ONE

The Hunt

1

The lobby of the fast-food restaurant was one of Joel Phillips' favourite hunting grounds.

It was on two levels, the upper floor designated for smokers. He sat nearly halfway down the main aisle of the ground floor. From this position he could see all manner of people filtering in and out. He carefully studied their different characteristics – the way they walked and talked, carried their shopping, pushed their prams, ate their burgers.

He watched, and waited for his match.

He had been in the local McDonald's for nearly half an hour and knew he would have to move on soon. It was nearly nine-thirty and he had yet to open his bookstore, *Pages*, in the centre of the small Cheshire town of Bradbury.

His cup was nearly empty so he drained it and headed to the counter for a top-up. He would drink the second cup quickly, and if nothing made itself apparent in the next ten minutes or so, he would have to leave for the shop, his active search for new prey over for another day.

He sighed as the young girl filled his cup with thick, black liquid.

The anticipation inside was burning him up, eating him alive. It had been so long since his last kill. He didn't know how much longer he could control the urge – if he could even wait for the perfect family. His need was desperate, driving him hard and torturing him.

He had to find them so that he could kill them, end their glorious bliss and find salvation once more for a sweet, short while, before the cycle began again.

Joel supposed, despondently giving up his search, that a customer in his bookstore might catch his eye. But that was unlikely; it had never happened yet.

He was still at the counter as the girl – her long blonde hair tied neatly back – placed cream and sugar beside his cup. He was lost in tired thoughts of the tedious day ahead, when, suddenly, he was certain that he had found his next victims.

'Can I take a couple of balloons for the children, love?' the man to his left enquired.

The guy was about thirty. His hair was slightly receding, but a thick moustache rested lazily on his lip, looking as if a rodent had crawled there, and then died. He was wearing a dark suit.

The pleasant counter girl nodded, but Joel did not catch her words as he watched the suited man help himself. One balloon of bright orange, and somewhere in the fields of helium there was . . . the man moved to another till where he stretched and reached for . . . a pink one, wedged in the straw dispenser with so many others.

A boy and a girl, Joel thought. I'd put money on it.

He picked up his cup with hands that were suddenly trembling, careful not to spill any of the coffee and draw unwanted attention to himself, and then moved back to his seat. In his haste he forgot the cream and sugar, but it didn't matter because as he sipped the hot drink he didn't taste it.

His day had suddenly taken a bright turn. He felt alive, his heart beating strong and fast at the certainty that he had found them again.

Joel watched the man negotiate a trail through the partly crowded lobby, saw him draw back with impatience as a woman with a baby buggy stepped out in front of him and blocked his way.

You don't like it here, Joel thought. Do you?

But the children . . .

The man found his mushroom seat in the kiddies' area. He actually looked embarrassed as he sat down and handed the balloons – which were attached to blue plastic sticks – to his two little children. Their faces lit up with excitement and huge grins.

One bright orange, the other a subtle shade of pink.

One boy. One girl.

One mischievous-looking son, and one lovely daughter, her blonde hair shimmering and long like that of the much older counter girl. There was a smear of red ketchup on her top lip. It looked so cute.

The woman – their mother, he correctly assumed, the man's wife – was plump. Not overweight, but not slender either as she probably had been once, before her maternal years.

Nothing was certain yet, as Joel was only just beginning his observations, but the man definitely did not look happy. He wondered if this reflected the state of their marriage. Could Hubby be having an affair? Would that make the family *more* perfect, because of the flaw? Joel thought it over carefully. Despite their strange love, his own parents had never slept with other people.

He couldn't hear the couple's conversation, but he imagined it consisted of the usual sort of exchanges.

The two children were having the time of their young lives, playing with cheap, breakable toys which had once been contained in now ripped Happy Meal boxes, hitting each other with their balloons.

The boy whacked their father playfully and the man snapped at his son.

Bastard, Joel thought, taking his time with the coffee now, knowing that he would have to stay a while longer. *Pages* would just have to open late.

You definitely don't like being here, do you? But your children – they love it.

Perhaps this was a rare treat. The mother seemed happy enough, and he guessed that she must frequent this place when doing her shopping. Joel couldn't remember having seen her here before, but then he was never looking specifically for a woman alone, or any one individual.

He spied on them surreptitiously, their father undoubtedly wishing he was elsewhere, their mother looking around, occasionally saying a word or two to the lonely lady on the table next to theirs, and the children, the sweet, beautiful children, enjoying their final days . . .

All blissfully unaware that they had been chosen.

Joel nearly missed them.

It was twenty minutes later, the hand on his watch slowly crawling towards the top of the hour. He had gone to the toilet, which was on the upper floor – noticing the smoke in the air – and had been shocked, when he came back, to see that the family were no longer in their seats.

He panicked, sweating quickly as he stood still at the bottom of the stairs, his eyes panning across the lobby, and then back again because he couldn't see them.

Where had they gone? *Where?*

'Excuse me.'

The woman behind him was impatient, trying to push by him as she came down the stairs.

'I said, excuse me,' she repeated.

'I heard what you said.'

Joel stepped aside and looked at her, gave her the lazy eye. She glared at him for half a second, but then looked away, unable to match the intensity of his stare.

You ever want to intimidate somebody, boy, just give them the la-zee eye . . . If only you knew who I was, Joel thought.

He turned back to the lobby and his heart missed a beat as he saw them, outside, passing by the window and out of sight.

2

Bad memories.

From a past he would rather forget.

Bad memories he chooses to see. Better those, than the bloody images he is creating now, and that will be with him for ever.

Bad memories . . .

He is still cutting, as he is now . . . cut, cut, cut . . . but for very different reasons. He is searching for the truth, for justice. He is helping to solve mysteries, instead of creating them. As a forensic pathologist working for the Metropolitan Police at Scotland Yard in London, he is at the forefront of any major murder or police investigation which falls into his district.

For now, though, it is the cutting he remembers, as he succumbs to a frenzy of hacking and slashing and stabbing.

In the brilliantly lit room of the post-mortem theatre, wearing a standard green surgical gown, he makes his first incision. This opening slit begins behind one ear, curves down to the sternum, and then around to the other ear. It is called the Opening Incision; the next one continues right down to the groin, over the chest and stomach.

He is never so precise in his murders. Cut, hack. Slice and dice. Time is short, so move fast. Kill, kill, kill. First the children, the boy and the girl . . . the ketchup displayed on her lip now red blood, then . . .

The preliminary incision enables him to dissect away the skin of the chest and neck quite easily – he literally peels it back up over the face on either side, covering the lustreless fish-eyes of the corpse. This exposes the organs of the neck; and then the chest wall as the dissection continues. It also reveals any subcutaneous bruising which might not have been apparent on the surface of the skin. With metal probes he deciphers the nature and depth of any stab wounds.

From the children's room he moves into the main bedroom

7

where the woman is handcuffed, naked and gagged. Her body is already bloody, swollen bruises forming. She is horrified as he charges towards her. She tries to scream, but he brings the knife up and plunges it down into her breasts, skin and flesh enveloping the blade.

He pulls the knife out as the gag muffles her cries, raising his arm and then bringing it down again, this time digging into her shoulder. Up, down. Up, down. Over and over . . . Suck, squelch and spray.

To examine the organs of the chest, he goes down through the ribs with bone shears. He removes the anterior wall of the chest and examines the organs in situ, *after which he may remove the heart, lungs, gullet and stomach, which he will then examine by further dissection from the back. From this he will discover any illness, the presence of drugs or alcohol, or any number of other foreign substances, such as poison, which might have contributed to the death.*

And let us not, he thinks, forget the smell *of death – a sweetish scent that clings to his clothes once the day's work is done.*

Truly, the smell of Death is sweet, *an exquisite aroma creating euphoria within him.*

He feels the knife glance off ribs and bone as he attacks the father, who is handcuffed to a radiator in the living room downstairs. He, too, is naked, his body already marked by various macabre wounds.

In the examination of all these victims, Joel knows that swabs will be taken from key sites. The vagina. The rectum. Her breasts. Their mouths. The Bradbury police would probably suspect that these are sex crimes from the nature and situation of the bodies, until the lack of relevant evidence proves otherwise.

He lifts the knife up and thrusts it down, in and out, with great pressure and strength. He impales the father again and again, long after he is dead.

He chances a glance out of the window, pulling the curtain back slightly. As always, he has killed by dawn's early light, streetlamps flickering out even as he watches for those few seconds.

He turns back to the room and looks at the dead man. One eye has been hacked out in the frenzy and his bottom lip is split wide open, the bloody gash cutting an inch-long rift into his chin. There are multiple stab wounds in his torso, arms and legs.

There is lots more to an autopsy, of course, but as he sits back on the carpet, exhausted, Joel chooses not to remember. The memories are bad, drawn from a time of corruption when his dark side, born in infancy, was maturing into an evil adulthood. He thinks about the bodies he used to touch, long after the morgue had emptied for the night, when he was alone . . .

His memories of the procedures from his past are a defence mechanism, enabling him to forget what he is doing as he kills.

After completion of any autopsy, there is the following legal requirement: he always has to reconstruct the body to an accept- able state for burial. He may need to insert glass eyeballs; a selection is always available in every mortuary. If he has removed organs for analysis, they must be replaced by packing, with news- paper, sawdust and sections of broomstick for long bones or spine. He then tightly stitches the body to hold it all together.

He smiles wryly, for two reasons.

Firstly, he no longer needs to bother with the time-consuming process of reconstruction.

Secondly, reconstruction usually took place in order to provide relatives and undertakers with aesthetically acceptable remains. In some circumstances, the appearance of a body has actually been improved by good reconstruction. That would be the case here.

Before leaving, he has one final objective.

He bends down to the man and – with difficulty – finds an unmarked piece of flesh. In this case, it is the left cheek.

He carefully begins to carve something into the skin. He will make exactly the same scratches somewhere on the surface of all the bodies, even the children's.

When he has finished, he slips out of the back door and down the side of the house to his car. No one has noticed him. It is just after six in the morning. By nine he will have been home and showered, before opening his store on time.

3

'Oh Christ.'

The sound breaking Tom's lips was barely audible, but Cindy saw Sarah look up from her cereal so she threw him a stern glance.

'Not at the table, love,' Cindy said, turning back to the sizzling bacon. She had lazily pulled her hair into a scrunchie and was still wearing her silk nightgown. It was Tom's turn to take the kids to school so she had all morning to get dressed.

'It's happened again,' he whispered.

Cindy glanced over her shoulder, her attention divided between the breakfast she was preparing and her husband's words; she saw it was not a national paper he was reading, but their own weekly, the *Bradbury Guardian*. She stared at his horrified expression as he read from line to line and suddenly knew what he'd been referring to.

She felt her stomach flip over, like it did when Tom drove too fast over a low, humped-back bridge. The greasy spatula she was holding fell from her hand and clattered on the tiled floor.

'Sarah, go and get your things for school,' she told her daughter softly.

'But Mummy, I—'

'Do it now!' Cindy snapped, and was immediately ashamed. She saw tears in Sarah's eyes and knew she shouldn't have spoken to the child so harshly. 'I'm sorry, sweetheart. Now go and play with your brother for a few minutes. Make him disappear or something. We'll drop in at McDonald's after school, buy you both a Big Mac and fries.'

Sarah's hurt expression instantly vanished at the mention of the treat she had lucked into, and Cindy managed a smile for her.

Sarah was fascinated by magicians and illusionists, and at the age of eleven she could perform clever tricks utilising sleight of

11

hand. *The hand is faster than the eye* . . . usually – for after a few repeated viewings, her family often worked out how she was doing her tricks, but never let on to their daughter.

The idea of making her younger brother Richard disappear appealed to Sarah. It would be a new trick to impress everyone. Especially if he disappeared for good.

The girl knocked her chair back away from the table, scraping it over the tiles, and rushed upstairs. If she couldn't make the lazy lame-brain disappear, at least she could tell him about the treat in store for them.

Cindy moved silently to her husband's side and gripped his hand. It was trembling slightly as he finished reading the report. She seized it tight to halt the motion, but instead the vibrations were like an infection and a shiver snaked down her own spine. She suddenly felt very cold in just her nightgown, even though the sun was pouring hot morning rays on to her back.

'Again – are you sure?' Cindy asked, finally holding his hand steady.

'Well, the police haven't come out and said as much, but it sounds like the Initial Killer again. It must be connected to the other families. The paper thinks so, anyway,' he informed her.

'How many people were killed?' she asked.

'Four.'

'Did . . . did we know them?' Cindy asked, swallowing deeply in preparation for a response she was dreading. Her voice was a crack in the sudden empty silence of the room, absent of the laughter of children.

'No,' Tom said quickly to put her mind at ease. 'It was a family called Napier from Marston.'

'Oh, Tom, what if we open the paper one morning and a photograph of our neighbours is staring back at us? I'm so afraid. Or what if one morning it is *us* the people of Bradbury are reading about?'

He stood and hugged her, held her close, felt her delightful beating heart. He loved her so much. He would never let anybody hurt her.

'It will never be us,' he told her, wondering if he could believe his own words. Who knew where this sick bastard would strike next? 'Never.'

Tom was out earlier than usual that morning, and he walked the half mile to the train station. Bradbury was only about twenty miles from Manchester, but he hated driving into the city to work because sometimes parking was difficult to find, and traffic was often bumper to bumper.

With each footfall he tried to think a little less about the new murders, but the photographs of the Napiers in the paper were seared onto his mind – like the after-image of the sun if you close your eyes after looking directly at it for too long. They were branded onto his corneas. He could do nothing but see them in the eye of his mind.

Sadly, he knew it would be a long while before he forgot them, for the images were a little too close to home for comfort.

The children, the innocent Napier offspring, had been represented by school photographs.

He remembered going to pick his son up from school on the day Richard had had his picture taken last year. The boy – then aged eight – had complained about how immature the whole scenario was, as the photographer, an old bald man with a sock called Slither the Snake hanging pathetically off one hand, had tried to make him laugh. The photograph was a testament to how the photographer's mission to elicit a smile had failed miserably.

Richard hadn't been impressed by Slither the Sock – with buttons for eyes, and a piece of red felt for a hissing, forked tongue.

Sarah, on the other hand, had loved Slither at first sight, and she would have been thrilled to take the woolly creature home. Her photograph was a happy delight to look at. Cindy had surprised Sarah that night with a makeshift version of Slither fashioned from one of Tom's old Nike socks. It had proved a great hit.

Tom reached the station just as a summer shower fell from the blue skies. The odd cold droplet hit him through the broken, Perspex overhang as he waited on the platform. The change in the weather reflected his morose mood. He closed his eyes and listened to the rain patter above.

He thought it would be for ever until he forgot the Napier children's faces. And for ever was a long time.

The train was delayed.

Half an hour later the rain finally abated and Tom thought about calling Mike at the office and telling him he was taking the day off. But then the guard walked on to the platform. 'She'll be here in a minute or so.'

Tom nodded slightly in acknowledgement, and then turned away. He didn't want the guard's company. The new murders would be the topic of the day; the first and last point of any conversation.

So the children in the newspaper, *the dead children*, had also been fooled by Slither the Snake because they were each a bundle of bright grins and sunny smiles, even in the dull black and white tones of the paper. He closed his eyes again, but could still see every single pixel of each picture.

One boy, and one girl.

Their parents had been photographed together, their faces huddled tightly into the single frame.

Jesus! Why was this affecting him so much? Why couldn't he shake off the images?

Only slight smiles were between the couple, but their eyes were sparkling. They looked very much in love.

It could have been us, Tom thought as the train rattled noisily into the station and a few birds took flight towards the sun. He boarded the nearest carriage and found a seat. *It might still be . . .*

The Napiers were the fourth family to be murdered in the past two years. About seventeen months to be exact, Tom thought. If the police didn't stop this guy soon, the Curtis family could be next.

Any family could be.

4

While Tom was making his laborious journey into the city, Cindy was silently cursing the morning traffic, annoyed with the children for fidgeting out of their rear seatbelts again.

They were never any trouble when Tom was driving, but whenever she was at the wheel and he wasn't in the vehicle, they took that as their licence to test her patience to its limits. Normally she would involve them in a word game or another activity to keep them occupied, but today she was lost in thoughts of Alan, her lover. She was late, and couldn't wait for her weekly rendezvous with him.

Halting in line at a set of traffic lights next to the station where Tom would have caught his train to Manchester, she took a second to look back.

'Fasten the seatbelts, you two,' she ordered.

'But Mum, they make us itch,' Richard whined.

The way they were behaving this morning, Cindy wished Sarah *had* made her younger brother disappear... and herself along with him. For just a few days, a month perhaps. A year, maybe. Say, until the time they were ready to move out.

'Yeah,' Sarah agreed, and began to fake scratch, rubbing all over. '*Itch.*'

Yes, and what a pile of horseshit, Cindy thought sarcastically. If you really wanted to, Sarah dear, you could fertilise the lawn with some of the rubbish you children spout. Naturally, she did not share this observation with them.

The lights changed and their progress was slow down the hill. Finally, she turned left and headed for their primary school, which was situated about a mile out of town. It began to rain again. The weather just couldn't make up its mind today, she thought.

When she reached the school she saw Jo Myers – one of the

15

teachers – out in the pouring rain, wearing a bright yellow rain-coat, with a hood to match.

The system for dropping off and picking up children usually went like a piece of cake. There was a long road in front of the school which forked off from the main street and rejoined it about 200 metres further on. This narrow splinter road was a one-way system.

There was always a teacher outside to make sure the busy mornings and afternoons went smoothly, and that no children were ever hit by some of the more impatient, selfish parent-drivers. Jo must have drawn the short straw today, Cindy thought, seeing the jam ahead. She was going to be here a while.

Jo spotted Cindy, waved, and began to jog over.

Sarah and Richard opened their doors and ran for the dry sanctuary of the school.

'Bye! Be good!' Cindy called after them.

Cars were stuck in a jam all the way to the exit ahead of her, and other vehicles were queuing behind her. There was no way she could get out quickly now. What a mess! Cindy glanced at the dashboard clock; she was going to be late, and Alan would not be best pleased.

'What happened?' she asked Jo through her open window, tasting raindrops.

Jo Myers was Cindy's age, thirty, attractive – even with her long hair bedraggled from the rain – and, as she made sure everybody knew when she was out partying, very single. She was a funny woman who never failed to put a smile on Cindy's face. They had been good friends for a long time.

'A dad tried his hand at dropping the kids off for a change,' Jo explained. 'Do you know what that means?'

They both rolled their eyes and laughed. 'In through the Out door!' they said in unison.

'Yeah,' Jo continued. 'I bet the mum was relieved, until she hears about all the trouble he caused.'

Cindy edged the car forward a few inches, and Jo walked alongside.

'What a moron. They just don't understand a simple system, do they?' Cindy said.

'They're men,' Jo replied, as if that should explain everything that ever went wrong in the universe. 'They don't have a clue. They have no souls, and I wouldn't be surprised if one of the bastards gets me pregnant one day.'

'You should slow down,' Cindy advised her friend. Jo had probably slept with more men than the two women had fingers and toes between them. And she was still going.

'You can talk,' Joe said, as the car crept forward again. 'How is Lover Boy, anyway?'

Cindy grinned. 'Probably very annoyed with me. I'm half an hour late already.'

Jo sighed. 'For the joys I'm sure he gets when he sees you, he should be able to wait until the end of the world. Oh no!'

Cindy followed her friend's stare all the way to the far side of the road.

The offending dad had climbed from his car and was angrily banging his fists on the bonnet of another. A large woman got out from behind the wheel and they began to argue. More horns honked as impatient parents waited; others left their vehicles to watch the dispute.

'I'd better go and stop them before World War Three starts,' Jo said. 'You know, they should just give us women all the weapons in the world and we'd sort this place out without a bodycount.'

Cindy nodded. Sometimes she agreed with her friend, sometimes she didn't. Mostly she just nodded and accepted the comments so that she didn't have to get into an argument.

Jo waved. 'I'll talk to you later!' she cried, and ran quickly to the quarrelling parents.

About fifteen minutes later Cindy was out of the loop. By that time Jo had gone inside and started her first class.

The warehouse where Alan worked was still a ten-minute drive away.

Cindy's heart beat faster as she thought about him. They had only slept together twice, and she was still nervous when they had sex. The tension probably added to the excitement.

As she drove, she fretted about the charade her life had become, but only one thought filled her mind. It made her feel guilty.

I'm free. Free for the day. Free at last . . .

The roads were clear and Cindy arrived at the warehouse where Alan worked the night-shift as security in under seven minutes.

As she reached the large building and parked, she knew that he would be annoyed and disappointed.

He liked to watch her walk in and wander the aisles as workers on the floor, sweating and hot, chanced quick glances in

17

her direction. From his console in a back room, he controlled concealed security cameras, and would make her their sole focus, the only star on the many screens in his office.

She liked to dress up for him, turn him on with sexy outfits, parade for the cameras and explore a part of her psychology she never knew existed until she met him. It excited Alan, as she was excited by the knowledge that somebody was secretly watching, admiring . . . a discreet form of voyeurism as she walked to his room at the back of the building.

Today, with Tom hung up on the morbid business of the Napier family murder, wanting to get an early train so that he would miss the rush – the predictable, bleak morning conversation; the shock of fellow commuters – she had been burdened with the responsibility of taking the children to school.

Because of the tailback there, she'd had no time to nip home and change. But she still looked reasonably good in casual tight jeans and a beige jumper, her hair falling down her back.

She caught the driver of a fork-lift staring at her as she walked by, and offered him a small smile.

What are you looking at? she thought. Give me time, and a little more patience than my sharp temperament allows, and I can look like a princess. *Even with these child-bearing hips.*

You're thirty already, she said to herself, and what have you done with your life?

She was attractive, with her long copper hair that cascaded over her shoulders like crystal water off a fall, piercing bright blue eyes, and a good figure despite fighting through the *joys* of natural childbirth twice. She was intelligent, too, but . . . she didn't know how much longer she could go on living this life, playing at Happy Families with a man she no longer loved.

Tom was drinking far too much these days because the research business he had founded with his old schoolfriend Mike Littler was going down the toilet. He was becoming more withdrawn, talking to Cindy less and less. He thought their marriage was a perfect and stable structure that could survive anything; only she could see it teetering, about to collapse like a house of cards.

Cindy thought about the failing research company, and wondered if she would have found more prosperity had she not dropped out of university to marry Tom and have his children.

She was not sleeping with Alan because she loved him, or because she wanted to hurt her husband. She was having the

18

affair because of the comfort it offered her. The feeling of being wanted and yearned for helped her through the bad time her marriage had become in recent months.

She had never realised that it might also become a self-destruct button for their imperfect wedlock.

As she waited for Alan, pouting at a camera like Marilyn Monroe, she acknowledged that both she and Tom were hiding from the problems in their relationship instead of confronting them. She felt sure in the arms of a lover, and he found solace in the bottle.

It was all wrong, she thought, and not how it should be.

When Alan left her bed that afternoon, Cindy was saddened, and wiped tears from her eyes. The sex was over, and all she was left with were old fears of deceit and a tired weight in her heart that she had once again betrayed Tom, taken another step away from him instead of a step closer.

She longed to have Tom in her arms.

Alone in their bed, she stared at the digital clock, as one minute flickered by and then another. And another . . .

When her mother had died it had broken her father's heart. Two years later his precious life was taken away from the world as he drowned in alcohol. He had left Cindy and Tom the family home, and whatever money he had saved from a lifetime's hard work . . . But now her husband was being claimed by that same beast.

She had to talk to Tom, stop him from drinking! She resented him for that. She couldn't lose him in the same manner she had lost her father. She also thought it was selfish of Tom to behave that way, when he must know how many painful memories he was dredging up.

She lifted the framed photograph of herself and Tom which lay face down on the bedside cabinet.

'Couldn't have you watching, could I, dearest?' she whispered to him, aware of the fresh tears welling in her eyes and falling, slowly falling.

19

5

After lying in bed for a long, slow hour Cindy suddenly came to life, changing the stained bedsheets and diving under a hot shower. Still with plenty of time to spare, she went to pick Sarah and Richard up from school, and – as promised that morning – took them into the town centre for a McDonald's treat, smiling because she liked the food too.

It was nearly five-fifteen when they got back and she discovered that Tom had returned early. She found him sleeping upstairs in his den – the attic room they had converted when they'd first moved in – four books stacked on his left, one fallen open in his lap. His wire-rim glasses had fallen down his nose and he was drowsing fitfully. She decided not to wake him because he looked so peaceful.

On the floor next to his chair was a half-empty bottle of vodka. She wanted to take the bottle and throw it against the wall, where it would shatter.

She descended the narrow flight of stairs which led down from the den. They had once planned to turn the attic into a fourth bedroom, for Richard when he was older. At the moment he was stuck in a boxroom while Sarah had all the space. It would have been a private domain in which he could pass his teenage years.

A private domain . . . That had instilled the first doubts in her mind. Who knew what Richard would get up to in there, alone, and then with girlfriends? And then Mike Littler came on the scene, and any doubts she had were set aside immediately because the attic suddenly had a new function.

Mike Littler was an old schoolfriend of Tom's, and a college buddy of them both. He was looking for a business partner. So, after a year of planning and preparation, *Little Researchers* had been born in the heart of Manchester . . . *to satisfy your appetite for knowledge* . . . with Cindy helping the venture out financially, offering them the last of her father's money. She was sure he would have considered it a good idea.

The attic had been converted when the company first opened. It was not really an office, although it contained a computer set-up with a printer and a modem which linked it to the database in Manchester. There were several bean-bags on the floor, and against one end wall in as tight a bundle as possible, was stashed all the junk that Cindy and Tom Curtis couldn't find a place for or bear to abandon on a skip.

Old toys and games. Some clothes in a black plastic binliner. A collection of books and movie magazines from Tom's childhood and teenage years. He still purchased the magazines, and months later would bring them up to store them with the others. Cindy wondered if the collection would ever be worth anything, or if it was just wasted wood pulp. A couple of hard wooden chairs completed the picture. The room was dusty and uncared for.

It must be a city of spiders, she thought, and shuddered at the idea of cleaning it out. *No thanks!* But it did need doing, as Tom mentioned every time he was up there working, staring dead ahead, past his monitor and at the junk – it staring back and seeming to laugh. *Still here, still here.*

The company had been open for nearly five years now, and *Little Researchers* was still recovering from the recession which had affected a lot of small businesses badly. They had been forced to move into smaller offices, and then Mike and Tom – with regret – had decided to lay off the staff. They could manage the existing contracts alone, and if too many came by in the future they could always expand again.

Cindy found the kids downstairs in the living room, watching cartoons. She switched the television off.

'Come on, you two,' she told them. 'No more TV on a beautiful evening like this. Why not go out and play for a while?'

'But Mum,' Richard whined, 'Wile E. Coyote was about to splat the RoadRunner with a giant boulder.'

'The dog would have ended up under the rock,' Sarah informed him. 'Always does. It's the law of cartoons.'

'A coyote is not a dog,' Cindy inserted.

'Cartoons don't have laws,' Richard argued, wondering how his sister could sometimes get things so wrong. 'But, does he really always end up under the boulder?'

'If the dog was real, he'd be roadkill,' Sarah smirked.

'It's not a dog,' Cindy repeated, but knew they weren't listening, so engrossed were they in their own conversation.

'They would have to scrape him up with a sponge at the end of each show,' Sarah continued, grinning.

Cindy wondered where Sarah got some of her more colourful phrases from. Roadkill? Scrape him up with a sponge? 'Roadkill isn't a very nice word,' she told her daughter.

'Well, thanks for ruining every RoadRunner cartoon I haven't seen yet,' Richard complained.

'Did you really think the dog was going to win?' Sarah asked, amazed at how stupid her brother could sometimes be.

'Yes, I did,' Richard responded honestly. 'He might have. You don't know.'

'Richard, get a life.' His sister gave him a pitying look. 'You're even dumber than I thought,' she told him, and then did a quick impression of the RoadRunner before racing off. 'Beep, beep!'

Richard quickly followed her out. Even playing with his sister was better than hanging about indoors with no TV.

Cindy looked after her children, still smiling at their idiotic banter.

6

Cindy spent an hour preparing something for Tom to eat, and then she went to wake him.

'Hello, love,' he murmured through clouds of fading dreams, rubbing sleep from his eyes. 'I'm sorry, I meant to have something ready for you. I just . . .' he stretched, yawning '. . . wanted to make a start on these first. Must have fallen asleep.'

She didn't mention the vodka, but could faintly smell the alcohol on his breath, and wondered if he had drunk the whole half-bottle before nodding off. 'What are they?' she asked, motioning to the books.

'Not a pleasant job,' he told her, and removed the book from his lap, putting it with the others.

She caught a glimpse of the cover. A bloody handprint. A knife. Something long and lethal-looking – a blade that was curved and sharp. A scythe, perhaps?

'Some journalist came to *Researchers* – said he had the ultimate idea for a serial-killer book,' Tom explained. 'I checked his name out with a couple of places, but nobody seems to have ever heard of him. It might just be a con, but while he's paying our current rates we can't exactly turn him down. He wants us to research the history of serial killers. Lazy creep can't do his own dirty work so he dumped the nasty on us. Mike and I flipped a coin. I lost.'

'But it's disgusting! Do you have to take this job?' Cindy asked, shuddering.

'We're still hurting from the recession,' Tom said. 'The guy is paying up front, and basically we need all the commissions we can get to stay afloat. I've had a bad feeling for a while now that the company is about to go under completely. I'm sorry, Cindy. Mike and me – we've wasted your money. I'm sure that's why I'm drinking so much. I'm really sorry, love.'

'It was *our* money, Tom. And you didn't waste it,' she told him, holding his arm. He was finally acknowledging that he was drinking too much. That had to be a start. 'I don't want the kids seeing these,' she warned him, pointing at the title of one of the books: *The Encyclopedia of Serial Killers*.

She had struck just the right note, Cindy commended herself. Nice and protective, caring and considerate. She might not love Tom any more – she believed the jury was still out on that one – but if one day she decided to leave him, she would take the children. Life would be unbearable without them, however much they sometimes drove her crazy. She would never let anybody hurt them, and couldn't imagine living without them.

She wondered if Tom would fight her for them if she did move out, or ask him to leave. Sadly, she suspected he would. The two children would never be without love.

'If we didn't have our own madman running loose round here, killing families, the material would be interesting, perhaps even border on fascinating. But right now . . .' he shivered.

'Tom,' she whispered. 'I'm scared.'

And suddenly they were holding each other tight, washing each other with wet kisses.

'He won't hurt us,' Tom promised, pulling her down on top of a large green bean-bag. 'We have too much going for us.'

Cindy indulged him, watched the ceiling as he entered her. She thought of Alan, and wondered why she was falling out of love with Tom. He thrust harder and harder. Tears welled in her eyes. Part of the trouble had to be because of the amount he was drinking.

As they finished, Cindy thought of the man out there killing families, and wondered how reliable Tom's final statement had been.

When they came down from the den and went into the living room, the meal Cindy had made for Tom was cold. Regardless, he began to chew on the mushroom pizza – leaving the chips – and switched on the television. He fetched a beer from the fridge and she hated the sound of the can popping open.

Why did he have to drink so much? she fretted for the thousandth time.

She looked out of the window to check on the children and then joined him on the sofa. She held his hand and he wrapped his fingers about hers lightly. There was still a spark, but why was the fire of their love no longer a raging inferno, only smouldering ashes? Could he know about Alan?

Then their fingers gripped even tighter as the inevitable report of the killings was rehashed on the local news. She could feel her nails digging into his palm, but he didn't pull away, although it must have hurt. It was then that she realised how much he loved her, and how hard he was going to fall if she ever let him know the truth – that she was sleeping with another man. *Not just sleeping, but doing the horizontal shuffle . . .*

She enjoyed the rare moment of quiet love between them and lost herself in Tom, who was a victim of her betrayal; he had done nothing wrong . . . *except the drink* . . . and was innocent.

The police appeared baffled by the Napier case. They could see no motive for the murders. Nothing had been stolen. A spokesperson said that detectives held every hope of catching the killer, but it was obvious from his stammering and flustered manner that he saw no clear paths ahead.

The police never used the phrase 'serial killer', although it seemed evident to everybody that the massacre of the Napiers was connected to the murders of the other families.

The officer on TV gave the same advice he had after the previous deaths, and Tom wondered whether it was word for word, only now the man's hair was slightly greyer, his eyes tired and lined with worry.

'Ensure, once you are inside for the evening, that all doors and windows are locked. Do not invite strangers into your home. Make sure that you know your children's whereabouts at all times. We will catch the person responsible for these horrific crimes, but we will only do so together.'

Tom remembered the television show *CrimeWatch*. What was it they said at the end of each broadcast? *Remember, violent crimes don't happen often, so please, don't have nightmares.* The truth, he thought, is that violent crimes happen so often that most TV channels feel it necessary to make shows specialising in them.

Cindy stood and moved to the window. Tom looked down at his hand. There were three fine tracks of blood on his palm.

Cindy saw Sarah and Richard playing with two of their friends in the park at the back of their house. She opened the window and leaned out.

'Richard! Sarah! I want you both in now!'

'But Mum,' Richard protested as usual, 'the ball's gone into old Barlow's garden.'

27

So that's why they were just standing about talking. All the children had the foolish notion that Roger Barlow, a WWII veteran with false teeth and a prosthetic leg, was a vampire thirsty for their blood. It didn't help that each Hallowe'en the old man opened his doors to the smaller children, under the supervision of parents, and then nipped down to wait for them in a coffin in his dusty cellar – even removing his leg for an extra thrill. The fright-feasts were always fun, but Cindy thought them a little too scary and was often reluctant to let Richard and Sarah attend them.

'I'll get it for you tomorrow,' Cindy shouted. 'Now come inside!'

'You'd best be careful,' Richard called, as they all walked closer.

'Yeah. I'll wear a clove of garlic around my neck,' Cindy said sardonically, and the children sniggered. 'I'm serious. Move it! Kevin, Lisa, come on in and I'll give you a lift home in a few minutes.'

They were close now, and Cindy heard Sarah whisper, 'We should call Childline. This doesn't happen to all the other children.'

'Our friends aren't called in this early,' Richard agreed.

She smiled at their comments as she closed and locked the window and then sat beside Tom once more. Their fingers linked together.

Better to be safe than sorry, Tom thought as he concentrated on the screen. It showed a shot of an empty house which, only days ago, had been full of vibrant life. But bringing the kids in wouldn't do any good.

This guy wasn't watching children exclusively, selecting them and following them home. It was the whole family he wanted. He might hurt the children before killing them ... Tom didn't want to speculate on the matter and, thankfully, the media had never supplied any details ... but Tom was sure it was the family unit this man was after.

The camera pulled slowly back, revealing a street that was empty apart from a few gathered onlookers. The estate looked like a ghost town, curtains drawn across windows, doors almost certainly locked. Most of those people were in shocked mourning, Tom predicted. But they were also scared, wondering how easily it might have been their home the man had chosen, how lucky they were to still be alive.

Cindy jingled her car keys. 'I'm taking the little terrorists home,' she told Tom when she heard the children enter through the back door, and kissed him lightly on the cheek. 'Back soon.'

'See you in a few minutes,' Tom nodded.

In their shock the neighbours were not aware of one thing. Tom felt sure of this, although he didn't know why; it was just a feeling. The family had been selected, *chosen* for their fate, like the other families. The neighbours had never been in any danger.

'Police have appealed to everybody in the area to come forward if they remember seeing anything in the past few weeks. Anything out of the ordinary, unusual or suspicious . . .'

As Cindy returned five minutes later and the door slammed shut, the news programme concluded. He heard the children run upstairs, shouting and giggling all the way, and listened to Cindy as she moved about the house, checking locks. Making them safe.

It didn't matter, Tom thought. He was sure it would be a while before another killing.

7

Even this soon after a kill, when he was not hunting, Joel had to stick to this normal routine. Be in the usual places at the usual times. Keep up appearances.

So, several mornings after he had killed the Napier family, he walked into the local McDonald's, picked up one of their newspapers and ordered a coffee. He sat and scanned the pages while he casually sipped the steaming drink.

Towards the middle of it – before the television and sport but after the big, main event news – he found a tiny, inch-long column about his own work. An unnamed reporter was speculating that there might be a serial killer loose in the Cheshire area. The police had released details of certain letters found carved into each body of the murdered families – S. F. and G. L.

He didn't pay it any extra attention, simply read it and continued on as though it didn't concern him. He had been in the papers before . . . *flashbulbs exploding in his face, blinding him. Reporters running up the steps, like a vicious pack of predators and he their prey. 'How did you know? What put you on to the knife?' He pauses, squints into the bright lights and holds up a hand. 'We were lucky,' he says. 'The fourth victim, Anthea Harrison, had a curved bruise under one of her lacerations. This was caused by the hilt of the knife. We . . . '* so this was nothing special. He read the television pages and gave the sports headlines a cursory glance.

He laughed slightly at the antics of Snoopy and Charlie Brown on the back page, and then returned the paper to the rack.

'No top-up today?' the kid standing behind the counter asked.

'No, thank you,' Joel told him.

When he got to his bookstore he opened the shop and then picked up the phone behind the counter.

His parents were staying with him, had been for a while and probably would be until the end. They were bedridden, very ill, and he didn't know how long they had left.

He was grateful that they had agreed to let him care for them in their final years, and that they had not preferred to be put in a home. He felt honoured; graced by their loving presence.

But it hadn't always been like that. He remembered, as a child, listening to them argue . . . *standing behind their bedroom door, wanting to go in and scream at them to shut up, shut up! And then running back to his bed, climbing beneath the blankets and crying himself to sleep . . .*

The next morning at breakfast-time he'd notice them exchange knowing glances. He had wondered what they did in the night to appease each other and make all the bad things right . . . and then one night he had dared to open their door and creep into their room, where he'd watched, unseen in a dark corner . . .

He closed his eyes as he quickly punched in his home number.

He was simply glad that they had learned to love each other again in their dying years, much as they had each morning after the vicious arguments. When the end came they would be in each other's arms.

'Hi,' he said to the answering machine. Neither of them could get to the telephone. He had the volume turned up loud so that they could hear him. 'It's only me. I'm at the shop. I'll take a break in an hour or so and bring you folks something to eat. Be good.'

He paused thoughtfully, and then put the receiver down. He liked to call them, reassure them of his imminent return. He would hate to be in their situation, helpless, as his victims were . . . dependent on him to end the pain.

He'd told them, as he had on the previous occasions, that he was going away on business for the night. There was no reason for them not to believe him. There was a lot of trust between them now. He finally knew all they had done to each other in the past, throughout his childhood. There had been a lot of hatred between them, and he had been influential in this final reconciliation. He had brought them back together. And they knew why he'd resigned from his job as a senior forensic pathologist working with the Metropolitan Police, helping to solve crimes.

The bruising made by the hilt of the knife leads to the discovery of the make of knife, and then to the identity of her killer. He studies the wounds, touches them, yearns to touch – and be touched by – her dead flesh. He puts down the scalpel and moves his finger between her legs until a part of his mind screams, 'Not yet! Not here!' and he manages to control his cravings for a long time, months, before another victim demands his attention and he knows that soon he must leave before his macabre habits are discovered, that he must get out of his job and away from all its frightening temptations . . .

The shop bell jingled and he opened his eyes, realised he was sweating. A beautiful woman walked in. Short skirt, long legs. He thought how sweet she would be dead, in his loving embrace. He had never had sex with a living female, and didn't think that he would be starting here.

'Can I help you?' he asked, quickly controlling his wild fantasies.

'No, thanks,' Jo Myers said, and walked up to a display of detective novels with a casual glance over her shoulder. 'I'm just browsing.'

Before he went to work in London, his father had joked that he had met a woman, that he was going away to have some fun with her. Surely that was better than them learning the truth of who he was, something they would never suspect, not even in their darkest, most beautiful nightmares . . . when they'd wake with the sweet stench of sweat washing over them, sheets gripped tight in clenched fists. Even then they would never come close to the truth.

'Do you have the new Patricia D. Cornwell?' Jo asked the middle-aged man behind the counter. At first he didn't respond, looked like he was having a great daydream. He might as well have been on another planet.

'I said, did you see the alien spaceship parked out back?'

He was still looking off into the room, staring at a point she couldn't see.

'There are little green men in it with Spock ears and bad breath, and—'

'I'm sorry, what did you say?' he apologised and looked at her. He was blushing, and almost stammered on his words. Jo thought he was sweet, even if he was a little old for her.

'The new Patricia Cornwell?' she asked tentatively.

'Sorry. I sold out straight away. You should try Dillons down the road,' he helpfully informed her.

'Right. Thanks. I'll do that. It's just, well, I walk by this place so often and it seems so small compared to their big building. I thought you might like my custom.'

He smiled, and she sensed he was beginning to relax in her presence. He was obviously taken by her, and she was surprised when her own cheeks suddenly warmed, turning a rosy red. She was pretty sure what he was thinking, and was having similar thoughts herself.

'I do OK,' he told her.

Jo looked him over, for the first time considering him seriously. He was handsome, even if he was old. *OK, older*. He looked about forty, fifty at the most. She was thirty. That made him sort of old. He seemed shy too, almost withdrawn, like a turtle; just his head poking out from his shell. He was so different from the men she normally dated, but something about him turned her on. She suspected he was more confident and assured than he was making her believe. She wondered if he was playing games with her.

'I'm sure you do,' Jo smiled. 'I'll try Dillons, then. Thanks for your help.'

Joel waved as the bell jingled once more and she looked back a final time. Now he could tell his father that he *had* met a woman. Perhaps one day he would introduce them. He wondered if he would ever see her again *The knife arcing down, down, down, ripping and tearing at the woman, who is kicking and screaming and then dead in his caressing arms . . .*

He could feel the talons of his insanity ripping at his mind, creating a bloody nightmare, like a savage knife through flesh.

A long time ago, when he was a child and had dared to look into the room of his parents, Joel had met another woman. She was a dark lady of the night, with dark ways and a dark soul. He was having an affair with her, a secret fling filled with violent, loving and memorable times.

Her name was Death, and she was his lover.

8

Cindy was dressed to kill, looking good and ready to party. It was Wednesday, the day of her regular date with Alan, and she had been looking forward to it all week.

Almost mercifully the days had come around quickly, even though there had been a couple of problems.

Tom seemed to be engrossed by his latest assignment for *Little Researchers*; he had spent most of his waking hours either in his den or at the office reading those disgusting books.

She had woken early on Saturday morning, before the sun, to find herself hugging a pillow, a rough facsimile of her husband's shoulders, enough to fool her while asleep.

She had climbed from the bed and pulled on her dressing gown before creeping stealthily along the landing, only pausing to look in on her children who were sleeping peacefully in their rooms. Richard actually resembled a human being, while Sarah was sprawled all over the bed, covers pulled from under the mattress, limbs dangling everywhere as she snored softly.

She went downstairs and found Tom in the living room.

'What's going on?' she demanded.

He was slumped on the sofa, some of those sick books at his side, a bottle in his hand. There was a glass on the floor but it was knocked on its side, a sliver of ice melting slowly within it. The bottle was nearly empty. He looked up slowly.

'Cindy,' he whispered guiltily. 'I'm sorry. I really—'

Cindy walked over and yanked the bottle from his hand.

'I've had enough, Tom. You hear me? This stuff is a killer. It killed my father, and now it's killing our marriage. Why can't you understand that?'

'I'm . . .' He paused, and she watched as he swallowed deeply, looking sick. 'I'm not rich, Cindy. Never have been. The business is drowning. We're going under. I wasted the last of your father's money . . . talked you into this crazy idea—'

'I gave you the money because I believe in you, Tom,' she said steadily. 'I think I still do. But this drinking has to stop. I won't watch you die like my father.' She turned and walked towards the door, but then came back, enraged, tears in her eyes. It was his behaviour that was continually driving her away. 'As for the money – I didn't marry you for money! I married you in the name of love . . . and . . .'

The anger left her like air from a balloon and suddenly she found herself deflated and in his arms. They were holding each other, kissing, weeping, making love . . . and all the time she was thinking: *how much longer can this go on?* She had to decide soon – either stick with Tom, struggle through these problems and make it work, or leave him.

Other than that night, they had only made love twice in the previous month. She realised mournfully that she felt no different with Tom than she did when she was having sex with Alan. And it should feel different. I'm married to him, *I should love him*.

Without his consent or conversation she had started to take the contraceptive pill again. She didn't want to have another baby with him, not while they were struggling financially and their relationship was in such a mess. It wouldn't be fair on their newborn.

The children had been good most of the week, although Sarah had been sulky about the new curfew her parents had set, the new boundaries for when they went outside to play. Typically, Richard had fallen in line right behind her, voicing his complaint and suggesting they should write to a place he had seen advertised at the cinema called Amity. Cindy didn't have the heart to tell him he meant *Amnesty*, and that they dealt with problems far more serious than childhood rules.

Sunday had been her sister's birthday.

She had celebrated it with a lonely visit to the church, lighting a single candle of remembrance. After sitting for a while in the silent, empty pews she took a bunch of summer flowers out to the gravestone where she cried for a while to herself.

At first the thoughts of Katie were nice memories, from a time when her older sibling was alive. She had been full of vibrant life and potential, a bright light of guidance and hope to anybody who knew her.

Only a week after she had been murdered, she would have been flying out to South America to help a charity organisation build a bridge. It had been an adventure she had been greatly looking forward to. A member of the charity group had come to pay his respects at the funeral.

Cindy stood before the gravestone and wept. 'It wasn't my fault,' she cried. 'It . . . God, I'm so sorry, Katie. I miss you so much.'

Slow spots of rain came down, and she looked up at the low, heavy skies. The wind picked up. She couldn't remember what had happened to Katie, but somehow, she knew she was responsible for her sister's death.

It came to her then: rain, cold rain in a black, starless night. She had been drenched and a man was . . . a man was trying to . . . but she couldn't see any more. It was as if the memory was trapped behind a door, one that would remain locked for ever.

After her visit to the churchyard on Sunday she had rifled through her photograph albums and found some good pictures of Katie. The photographs all depicted her sister in various poses and action shots: partying, rock-climbing, modelling new outfits, running and dancing. They all had motion and vitality. They showed her *alive*. Then she'd written a letter to the prison where her sister's killer was currently residing.

The letter she sealed in an envelope with the pictures suggested he kill himself, as each one she'd sent did.

Cindy didn't know whether he received the letters or not. She doubted it. The prison – all prisons – must surely have some kind of system to protect their inmates. But it felt good just to mail them, to know that she was still doing something to help her sister even though Katie was gone.

Gone was such a better word than dead.

Yesterday evening, Jo Myers had telephoned, and the two women had gossiped for an hour. Apparently, Jo had met a new man, although she wasn't sure about him. *I mean, we haven't gone out or anything . . . yet*, Jo had giggled and Cindy suspected she'd had a drink or two before calling. She said he owned a small bookstore in the town centre, and Cindy promised to look in and give Jo her verdict of him.

This morning there had been no more bad news in the *Bradbury Guardian* – no more killings, anyway – so Tom had caught his usual train after dropping the little monsters off at school. That had left her time to dress up tartily for Alan. Tom had left his car at the station, so she headed for her secret meeting in her own blue Ford.

When she reached the warehouse, she sauntered up and down the aisles for Alan, knowing exactly where the cameras were, parading her body for him. Her legs were wrapped in a short, tight skirt, her body covered by a diaphanous top through which the flimsiest of Wonderbras was visible. Lace and stockings. High heels.

Just what she knew he liked.

Alan met her eagerly and grabbed her hand. 'Come on,' he told her urgently. 'Let's go.'

They were driving into the town centre when his hand moved from the relaxing position on her leg, further up her skirt, over suspenders and—

'Hey, hey, hey,' she said, and quickly pulled into the side of the road. 'Slow down, tiger.'

'What's wrong?' he asked resentfully.

She gently lifted his hand away from her legs. He had a muscled body and arms that bulged, stretching the sleeves of his shirt. He spent as much time in the gym as he did in work, was strong and could handle several men in a fight – or so he often boasted. He would do anything for her, and also had a brain the size of a pea. A small pea at that, Cindy thought.

'Anticipation,' she told him, and climbed from the car. The truth was, she didn't know if she wanted to have sex with Alan again. He also got out of the vehicle. 'You should be savouring these moments.'

'I do,' he said flatly, not really sure what she was talking about.

'The tension. The build-up. You think I put all this on, get all made-up, just so you can rip it off without a second thought?'

'Cindy, what is all this? You know I think about you all the time,' he told her, and they began to walk towards the shops.

They had only been into a couple of stores, Alan following on her heels like a dog, becoming more and more frustrated, when she decided to check out the next man to be lined up in Jo's sights.

They entered the small store named *Pages* and she picked up the odd book, having no intention of buying anything.

A man appeared suddenly at her side, startling her. 'Can I be of service?' he asked.

9

'What did you do to them?' Detective Inspector Ian Knox asked as he sipped from his chipped cup of coffee. He pulled a face at the taste – it was tepid – and handed the cup to a passing constable.

'I told you!' the male voice screeched down the phone line. 'I killed them! Killed them all!'

The man began to laugh and Knox whipped the phone away from his ear as the constable returned with a steaming cup. 'Thanks,' he whispered, and then turned to Lewis who had passed the call on to him. *I've got a right one here*, he mouthed.

'Yeah!' the man continued. 'You listening, copper? I did them all!'

Why was it, Knox thought drearily, that whenever something bad happened, all the loonies came out to party? Why couldn't they just seek attention when it was quiet and nothing was happening?

'Did you murder the dog, too?' Knox asked politely. He picked up a framed photograph of Lucy and stared longingly into her eyes. He had recently lost all his passion for the job, as he had life. *Not long now, my dear*, he thought.

'Killed their dog, their goldfish and their fucking pet turtle!' the voice boasted.

The only pet belonging to the Napiers was a dignified yellow Labrador called Thief, who had been put to sleep a fortnight before their deaths. There was a remote possibility that the caller was being sarcastic, but Knox suspected he was wired on drugs and had nothing at all to do with the case. It was just another crank call.

There was too much rottenness in the world these days – never mind Denmark – and Bradbury seemed to be harbouring more than its fair quota. There were too many lunatics residing in the town. It was as though there was a full moon hanging over them every night.

I can't do this for much longer.

He put the picture of Lucy down. 'How did you kill them?' he went on conversationally.

'I cut them! I stabbed them!' the man screamed, and then laughed like a hyena braying.

Knox shrugged, and finished the coffee. He nestled the phone between his shoulder and ear before unwrapping a chocolate bar. He was giving up smoking and the chocolate seemed to help. He didn't know why he was quitting now.

The more he smoked, the sooner he would die. The sooner he would be reunited with Lucy.

It was a bitter irony that she had wanted him to quit before she'd passed away, and only now could he find the discipline to grant her that wish.

Not long, my love.

He just wanted to do that one last thing for her.

'Hey, loser! You still there?'

Knox swallowed the last of the chocolate bar and tossed the wrapper at the bin. It bounced off the rim and landed on the floor. He never usually missed. So far the caller hadn't told him anything that had not been in the papers. Time to put a hole in the story the size of the Grand Canyon . . . *Lucy had always wanted to visit the Canyon, had always said that their problems wouldn't matter out there . . .*

'What did you do to their skins?' Knox asked.

'I told you, whore. I cut them up!'

The crank was one amongst many. Knox was becoming bored with them all wasting his time. 'What did you carve on to their skin?' he persisted.

'S. F. G. L.,' the man said with almost rehearsed precision, and then he was screaming like a banshee once more. 'The press got that right! S. F. G. L.! I'm the Initial Killer!'

Wrong again, Knox yawned, but it wouldn't hurt to pull this arsehole in and get him taken off the streets for a few days. 'I'll have to take your name, a contact address and a daytime telephone number in case we need to—'

'Hey, fuck you!' the man squealed, and Knox winced, holding the phone away from his ear again. 'I'm the Initial Killer. Catch me if you can! Your mother sucks cock! Your wife gives billy goats blow jobs and eats the—'

Knox slammed the phone down, his hand trembling. His temples were suddenly throbbing and he rummaged through the mess on his desk until he found a container of Paracetamol. He dry-swallowed a couple of tablets.

The press were right about a lot of things, but they had got one thing wrong. Due to the police deliberately withholding information, no one except they themselves knew what the Initial Killer carved into his victims' flesh. This gave them a safeguard against such calls, made it a little easier to check them out.

In this case, it was the symbol of a heart separating the two sets of initials.

Knox remembered the afternoon when the autopsies of the Napiers had been been conducted. Simply because of the horrific situation of the bodies, they had suspected the same killer who had murdered the other families. The forensic pathologist – a man named Malone – had offered conclusive proof that a serial killer was on the loose in Bradbury.

'Look,' Malone had told Knox. 'Each body has the initials carved into it, even the children. Plus that damn heart.'

'So Chummy is up to his tricks again, Doc.'

"Fraid so. He really had it in for these people,' Malone said sombrely, and he lifted the arm of the little boy. 'Look at this.'

Cut into the underside of the arm, just beneath the elbow, were two sets of initials. S. F. and G. L. They were separated by a tiny heart.

'I found the same on each body,' Malone sighed. 'On the left buttock of the woman. The left cheek of the man. The bottom of the little girl's right foot. We've got a very bad man out there, Knox. You must catch him.'

'I know,' Knox had whispered. 'Believe me, Doc, I know.'

PART TWO

By Reason of Insanity

1

It was incredible how it happened.

Joel was putting out some stock in *Pages* when he first picked up traces of the scent. He walked around the shelving and spotted her at the end, wearing too much perfume, a looming hulk at her side.

He recognised the scent as Coco, and he saw this through the eye of his mind in a flash... *the woman, naked, bleeding, her aroma – Coco – gorgeous as it washed over him...* It had to be more than coincidence that this beautiful female was wearing the same perfume as the Napier woman; and also wearing it heavily, as the other woman had.

He stepped up silently behind them. 'Can I be of service?' he asked quietly, overwhelmed by the sudden certainty that he had found *the next ones.*

'No. I was just looking,' she told him pleasantly.

Then she turned and walked out, the hunk trailing behind her, leaving him with only her scent. He drowned in it. *The knife is in his hand and he tickles the bottom of her feet with the tip of it. She tries to scream but her voice is suffocated by the gag, and he laughs and laughs...*

He realised from the way she was dressed, overtly displaying her sexuality, that she was probably wearing the perfume a tad heavily for the sake of her male companion. Neanderthal Man might not be her husband.

He had to find out.

Joel quickly grabbed his jacket and went after them, forgetting to lock the shop door in his haste and having to dash back and do it. He spotted them.

It was definitely Coco she was wearing. It was burning the insides of his nostrils. The scent had to be a sign.

It was fantastic. He was not even on a hunt, hadn't been searching for prey. It had merely happened.

His heart was beating fast with excitement and he tried to relax. She still had to qualify, he told himself. She might not be perfect. There was logic behind his insanity. He didn't just kill on the whim of a moment.

But he had already decided. If she wasn't married, didn't have children, then he would take her anyway, to satisfy his own dark desires.

He stopped as he watched the couple walk down the side of the library. They crossed to the car park and he turned and ran for his own vehicle, which was parked at the back of his store. He must not lose them.

Joel had never chosen an individual person until now. He usually worked from groups, observing, selecting, seeing what he liked, *what had to be destroyed*, and then began to stalk them. He'd learn everything he could about them before . . .

He dropped his keys as he fumbled with the car door. Quickly, he scooped them up. He was sweating as he started the engine.

This time it was different, and he was playing outside his own rules. She had to be married, have children, he thought frantically. If she didn't he wasn't sure how he would proceed. Would he take her to quench his sexual thirst? That would be a shame, because he was certain that the other woman he had spoken to in his store was destined to become his next dead lover.

He fervently hoped that the Coco woman would fit his deadly agenda. He yearned for it. Longed for the night some time in the future when he would murder her and her perfect family; her husband and all her children.

She had to be the one.

Urgently, but not daring to break the speed limit, he followed the one-way system around the shopping precinct. Please don't let me miss them, he prayed, and drew up outside the car park behind the library.

He rummaged through the glove compartment and pretended to consult a map, secretly watching each car as it pulled out, checking the occupants, searching for his new prey. He was a hawk in blue skies circling for a tiny mouse in the field below. He had absolute power.

Joel sighed as another vehicle exited the car park. Once more it was not the woman. He wished he'd thought to check her finger. Had she been wearing a ring? Was she married?

Questions, over and over, gnawed at his mind.

Then he saw her, the man leaning over to kiss her neck as they drove away. He let a car come between them and then pulled away from the kerb, following from a distance where they wouldn't see him.

It wasn't long before the car pulled into the driveway of a big detached house and he parked on the opposite side of the street.

Joel watched as the couple climbed from the car. As they approached the front door the man began to pull at her blouse. The Coco woman struggled with the key as she tried to fend off his advances. Joel caught her expression; she was glancing about nervously as she eased the door open, obviously afraid they might be seen.

He smiled.

Her behaviour was deceitful. He was certain that this man was her lover, and that she was married, frightened of passing neighbours seeing her with him.

Joel looked upstairs and after a few seconds, as he'd anticipated, her face appeared at a window. She looked out for a moment, once more checking up and down the street. She didn't notice him. The cups of her black bra were pushing her breasts up, enhancing her cleavage, giving the man more to behold. He could see her tanned, flat stomach and . . . then she pulled the thin summer curtains shut, and their illicit passion was hidden from the world.

He was alone.

It was an affair he was witnessing. The man had been careless and frantic, typical of a passionate lover, whereas she, the guilty wife, was cautious about what the neighbours might see.

Joel remembered looking into her eyes in the store. They had been scheming eyes, and he imagined how they would look in a few weeks' time, when she was handcuffed and at his mercy. *The Napier father pulls at the cuffs. Sobs. There is no way he is going to get free. He's begging for mercy and Joel hasn't even started to hurt him yet.*

Then Joel saw her again at the window, a silhouette behind the curtain. Her body was full, but slim. She turned slightly and he saw petite breasts in shadow, nipples erect, and then they were gone and it was her back facing him, her tight arse.

Yes, he thought as he watched her dance for him. *You are the one.*

Joel felt the same excitement as when he was selecting the

47

last family: the moment he had seen ketchup covering the little girl's top lip. It was an exquisite feeling as he watched the Coco woman move away from the window, her image fading. It wasn't sexual. It was something more than that, a secret knowledge deep inside.

Joel smiled. His hands were trembling and he was sweating. Only he knew the horror he would soon bestow upon them – her, and her perfect family; they who had all he had ever wanted.

2

When the sex was over, their rapture drained, Cindy and Alan lay together, wrapped in sheets, cocooned from the world. Unaware that a stranger was watching, waiting . . .

Alan casually began to tap out a cigarette from a packet.

'What are you doing?' Cindy snapped, snatching it from his hand. 'Neither of us smoke. What if Tom smells it in the air, or something?'

Alan sighed. Sometimes Cindy could be more trouble than she was worth. 'You never smoked?'

'Yeah, when I was a kid, at school. Back then I did a lot of bad things,' she told him, and paused, tears welling in her eyes for a second as she remembered Katie. Her sister had saved her from something bad, something terrible, she knew that much. *It was my fault.* She shook her head, blinked the tears back. 'I never cared much for smoking, but it was fashionable amongst my peer group. I argued with my parents about it, and my big sister, just to look good in front of my friends. A typical rebel, that was me. Then I met Tom and—'

'I didn't know you had a sister,' Alan said, diverting the conversation from his rival.

'There are a lot of things you don't know about me.'

'OK, OK,' he said quickly at her blunt response. He held up his hands defensively. 'Did Tom make you give up?'

She waited for a few seconds, wondering whether she actually wanted to talk to Alan. She didn't use him for conversation. The sex had been good, but now it was over and nothing had changed between them. She didn't love him and never would.

She sighed. So much was wrong in her life.

'No. He would never force me to stop. He's too nice a guy. God only knows how he ended up married to a bitch like me. I told you, I didn't really care about smoking. Tom had never touched a cigarette in his life, so it was easy to give up.'

'How did you guys meet?' Alan asked.

'What is this? *Twenty Questions?*' she said irritably, climbing from the bed and walking over to the window again. As daylight struggled through the thin material of the curtain, Cindy imagined what her silhouette must look like to any people outside. She was grateful that nobody had a reason to be watching.

'Hey, I'm just curious about the competition,' he grinned cockily.

Competition? She turned as he stared at her, open-mouthed. He was virtually drowning in his own drool. Enjoy what you see, she thought. This will never be yours. It isn't some game, with my body as the prize.

She let the comment pass; let him believe the fantasy he'd created for himself. It didn't hurt her to feel wanted. Let him believe that one day she would walk out on her husband for him. Though if she ever did leave Tom, it wouldn't be for Alan, for whom she had only one use.

'University,' she told him, and pulled a wrap on. She didn't want him looking at her, it made her feel dirty.

He laughed. 'You went to university?'

Her smile was thin. 'Yes. Anything wrong with that?' she snapped. 'Look, I've got things to do and I know you want to go home and catch up on your sleep, so . . .'

'What? Are you throwing me out already?' he protested.

'It's time you were gone,' she repeated, pointing at the door.

Cindy watched Alan dress without speaking. She didn't have to tolerate people making fun of her.

He tied his shoelaces and looked back from the door. 'Will I see you next week?'

'I don't know,' she shrugged, and turned away. She heard him thunder down the stairs and then the sound of the door slamming.

She wasn't some bubblehead who had flunked out. She had dropped out of her studies when she became pregnant with Sarah. Tom had proposed to her. He had whisked her away to the Scottish Highlands for a weekend, where she'd accepted his offer of eternal matrimony, always believing there would be an opportunity to take up her studies again in the future.

Eternal, she thought solemnly. *Until death do you part . . .*

That was how the sacred vow went, and she'd sworn it. Yet here, at the first signs of trouble in her marriage, she was looking for solace in the arms of another man instead of facing her problems.

Cindy wiped tears from her eyes.

She decided never to see Alan again.

A year after the birth of Sarah she had fallen pregnant with Richard. Mothering had become a full-time prospect. Tom was a good husband, and she realised now that she only resented him for two reasons. One, the opportunities their marriage had taken away from her, and two, his drinking.

The affair with Alan could not be allowed to jeopardise her marriage. She was crying and only now acknowledged how much she loved Tom.

When he'd proposed he had promised to always care for her, and look after her. He had never broken his word. But with *Little Researchers* failing, she thought, Tom must be under great pressure. And that could be one of the reasons for his drinking.

She had to talk with him about that. She had married him because of who he was, not because of what he might one day give her.

Cindy wept. She loved Tom, had to tell him that, show him, before he drowned himself in a bottle as her father had done.

Joel had been waiting outside the house for about an hour and a half when the man stormed out. He was a big individual. He slammed the door and walked angrily down the driveway, stopping to glare up at the veiled window. His body language gave Joel a rich mine of information.

Then the man removed something from his pocket and placed it against the side of the woman's blue Ford. He walked alongside the vehicle, scratching all the way. At the end of the car he bent down. He glanced once more up at the window, checking he wasn't being observed, and then spent a minute scratching at the smooth surface of the car, just above the hub of the back wheel.

He stood, walked out of the driveway and crossed the street. For a few seconds he was walking directly towards Joel, looking at him through the windscreen.

He's going to recognise me, Joel thought in a panic. Remember me from the bookstore.

The woman's lover was at the car now, approaching his door, stepping closer. *Think! You need an excuse for being here!* But then the man walked by, off up the street.

Joel breathed a long sigh of relief. He waited a moment, and then got out of the car, deciding to follow her lover on foot. There

51

was a story to know here, one he would surely hear soon through sobbing tears and screams of pain.

It would be far too conspicuous to follow the man by car, so he matched the lover's pace step for step at a distance of about a hundred yards.

Twenty minutes later, Joel watched the man enter what he presumed to be his home. Hurrying past now, he got a glimpse inside. Cheap carpet. A table with a vase of flowers upon it. Telephone. An old voice, female and frail. 'Is that you, Alan?'

The walk had been uneventful and he had learned nothing except for this address; one he would probably never need. Still, he made a mental note of the street name and house number just in case.

He returned to his car, hoping fervently that the woman had not yet left. He wasn't disappointed; the Ford was still in the driveway.

He got back in his car and settled down to wait again. He wanted to go and look at the Ford up close, see what Alan had scratched above the wheel. But it would be too risky in broad daylight.

Whatever happened for the rest of today, he decided he would return tonight.

3

That afternoon, as Tom read the latest edition of the *Bradbury Guardian* in his office at Manchester, he remembered the beggar he had seen on the street earlier.

The sun had been struggling through the clouds and the man, he wasn't much more than a teenager, his hair straggly and dirty, his eyes dark and baggy, wearing clothes that were ripped and ragged, had held a piece of torn card at his feet as morning people entered Burger King, ignoring him.

There was writing on the card in a thick, smudged marker. Tom thought it was an extract from the Bible.

NEVER DEPRIVE A PERSON OF HOPE BECAUSE IT MIGHT BE THE ONLY POSSESSION HE OR SHE HAS

Tom had dropped a couple of pound coins into the man's polystyrene coffee cup to a grunt of thanks.

As he read the *Guardian* he thought about that beggar, and the message on his card. The editor of the *Guardian* obviously had the same idea, for the front-page story concerned a local school's production of *A Midsummer Night's Dream*. There was also a banner proclaiming that photographs of all the contestants for this year's Miss Bradbury competition could be found in the centre pages.

Tom glanced at the editorial. The editor wanted his readers to know that there was more to Bradbury than the evil of one human soul.

It would have been a nice message were it not for the short article which had been relegated to page four. A veterinary surgeon had come forward with information that Mr Napier had brought the family dog – a yellow Labrador named Thief – into his surgery a couple of weeks before their deaths. The animal was severely mauled, possibly from a road accident, and the vet had been forced to put him to sleep.

The man said he would have come forward sooner, but he had been in France on vacation with his family.

Suddenly, Mike Littler opened the office door without knocking, and Tom nearly jumped out of his seat with shock.

'We got it!' Mike declared jubilantly. For the past month he had been schmoozing an independent television production company who were preparing a series for the BBC. 'We got it!'

Mike grabbed his friend's face and gave him a wet kiss on his forehead.

'Save it for Danielle,' Tom grimaced, wiping his face. 'You mean it?'

'We got it!' Tom was beginning to wonder if these were the only words in his friend's vocabulary, when Mike continued: 'You know what this could do for us? This could be just the start. We can get bigger premises again, and—'

'We could pay some bills,' Tom interjected.

'Yup, that too. But this could be e-fucking-normous! What's up? You don't seem to be sharing my excitement, pardner.'

Tom grinned for a second. Mike could sometimes sound like a bit player in a cheap television Western.

Tom put the paper to one side. 'They were stalked, Mike.'

'What?' Mike was confused. 'I bought a bottle of bubbly. Phone Cindy and get her over here and let's celebrate! What are you talking about?'

'The bastard who killed the Napiers,' Tom said in a dull voice. 'He did the Cusacks, too, and the Fosters and one more family before that. He's picking them, Mike. He's selecting his victims and torturing them. It's not random – I know it.'

'Listen, we have the police for stuff like that. Sure you haven't been reading too many of those blasted books? Damn morbid if you ask me,' Mike said. 'Why not give the bloke his report and get rid of him?'

'Yeah. Give me a week or so. After reading about this vet I want to check a few things out in one of the books first.'

'What vet? What is this – one of those cheap do-it-yourself television detective shows? We're researchers, Tom. That's what we do. Let the police do their job, and we'll do ours, OK?'

'He's picking his victims and stalking them, Mike,' Tom insisted.

'The police will know that.'

'But *nobody is safe* – don't you understand that? Unless, of course, you're single,' Tom said feverishly, and saw Mike smile slightly at his marital status. 'He killed the Cusacks' cat before he came for them – don't you remember how it was reported a couple of weeks before their deaths? The police later speculated if there was a connection.'

Tom was suddenly grateful that they had never allowed Richard or Sarah to have pets. Silence separated them for a minute. Mike's enthusiasm for celebration seemed dampened.

'Did you see the papers yesterday?' Tom demanded.

'I glanced at the TV pages. Why?'

'A man named Ryan Stowe was executed in America. He raped, tortured and killed seven young girls. Something went wrong with his lethal injection. Apparently he really suffered, gagging and slobbering. It started a whole new debate raging about the death penalty.'

'So?' Mike asked impatiently.

'I'd never really thought about the death sentence before,' Tom said slowly. 'I took it for granted that it would never affect me. I think I would probably have always voted against it, even taking Katie's death into account. It always seemed so barbaric.'

'There'd better be a point to all this,' Mike said half threateningly.

'But after reading some of this material . . . it was like an eye-opener. When somebody is murdered, it isn't the same as dying naturally,' Tom struggled to explain. 'It's about pain and horror; the difference between dying when your card comes up and dying at the hands of another man. It's a whole different ballgame. It's about fear. This maniac deserves to be hanged, Mike.'

Tom removed his wire-rim glasses as the cork exploded off the bottle of champagne. 'No trial. No jury. No appeals. He should be sentenced to death.'

4

'Mother! Father!' Joel called from the bottom of the stairs as he stuffed half a sandwich into his mouth. 'I have to go out tonight. Just for an hour.'

He finished the smoked ham sandwich and walked into the living room, where a black sweater was draped across the back of a chair. He pulled it over his head, working his arms into the sleeves as he went up the stairs. With both his parents being ill, he acknowledged that it wasn't such a clever idea to have them on the upper floor, especially since the stairs were so steep.

He looked into their room. 'Is BBC2 OK?'

'I want ITV,' his mother informed him, and he obediently crossed the room and changed channels on the old black and white portable. The picture was fuzzy, and there was a constant hissing beneath the soundtrack.

'Yes,' his father concurred. '*Magnum* is on in ten minutes.'

'That Tom Selleck,' his mother whispered sexily. 'He could—'

'I don't want to know what he could do,' his father told her.

'More than you ever could,' she teased him.

Joel listened to their flippant banter and decided enough was enough. Everything was better between them now, and he wanted to keep it that way. 'If you two keep bickering, I'll turn the television off.'

They fell into a well of silence.

'Good,' Joel told them. 'Enjoy the show. I'll be back soon.'

He left the room, collected his car keys from his own bedroom across the landing and jogged down the stairs.

As he was driving to the woman's house he thought it was strange that he could still hear his parents' voices. It was as if they were sat in the back of the car, and a couple of times he looked over his shoulder to check.

Don't be stupid, he told himself. *They haven't got out of bed in years.*

He concentrated on the voices as they began to talk about the woman he'd spoken to in *Pages* the previous week – the customer who had asked for the Patricia Cornwell book. How could they know about her?

'When do you think we'll meet her?' his father asked his mother, even as Joel could hear the *Magnum* theme tune, that heavy guitar riff – he could almost see T.C. swooping over the islands in his helicopter – shrouded in static from the bad reception.

'I don't know,' his mother responded. 'What happened to the last one?'

The voices, he finally decided, were coming from inside his own head. He'd heard them before, but never so clearly or vividly. Perhaps he was psychic, Joel thought, and then continued to listen.

'. . . useless to him,' his father was saying. 'I think he buried her.'

Joel swerved the car in shock, and a horn sounded behind him. How could his father know that? How much did the old man know? What had he seen? Behind the wheel, the car under control again, he began to sweat.

'Not in my rosebushes?' his mother gasped. 'That's disgusting!'

'Your rosebushes are all dead. He hasn't tended the garden since we arrived here. Besides, it wasn't so bad,' his father explained. 'He killed her before he buried her. She was a sweet little thing, too.'

Joel gripped the wheel tightly. He never tidied the garden, but how could his father know that? Could they *all* be psychic, picking up on each other's thoughts and conversations?

'Just once I wish he'd bring a man back here,' his mother sighed. 'One like Tom Selleck.'

Five minutes later he eased the car to a slow stop two houses down from the familiar property. He opened the glove compartment and pulled out a flashlight. He clicked it on and off, testing the batteries, the light casting a ghostly glow over his face.

'Boo!' he whispered, staring at his reflection in the rearview mirror, and laughed.

His parents had remained silent since his father's portentous revelation. He wondered if they were sleeping. Or if they were making love. Did old people have sex? Did they enjoy it? It would probably be over very quickly, while their actions would be very slow.

He smiled as he climbed from the car. It was good if they were making love. They had argued a lot when he was a child. He was glad they had found salvation in their final years.

He looked at his watch. It was nearly midnight.

As he reached the bottom of the driveway which led to the family he would soon intrude upon, he cast the psychic powers he believed he possessed into the dark lake of the night.

He could hear nothing. No ripples.

Perhaps his parents had found a way to exclude him from their minds, keep their conversation secret. He had to find out how much his father knew, and how much of it was merely suspicion. How could the old man have seen into the garden, without having psychic abilities?

Joel looked up at the window, where earlier he had seen her delightful figure. The curtains were closed, and no light crept through the cracks or seeped through the material. The lights were out, as they were all over the house.

Everybody was asleep.

Stealthily, yet confidently, he moved up the driveway. He couldn't see much in the darkness, but he wore it like a cloak, aware that it concealed his presence from any prying eyes.

Halfway along, he spotted the rosebushes in the garden. After his parents' conversation he knew his mother would like them, so he bent down and broke the stem off one. When he reached the Ford he crouched next to it, on the side away from the house. He smelled the rose; its fragrance was the sweet scent of Summer.

Joel checked the house. There was still no light, no movement. There was nobody to see him.

I am shrouded by the night, walking in its shadow.

He turned to the road. Nobody was about.

He clicked the torch on and shone it on to the side of the vehicle so that its illumination was minimal. It only took him half a second to find what he was looking for.

There was a thick scratch, revealing silver metal under the sky-blue paint, that ran the length of the car, and just above the back wheel were three words that gleamed in the light of his torch.

FUCK YOU BITCH

So, 'Alan' *was* her lover, Joel thought to himself. And from the anger he had witnessed earlier, the act of vandalism to the car and these words of hatred, he was sure that the Coco woman had ended their affair that very afternoon.

It was just after midnight when Tom awoke. He left the bed and walked to the window, where he stood and stared at Cindy's sleeping figure. His wife was beautiful, even in slumber.

He sighed deeply. He was risking losing her because of his drink problem. At least he was recognising he had a problem – that had to be a start.

He watched the rise and fall of her chest, the quilt that covered her undulating like waves on a dead calm sea.

I don't want to lose you, he thought. The business was back on its feet . . . almost, anyway. The prospects of *Little Researchers* had not looked so big in quite a while. The new contract Mike had been working on was a done deal, and they were on the up and up.

Tom had been born into a poor family, and had never known the kind of money – and the benefits it can bring – which Cindy had always taken for granted as a child. He had been shy as a teenager and when his friends at university had learned of the crush he harboured for Cindy they had pushed him into asking her out.

He studied her now, marvelled at her gorgeous face, her supple hands, slender arms and soft shoulders, and was suddenly overwhelmed by an unrelenting feeling of love for her. He wanted to wake her, share the powerful emotion, but she looked so tranquil and at peace that he dared not disturb her.

I love you so much, Tom told her silently.

When he was younger he used to watch her from afar, afraid of even joining her in conversation for fear of destroying the dreams his imagination conjured up for him. He knew her to say hello to, and that was about all. He had no idea that she found him attractive, too, nor that her friends were always teasing her about him.

He was surprised when she accepted his offer to go out . . . *you know, just for a laugh* . . . and when the fun night had turned into a romantic date accompanied by moonlight he had been silently disappointed by her reticence.

He grinned now as he reminisced.

Cindy had been alone in a booth at the library. At the behest of a couple of female friends, whom he could trust and didn't mock him like the guys, he had been encouraged enough to ask her out. He had sat opposite her, and didn't even bother with small talk. Diplomacy and subtlety were not his strongest suits, and he stuttered and stammered his way through a sentence.

'So, I was just wondering, like, do you want to, you know, maybe do something Tuesday night?'

Good going, Tom, he remembered thinking. Very assertive. It had been late in the afternoon. He had gone to the library in search of a book called *In Cold Blood* which he needed for English, and had seen her by accident. She was wearing a pair of tight Wranglers, and a cotton shirt. Her hair was short, back then, and she had worn little make-up. He had popped the question before he had a chance to think what he was doing and lose his courage.

Cindy looked up from her book. 'Oh, hi, Tom. You say something?'

'Me? Oh no. I was just looking for—'

'Tom, I'm teasing,' she smiled. 'I have Computer Club on Tuesday evening.'

'Is that: I have Computer Club on Tuesday and I wish this jerk would leave me alone? Or: I have Computer Club on Tuesday and this guy isn't so bad?' Tom asked.

'How about Saturday?' she suggested.

'You're asking me out?' Tom had blubbered. He must have come over as such a geek, he thought now.

'Yeah,' she laughed. 'What's so amazing about that?'

When he'd tried to kiss her though, at the end of the evening, after walking her home through Verdin Park, she had slowly pulled away.

'I just need a friend right now,' she told him.

So, for the next two years they had been the best of friends, on the phone every day, making each other laugh all the time. He worked hard in part-time jobs for those two years so that they always had money to go out, and he could keep up with her lackadaisical attitude towards finances.

He knew she had never known how much of a struggle that had been, and he hoped she never found out.

At the end of summer term they went on holiday to Greece. The first night there Cindy told him what had happened to Katie, although she couldn't remember any specific details. They had found a secluded beach and made love, drowning in the moon's lambent glow as warm waves lapped over their bodies.

He felt a sharp guilt, knowing how much pain his incessant drinking must be causing her. After her mother and sister had died, alcohol had slowly claimed the body and soul of her father.

'I'm so sorry,' he whispered, looking at her tranquil figure. 'It ends here.'

Tom looked up as the neighbour's dog began to bark. The hound disturbed them so many times at night that Tom felt sure the animal thought it was a wolf baying at the moon. He pulled the curtain aside and opened the window wider.

'Go to sleep,' he hissed into the darkness.

But the dog continued to bark. Tom could see the fence outside wobble slightly in the still night, and sensed the dog scratching the wood there.

Cindy rolled over, and he let the curtain fall. He left the bedroom, deciding to go down and throw the mutt some leftovers so that the rest of the world might get some sleep before sunrise.

5

The first thing Joel knew about anybody being awake in the house was when the front door opened just as he was about to steal away. He froze. A man yawned and stretched in the door-way before stepping out.

Joel ducked quickly behind the car and scampered along its side to the front of the vehicle; he crouched down and stayed low. He dared to peek through the windows of the Ford and could see a shadow figure come from under the porch-light, and walk by the back of the car to the high fence. He was carrying something.

As the man reached the fence, Joel moved around the front of the car, keeping the vehicle between them.

The dog next door continued to bark, sensing his malevolent presence.

Earlier, Joel had been tempted to climb the fence and kill the dog. Silence its yapping for ever. But he had already been preparing to leave when it began to bark, so he had no true motive to murder the animal.

'Shut your barking face up,' the man whispered harshly, and tossed something over the fence.

There was a soft thump as the object landed, and Joel listened as the dog ran to the sound. Then slurping noises came from behind the fence, and he realised that the woman's husband must have thrown the dog some kind of food to shut it up.

Joel smiled. Less messy than killing it, he thought.

'Go to sleep,' the man told the dog firmly, and turned at the fence, looking around.

Joel ducked again, almost dropping the torch. His heart beat hard, pounded in his ears. Now that he had found the perfect family once more he wanted to sneak up on the man, stab him over and over. Destroy their happy bliss.

He almost stood up, but the sudden whisper of his father shocked him, left him frozen.

'Stay down, boy.'

Joel began to sweat with the fear of being discovered. He was not ready to kill again. He twisted the torch nervously in his hands, careful not to switch it on by accident.

Eventually, the man returned to the house, yawning loudly. His back was to Joel, who smiled. He wanted to race over and club him on the head, bludgeon him with the torch. Steal their perfection.

'Not yet,' his father ordered sternly.

The woman's husband didn't turn at the sound of the voice. As the door shut, the porch-light went off and Joel listened to the locking mechanism.

He waited in the dark.

Perhaps his mother and father – his father in particular – were the psychic ones, Joel thought. They were tuned into the wavelength of his mind and brain, could send signals as well as receive them. That would explain how they knew everything.

Joel gave the man twenty minutes, and then decided he would be back in bed again, sleeping soundly. The dog had finished eating, and it too had fallen into a deep slumber.

He moved stealthily down the driveway, and then returned to his car.

His father was right, of course. His father was always right. Joel would not kill the man yet. He had to learn everything about the people in that house, and then he could torture them, show them how wrong they were in their happy little world.

They could not have what he had yearned for throughout his childhood, and only found now, in his parents' last years. He had to take it from them . . .

6

Standing at the window that night, studying his wife, Tom had realised that it was not some game he was playing. Sneaking down in the dead of night for a drink, each mouthful hurting her more than he could ever have known.

As he woke the next morning, rubbing sleep from his eyes, he was grateful to find that he still held to that conviction: his drinking had to end. He was betraying Cindy and the children, too. He had to stop before it destroyed their marriage.

Clad only in his Scooby Doo shorts, he went downstairs and opened the fridge. Inside there were four six-packs and a couple of bottles of cheap wine. They had some good stuff in the cellar, left by Cindy's father. He would keep that for guests, or in case Cindy ever wanted a sip – which he knew was most unlikely.

He started with the wine. He took out the bottles and found a corkscrew in one of the drawers under the sink. He pulled the corks out carelessly, not bothered that tiny pieces fell into the clear liquid and floated there. He had no intention of drinking it.

Tom poured both bottles of wine into the sink, watched the liquid as it twirled down the drain.

Then the cans. Popping them open one by one, the alcohol frothy as it washed away.

'What are you doing?'

He turned at the sound of his wife's voice. It was early, and her eyes held slight bags under them. Her hair was a mess. She looked great.

'It's over,' he told her, and grabbed a small pair of sunglasses from the windowsill. They were Richard's, and a tight fit on his face, but the sun was shining directly into his eyes through the window above the sink. His head was throbbing.

He looked down at the sink as the last of the alcohol disappeared. He already missed the taste and wondered how long it

65

would take before that feeling abated. He hoped it wouldn't be long.

Cindy watched, tired but amazed, as he dropped the last of the empty cans into a black binliner, and then carried the bag into the back garden and placed it by the bin. He padded barefoot back inside.

She grinned, could not believe he was serious. That he was going to stop, just like that. Cindy laughed. She remembered the day he'd asked her out. She smiled. She loved him so much.

'This isn't funny,' he told her, a painful headache forming above his right eye. He hoped it wouldn't last, that the headache wasn't how it felt to be sober. It had been so long, he couldn't remember.

'It is, my love,' she said, smiling sweetly.

It was time to get on with her life, Cindy thought. This was it. This was all she had, and it was more than she'd ever hoped for. Two beautiful children and a loving husband who was a great father to them. A man who could be funny and charming when he wanted to be; good in bed, if she let him be.

There would always be time for her studies, to get her degree, now that she had broken it off with Alan.

For a brief second Cindy silently mourned the days she had let slip through her fingers as she had sex with a stranger, or whiled them away watching gameshows and soaps.

'Your shorts,' she gestured with a grin, telling herself that this was not a time for lamenting, but a moment of celebration. She loved Tom. He was so much more than she deserved after her betrayal. She would never let him go. 'Scooby Doo. When we first made love on the beach, you were wearing Scooby Doo shorts,' she giggled sexily.

'Hey, no shame,' he told her, and they stepped closer.

She removed the glasses from his face, revealing eyes like her own, wet with tears.

'I made you wait so long for that night,' she remembered, and a couple of tears slipped down her cheeks. 'I can't believe I almost lost you, Tom.'

'Let's go back upstairs,' he said, and through her tears he could see her eyes sparkling like diamonds. He realised sadly how long it had been since he'd seen such life in them, how much he had missed her.

Cindy held his hand softly and led him upstairs.

Tom's last thought before they made long, slow love was that

66

there had been something wrong with their marriage. Somehow they had managed to slip onto separate rails. But whatever had happened, they were back together again now, on the same tracks. Back together until the end of time.

When they came down over an hour later, the children were dressed and had prepared their own breakfasts. The mess they had made in the kitchen – spilt milk and sugar on the counter, crushed cereal on the floor – was not so cool, but it could be cleaned up later.

Tom found Sarah and Richard in the living room, and was gratified to see that, for once, they weren't sitting glued to the television screen watching cartoons.

Sarah was practising a new card trick, one he was sure they would all be dazzled by in a few days. Richard was reading a gory comic, something about *Aliens* and *Predators*. Neither seemed too concerned that they were late for school.

Cindy came in with two glasses of fresh orange and a Snickers bar for each of the children. She passed the chocolate out and handed Tom one of the glasses. He sipped it, surprised how good it tasted without the vodka.

Sarah looked up as she finished her chocolate bar. 'Are we going to school today?' she asked hopefully.

Richard glared at his sister over the page of his comic. Sarah could be such a panic merchant. He was happy with the knowledge that they were not in school, but she had to push the subject, afraid that any second they might be shipped off into class. Richard took each second as it came.

'No,' Cindy told her.

'Good,' Sarah grinned, returning to her trick.

'We're going to Alton Towers for the day instead,' Tom told them.

At this Richard lowered his comic. His friends had all been to Alton towers in Derbyshire, and always came back raving about the place, bubbling over with tales to tell. It was a place of magic, full of rides and thrills, fun and scares. Laughter. It was a good place to visit if you were a child.

'What's Alton Towers?' Sarah asked.

'It will be good,' Richard assured her. 'We're gonna have some fun.'

And they did, not coming home until late in the evening. It was about seven, and the children, exhausted from the events of the day, were sleeping soundlessly in the back of the car, buckled into their seatbelts since Tom was behind the wheel.

It had been a good idea to come out like this, Cindy reflected as they returned to Bradbury. A good, bright day for a new beginning.

The children had laughed a lot, eaten ice creams and hot dogs, all the things that were bad for them, all the things that helped make such places full of joy. They had watched the shows and got drenched on all the water-rides. Poor Sarah had looked like a little water rat after the log flume.

Their parents had left the children alone three times during the day, and at first Cindy had been concerned – while they had run off to the nearest arcade, from which sounds of alien destruction, cars racing and virtual-reality robots doing battle emanated – their pockets jingling with change, not sharing her worry.

But then Tom had assured her that the man who was killing families seemed to be operating only in their part of Cheshire; and anyway, he was not looking for children alone.

'How do you know that?' she'd asked anxiously as they queued for the Nemesis. The other two rides the children had missed were the Corkscrew and the Thunderloop; Tom had deemed them all too frightening. Richard had moaned a little, looking for adventure as always, but Sarah had seemed positively happy that she didn't have to go on the rides.

Cindy was glad that she and Tom had the chance for a few minutes alone now and then.

She laughed quietly as she thought about the day. Tom had been afraid to go on the high swings, a fact which Richard and Sarah – with a little encouragement from herself – had teased him about endlessly. She looked at their cute faces in the back; at least until they had fallen into their deep, pleasantly quiet sleep.

'You have to understand something,' Tom had explained as they moved forward a few paces and saw a bright sign which read: TEN MINUTES FROM THIS POINT. The Nemesis had been great fun, preceded by morbid conversation. 'The man who is killing these people – he's selecting them. He knows who they are, what they do, where they work. All about them. Every detail that counts. They're chosen. Unless you're single, you could be next.'

'At least Jo's safe then,' Cindy responded. 'How can you know all this?'

'I'm not sure. There was something in one of those books I've been reading – something about *stalkers*. They like to torture people; both physically and emotionally. That's what they do. It thrills them to try to make contact with the people they intend to kill. Do you understand what I'm saying?'

'How do you know this guy is one of these stalkers?' she asked.

A mother in front turned her head, disgusted by their conversation, and shuffled her young son forward, out of earshot.

'He tortured the Napiers' Labrador a couple of weeks before their deaths. The poor animal had to be put to sleep. The Cusacks' two cats went missing six days before their deaths. Do you see what I'm getting at?' he asked.

'He kills pets first. We don't have any animals. What's your point?' she insisted.

'You don't see it. We have to be careful, Cindy. *We must be careful*. If we make any new friends, until this is over, we have to watch them closely.'

'That's insane.'

'He – or she – could be anybody, Cindy. And he or she could be watching anybody. Even now. I don't think it's going to end until somebody stops him or her. I've got a terrible feeling about this killer.'

Cindy tried not to laugh. Perhaps some of what Tom said had a certain logic to it, but he sounded so melodramatic.

'You should tell the police about your *terrible feeling*. It might help them. But then again, maybe it was just something you ate,' she said playfully.

The conversation had been the only dark point during the whole day, and after it she had at least been certain that nothing would happen to Richard and Sarah while they were together in the arcades. At last not at the hands of the Initial Killer.

But there were a lot of bad people in the world, and a part of her still worried silently as . . .

. . . *they were clinging to each other, wind catching their hair; rushing through his short cut and blowing her long locks back, tangling them as she screamed. Their car rocketed by people standing in line as they sweated spent adrenaline. Is this how he feels when he kills? Tom thought, his heart hammering* . . .

Alton Towers was a playground for the young and young at heart – there was even a sprawling garden for those who felt their age and needed a rest from the breakneck pace. They had wandered there and Tom had gripped Cindy's hand lightly, told her everything was going to be all right as the children ran ahead, kinetic energy hitting overload.

It was a good day to start over, Cindy thought now as they arrived home. She smiled and kissed Tom's cheek before waking the children. A good day.

7

It was the first day Joel learned anything about the family, and
the Coco woman's life, apart from what was obviously a jealous,
secret lover. After reading what had been scratched into the side
of the car, he was certain that she had ended the affair.

After leaving the driveway last night he'd waited a few
minutes to see if the husband would come out again. He never
meant to fall asleep in his car, and when he woke bleary-eyed the
next morning it was nearly nine. As far as he knew, there had
been no more activity from within the house.

He looked over his shoulder after rubbing sleep from his eyes.
Their Ford was still in the driveway.

He sighed and his heart dropped. The primary school was a
good fifteen-minute drive away, so if she had young children she
would be currently taking them in. The couple must be childless.
He was disappointed, because until now everything had seemed
so right.

He decided to go home and shower before opening *Pages* for
the day. Customers had been complaining about the erratic
hours of business. If he wasn't careful, he'd wind up broke. He
inserted the ignition key and was twisting it when the front door
opened.

They ran into the garden like a light into the darkness of his
mind. Two children. A giggling girl of about eleven, and a
younger boy who was shouting something, sending his sister
into a fresh bout of hysterical laughter. How beautiful you both
are, he thought, dazzled. And how perfect the family suddenly
was.

The mother came out next, the woman who had first caught
his attention and brought him to this delightful place. She was
wearing a white summer dress and sunglasses. He smiled. She
looked even better than he remembered.

He watched as she wandered over to her rosebushes, inspected them for a second and then motioned for the children to join her. She pointed accusingly, and the pair seemed to protest before running back to the car. Joel smiled, aware of the blooms on the seat behind him. She thought the children had damaged her sacred roses.

The father came out last, and because the rest of the situation was so perfect, Joel's disappointment was only mild. In the night the man had looked big, his shadow figure strong and well built. Joel had even been slightly afraid of being discovered.

But now, in broad daylight, he could see that the man was tall, perhaps a tad under six foot, and slight. He had a natural build, and didn't bulge with muscles like his wife's over-developed lover. He wore round wire-rim glasses.

The husband moved gracefully, turning quickly to lock the door and then jogging over to the garage. In jeans, T-shirt and running shoes he looked casual, yet handsome. He was young, and a good match for the mother.

'Come on, kids. Mum's taking a break from driving and I'm at the wheel,' Tom told them, and they climbed into his car, the children apprehensive because of the seat-belts.

Joel smiled, all his doubts forgotten.

The bad memories began to haunt him again.

Standing beside the body of the clothed woman, rain pouring into his face as he looks into the sky, clouds thundering overhead in a strong wind . . . it's a nasty one, somebody says. The field is slick with mud. He bends over the corpse . . .

A long time ago, he used his skills and knowledge to help the police. Later on, he used them to evade the forces of goodness, and to help camouflage his bad deeds.

Rigor mortis – or rigidity – is first detectable in the face and fingers about an hour after death. It then extends to the whole body in four to six hours, depending on the temperature. The body remains in this state until the muscle tissue begins to decompose. Rigor gives a very approximate measure to the time of death.

She has been dead less than six hours, her body either left here or dumped, the heinous crime taking place elsewhere. He informs the police of this and continues to work on the body, rain slashing into his face, a chill wind biting his red-raw cheeks. How did you come to be here? he thinks.

That last thought was the rigor mortis of his mind. Soon afterwards, the decomposition of his thought processes began to set in . . . the rot. He became attracted to the bodies that were deposited on his morgue slabs, and fascinated by what type of tool formed which type of wound, how a person could end up in such a bad way.

That sweet, morbid enchantment, coupled with the bad headaches . . . Somewhere behind a bright, blinding door of white light in his head was the answer to why he hated these perfect families so much, why he was driven to kill them.

He dared not open the door. The demons of his mind were evil and malicious, and even he was frightened of what he kept imprisoned within the sealed room.

He was learning now, their car reversing slowly out of the driveway, learning as he had back then . . .

He checks under her nails for vital clues, isn't disappointed when he finds fibres, traces of dry blood. It is possible she has scratched her killer and they will identify him from the blood. He then looks for signs of hypostasis – livid discoloration of the flesh caused by blood draining under gravity to the lowers parts of the body once circulation has stopped. Somebody tells him the police have already picked up a suspect. They are going to solve this one, he thinks . . . and wonders if he could succeed where so many others fail . . .

The family slowly accelerated away and he obeyed the primal, bad instinct in his mind to follow. He had to watch and study them. These next days would be valuable lessons in the life of the perfect family – who their friends were, how often they went out together or just the parents, leaving their children in the care of a babysitter. A stranger in their home. He had to know about all their hobbies and habits. Their joys. Their strengths and weaknesses.

His knowledge of the mother's affair was his first weapon.

Slow down, Joel thought as he approached the junction of the main road. The last thing he wanted was for some nosy neighbour to report his licence plate to the police for speeding through the suburb.

He drove casually, stayed calm, tapping on the wheel in tune with a song on the radio. *Everybody Have Fun Tonight*, by a group called Wang Chung. He laughed quietly. The song seemed so well suited to certain nights in his life – another of which was on the agenda. He might adopt the song as his very own personal theme. His anthem.

He would tell the father about the affair his wife had been having and turn the couple against each other, make them hate each other. Suddenly the light from the door in his mind flared a dazzling white and his head throbbed ... *they hated each other* ... and he held his brow with one hand for a second until the pain ceased ... *even as their deaths were imminent, as sure as the rising sun, they would loathe each other.*

So this is why the children are not in school, he thought later that morning.

The parents had let them have a day off so that they could enjoy all the fun of Alton Towers. It would be a day of joy for them all, and a day of surveillance for himself. As if he were the one in school, while they were playing truant.

When he joined them in the entrance queue he watched the children playing tag, chasing each other around the spacious car park. Once more he caught her scent. The fragrance was Coco again, the same perfume the Napier woman had preferred to wear, and at once he was lost in the brief memory it generated.

An ornate dressing-table in a spacious bedroom, adorned with various make-ups, perfume – Coco – and jewellery. He lifts the Coco bottle and pours the golden liquid over his surgically gloved hand. It dribbles down his arm and on to the carpet as he walks over to the unconscious, naked mother. He slowly moves his finger across her breasts, surprisingly gently considering her battered state.

She stirs groggily.

'You have to smell nice,' he says fussily.

He smears his hand over her breasts. Her eyes are wide with terror.

'You have to smell beautiful,' he tells her.

'No ...' she whispers and tries to struggle away. She pulls hard, but can't move. The handcuffs hold her in place.

'You have to smell nice!' he screams, losing control.

He goes back for the bottle of Coco and smashes it into her face, leaving shards of glass piercing her skin. Lethal splinters.

Joel looked up. The perfect family were walking away from him. The father placed one arm around his son's shoulders, and locked hands with his wife.

The best times were when they left the children alone.

Each time the parents went to stand in line for one of the scarier rides, the father would pass them a handful of coins or a note. Joel lingered, eavesdropping in the background as they promised to return in no longer than fifteen minutes, and then ran to the nearest arcades.

Joel would follow slowly, keeping them in view, eating ice cream, letting it melt slowly in his mouth, savouring the taste as he savoured their proximity.

He played games in the dark rooms, listening to the electronic sounds, always losing as he concentrated on the children. Sarah was better on the loud machines, but Richard enjoyed the basketball hoops and the remote-control cars and boats.

In the Haunted House ride – while their parents waited outside – he managed to get into the same car as them, seated behind. He had waited patiently, letting his courage build up, and then, as bright ghosts raced overhead out of the pitch blackness, he whispered, 'Duck!'

For a moment his heart beat faster with nervous energy as he spoke the single word. Blood raced and perspiration seeped through the pores of his skin. After that, it was easy.

'Watch out!' he called.

'Are you scared?' he asked them, disappointed that he did not elicit a response.

Adrenaline had rushed through his body, breaking floodgates down, and he knew that if he was sat next to them they would both be clamouring to hold his hand, to distil their fear with his protective adult presence.

After the ride he waited for a moment, let them run ahead to find their mother and father who were waiting patiently.

Joel melted into the crowds and watched Richard look back, searching for their guardian from the ride.

Joel had smiled and laughed.

The boy could not see him, even though his eyes contained a thirsty hunger for them all.

8

One of the teachers at the children's primary school was a large, brooding man named Geoff Pritchard. When Jo walked into his home – only a few doors down from Cindy and Tom – she was surprised to see that his wife, Mary, was an equally strong-looking woman.

Mary shared a lot of similar opinions towards men as Jo, and Geoff had been trying to get the two women together for months, but the other teacher had always been reluctant to accept his invitation. Pritchard always seemed to be goofing around with the two other young male teachers, and until this evening Jo had pigeon-holed him in the same category as Cindy's lover Alan – a well-meaning moron who loved a good game of football as much as the woman in his life.

Geoff Pritchard had no hope of getting Jo to join in a conversation, never mind go to his home for dinner. But then the headmaster had partnered them to organise a charity event with the PTA, and Geoff had used this as an excuse to get Jo and Mary together.

Jo had imagined that Mrs Pritchard would be mousy and timid, obedient to Geoff's every command. She was wrong, and glad that she had allowed herself to be cajoled into the evening.

Nothing better to do, had been her attitude; and anyway, one night in the company of Pritchard discussing ideas for the charity event and in the presence of his wife, would be better than several isolated occasions after school hours.

Earlier in the week she'd contemplated asking the owner of the bookstore out, but – untypically – had lost her bravado at the last second. Outside the door of his shop she'd found herself with butterflies in her stomach and jitters in her hand as it trembled on the door handle. *Get a grip, girl*, she told herself fiercely.

Cindy had phoned earlier this morning, and told her that she thought the bookshop guy looked weird and too old for her. Cindy had also confided that she'd finished with Alan, before cancelling plans to go and see a movie with Jo. Her friend could guess what she would be doing with Tom instead. She was glad that Cindy was getting her life on the homefront sorted out – although it was a shame about Tom. Jo wouldn't have minded a shot at him herself if Cindy had decided to end her marriage – strictly in the spirit of *use 'em and abuse 'em*. Jo had Tom filed under Intellectually Handsome; not good Hunk value, but not ugly either.

Now Geoff Pritchard began to clear the table as she and Mary went into the living room. Mary was an attractive, strong-willed woman. Jo believed the foundations of a good friendship had been formed over the dinner-table.

'You've got him trained well,' Jo giggled as they sat down. 'I think I've had too much wine.'

'Nonsense,' Mary told her, but still mouthed the word *coffee* to Geoff as he returned for the last of the dishes. 'You can never drink enough good wine. Did Geoff tell you he prepared tonight's meal?'

'He cooks too?' Jo gasped – definitely had several glasses too many, she thought – and Mary laughed politely.

Geoff was obviously St Domesticus, Jo thought, and realised she had misjudged him badly. She would apologise to him tomorrow for her standoffish attitude in school.

Geoff walked in bearing a tray with cups of coffee, cream or milk and sugar or sweeteners – and a variety of biscuits arranged upon a plate.

'You're a lifesaver,' Jo told him as he handed her a cup.

Geoff joined them and when Jo glanced at her watch over an hour later it was creeping towards eleven.

'This has been great,' she told them, 'but I really should get going.'

At the door Mary insisted that Jo call her some time. 'It makes a change having a woman in here, instead of sweaty men playing poker or talking and watching sports. I enjoyed our conversation.'

'Me, too,' Jo said, and tripped on the step. She was still a little tipsy.

'Are you sure you don't want a taxi, or a lift home?' Geoff enquired. 'You don't look fit to drive.'

'I'll be OK,' Jo told them, fumbling with her keys and dropping them. When she picked them up her hair fell in front of her face. She shook her head violently and then brushed the long locks back with her hand. 'I'm not drunk. Just a wild feminist looking for a guy to beat up. I'm going to have a headache tomorrow, aren't I?'

Geoff and Mary nodded, both smiling sympathethically.

'Whoops,' Jo whispered, and waved as she walked off down the street.

As Jo hurried towards her car she noticed that Cindy's Ford was in their driveway, but now Tom's Volvo was keeping it company. As a courtesy since she was in the neighbourhood and their lights were still on, she decided to pay them a visit.

She was grateful that Cindy answered when she knocked on the door because she wanted to get the lowdown on why her friend had dumped Alan.

'Because I love Tom,' she told Jo honestly.

'Who is it?' the man she loved called from their living room.

'Your favourite feminist,' Cindy called back.

'Yeah!' Jo shouted. 'So you'd better stay back because we are talking about one seriously drunk woman here!'

'Hi, Jo,' Tom replied.

'That's all?' Jo hissed, even though she knew Tom wouldn't be listening to their conversation. He was too much of a gentleman for that. 'No fetishes that turned you off? Nothing juicy?'

'The only juices involved are Tom's,' Cindy smiled sexily, 'which I intend to taste as soon as you have gone.'

Jo gasped. 'That's a not-very subtle hint for me to exit stage left. Are the kids OK? I noticed they weren't in school today.'

Tom appeared in the vestibule. All he had on was a pair of Goofy and Pluto shorts and an erection that made them tent.

'Oh,' Jo said, dumbfounded. 'Hi, Tom.'

'Hello, Jo. The kids are fine and I'm sorry but I think I'm going to steal my wife away from you now. We have to make love.'

'No problem,' Jo said, and looked at Cindy as Tom wrapped his arms about her and began to unbutton her blouse. 'I'll phone you soon.'

On her way down the path, Jo spotted a car pull up in front of her friend's house, the exhaust plume blue in the night. At first she thought Cindy and Tom were going to be interrupted by another late visitor, but then the engine cut off and nobody

79

emerged from the car. The vehicle was still in the night.

As Jo walked by, heading for her own car, she glanced into the window.

She was surprised to see the man from the bookstore behind the wheel, unwrapping a bag of chips in his lap. He looked up and smiled. She returned the gesture nervously and went on her way.

Joel watched the woman walk away, her heels high, her skirt short, revealing long legs. He had seen her teetering down the driveway when he'd drawn up and had quickly pondered whether he wanted to be seen by her or not. He decided it was all in the hand Fate was dealing him, so he left it to chance.

It was a nice coincidence that she knew the family. As best he could see, they didn't have any pets; no cats or dogs, nothing worth killing. Nothing they would truly miss . . . but they had this friend, a woman who must be close to them to be calling this late.

A woman he could also get close to.

His head began to ache slightly and he saw the door in his mind burning bright. He knew the intrusion on his concentration meant that his mother and father were watching and listening again.

'She's nice,' his father said sibilantly. 'Very pretty.'

'Now don't you go touching her,' his mother chastised. 'I like my rosebushes the way they are. I don't want another body planted amongst them.'

'Relax,' Joel told them both calmly.

He looked mournful as he finished his chips. Even though they were all cheerful and in love, his mother would never be happy. She would always moan and complain about something, anything and everything. It used to drive his father insane until he . . .

. . . *the door was slowly swinging open, the bright light dissipating, no longer blinding him so that he could see the horror within* . . .

Joel closed his eyes to the pain, and the headache began to fade, the door to shut once more. He had forbidden himself to ever open that door and look inside. Because of the pain and the headaches he associated with it, he sensed that something nasty was waiting within.

Something unspeakably bad.

9

The next day Tom and Cindy spoke to the police twice.

On his way out to work in the morning, Tom noticed the writing on the side of the Ford when his own car refused to start. The sunlight gleamed sharply off the scratches:

FUCK YOU BITCH

The words seemed to be directed at Cindy. He decided to catch a later train and went back inside. He told her about the marks and called the police, remembering the night he had thrown leftovers to the neighbour's dog. He had felt certain then that somebody was watching him; the hair on the nape of his neck had been prickling.

Cindy went upstairs to dress when Tom told her that a constable would be calling by in about twenty minutes. As she pulled jeans on she cursed Alan, and prayed he would not cause any trouble between her and Tom.

Sarah and Richard thought it was great that yesterday they'd had an extra day off, and this morning their dad had told them they would be going in late. Tom didn't know whether the police would mind him using the vehicle before they arrived, or whether they would want to inspect it closely.

A police car pulled up outside nearly an hour later.

Sarah looked out of the window, and feigned horror. 'They've come for you,' she told Richard. 'The Parent Police are here for you.'

'What? Who?' Richard asked, gullible and as susceptible to her pranks as ever.

'I heard Mum and Dad talking about you. They asked me to make you disappear but it didn't work, so they must have called the Parent Police.'

Richard looked outside. The policeman was approaching the door. He ducked down, worry on his face. Sarah went in for the kill. 'He's going to take you away and lock you up until you're an adult.'

There was a knock on the front door and Sarah ran to answer it. She was facing the policeman's waistline when she opened the door. Either he was very tall, or she had a way to grow yet.

'Good morning. I'm— Oh,' the officer said, surprised. 'Hello down there. Are your—?'

'Yes, he's through there,' Sarah said, and pointed to Richard who was attempting to creep from the living room. 'You can have him for ever.'

Richard ran straight to the bottom of the stairs. He stopped on the first step and looked back at the policeman who was staring at him with deliberate intent.

All his life the uniform the man was wearing had been a sign of safety and assurance. The men and women who wore those clothes were supposed to help. His mother had even told him to go to one of these people if he was ever lost, or to ask any adult for directions to the nearest police station.

Those commands were right up there with some of the biggies. *Don't talk to strangers.* (If he couldn't talk to strangers, how could he get directions to the nearest police station?) *Don't get into a car or accept sweets or gifts of any kind from a stranger. Don't pick your nose at the dinner table, and definitely* don't *eat what comes out . . .*

But now Richard knew the truth.

'You're not taking me!' he screamed at the officer of the Parent Police. 'I'm not going anywhere!'

Tom came down the stairs as Richard raced up them, his face stricken by panic. He saw Sarah collapse into a fit of giggles.

'You playing jokes again?' Tom asked her as he reached the vestibule.

Sarah nodded guiltily. Terrorising her younger brother was her second favourite hobby, after magic.

'Go and tidy up the breakfast things,' Tom told her wearily, and he looked at the uniformed police officer as she ran into the kitchen. 'Sorry. You know how children can be.'

'Yes,' the officer nodded, but it was obvious from his expression that he didn't have a clue. 'I'm PC Collins. I'm calling to check on the vandalism reported to your car.'

'Tom Curtis,' he introduced himself and shook the man's hand.

82

'I'm sure you saw the car when you came up the drive.'

They walked out to the Ford, and Tom guided him around the back of it. He pointed above the back wheel. It made Tom seethe that somebody could write something so malicious and hurtful towards his wife.

'Rather nasty piece of work, isn't it?' Collins said, bending closer to inspect it, and noticing the long scratch that ran the length of the car. 'Almost personal.'

Collins looked up to the window where Tom's wife was leaning out and watching them. She was an attractive woman.

Tom nodded. 'You want to come in for a coffee?'

'No thanks, I'm a tea man myself. Besides, I'll have to get back to the station. We've had several reports of drunken teenagers in this area over the past few weeks. Perhaps they're responsible. Or a couple of graffiti artists who are working the suburbs, spraying cars.'

'Maybe they ran out of paint,' Tom joked, but the constable didn't smile. 'You don't think it could be the guy killing families, do you?'

The policeman seemed to almost sigh with exasperation, as if everybody with the smallest complaint asked the same question.

'No, Mr Curtis. Just kids having fun, although it does seem strange that the comment is directed at your wife.'

Tom looked into the police constable's eyes and could sense what Collins was thinking. *Almost personal . . .* My wife isn't like that, Tom thought. Cindy doesn't sleep around. But he could tell from Collins' expression that the constable had made his mind up and come to his own conclusions.

'I'll file a report,' Collins said, and began to walk down the driveway, 'and we'll look out for the culprits. But I wouldn't expect too much, Mr Curtis.'

'Well, thanks,' Tom whispered sarcastically, out of earshot, as Collins climbed into his car. 'With you working the case I won't expect anything.'

Cindy watched their exchange from the bedroom window. She guessed what was being said, after the constable had leered at her. When she saw Tom's disillusioned expression as the police-man walked away she knew that nothing had been accomplished.

She smiled and waved at Tom as he came up the drive, and then turned back into the room.

It was probably for the best that the police weren't going to find anything. She didn't want them somehow tracing the marks back to her former lover.

She had no intention of telling Tom about Alan. It was a bad time in their marriage that they had managed to overcome, and all she wanted to do was put it all behind her.

Damn you, Alan. You'd better not make any more trouble.

10

Their second visit from the police came after the sun had set and the moon was claiming the land.

At first when the man at the door identified himself as a police officer, Tom thought they must have some news about the car, that the police had perhaps even caught the person or people responsible. But it turned out that the purpose of this second visit had a far graver basis.

'Yes?' Tom said when he opened the door to the stranger. He was a big man, slightly overweight, with a strained expression on his face, and when Tom learned who he was he decided the permanent frown had to come from the stress of his work. The man looked worn out, ready to fall asleep on his feet.

'I'm Detective Inspector Ian Knox,' the man said, automatically removing his wallet and showing identification.

You have it all to look forward to, Constable Collins, Tom thought gleefully.

'That was quick. Constable Collins wasn't very hopeful,' Tom told the detective. *Or helpful.* 'Would you—?'

'I'm not here about the car, Mr Curtis,' Knox said shortly. 'I'm here to see Cindy.'

That was the first clue Tom had that something bad had happened; that somehow Ian Knox knew his wife. He had called her Cindy and not Mrs Curtis.

'Come through,' Tom said, and stood aside. He closed the door and was about to show Knox through to living room when he saw that the police officer had already walked in. He wondered if the cop was gifted with some kind of sixth sense of direction.

Cindy was watching television with Sarah and Richard.

'Good evening, Cindy, I'm—'

Cindy turned at the voice and finished the sentence when she saw who had come to visit them. 'Detective Ian Knox!' she blurted out, her face beaming as she stood to hug him.

85

Tom saw that her hands were strong and tight on his back. Cindy was obviously close to the police officer.

'Detective *Inspector* now,' he corrected her, as they separated.

Richard looked back from the television at this line, and then to Sarah. 'Is it—?'

Sarah nodded confirmation.

'Go and play upstairs for a while,' Tom told the children.

'All right, Dad,' Richard said hastily, already on his feet. As he passed the Parent Police he formed his fingers into a protective cross. 'You're not taking me anywhere.'

Sarah giggled after him.

'You have children now, I see?' Knox observed, looking quizzically at Richard.

'Yes,' Cindy nodded, beaming proudly. 'Who would have believed it all those years ago?'

'Some people actually think those two are alien beings in disguise as human siblings,' Tom joked. 'I personally believe the nurse dropped them on their heads when they were born.'

'This is Tom Curtis, my husband,' Cindy told Knox, and the two men exchanged a strong handshake.

She looked at Knox and, despite her struggle against it, found herself remembering images from the past.

It had been years since she had last seen Ian Knox. He'd led the investigation to apprehend Katie's killer. Knox had been determined to catch the man, and she had learned from another officer at the time that his wife had once been . . . the victim of a similar attack to the one suffered by Cindy. She fought back tears and images that she had not dared look at since Katie's death. Knox had wanted the man badly, and for a few months he and Cindy had become close friends.

Knox seemed much older now. There were more years and experiences carved into his stone face than had actually passed. His hair was flecked with grey; it looked unkempt. His eyes were wrinkled and tired. Lifeless, Cindy thought. His moustache was gone, but he hadn't bothered to shave in a few days. His stubble was grey. Nor was he as lean as she remembered him being; his muscle had turned to flab.

Detective Inspector Knox looked a lot older than he should have done.

Knox sat down and Tom turned the television off, before leaving the room and coming back with three cups of coffee and a variety of biscuits.

'How are your children?' Cindy asked when they were all sitting down, steaming cups in their hands.

'Bob and Henry are fine. Bob's at John Moores University in Liverpool and Henry has a kid of his own now, little critter called Carlisle.'

'That makes you a grandad!' Cindy laughed jubilantly.

'I hate that word,' Knox smiled. 'It makes me feel so old. Henry is the most irresponsible parent I know.'

'And Lucy?' Cindy asked.

There was a short pause. Knox finished a biscuit before answering. Tom expected something bad.

'Lucy is dead, Cindy,' Knox said and swallowed deeply. Those words never got any easier to say. The pain never eased. 'She died of breast cancer a couple of years ago.'

Cindy's hand reached to her mouth, and then gripped Ian's arm gently. 'No,' she gasped. 'God, I'm so sorry, Ian.'

'She fought long and hard. I took . . .' Ian paused as tears welled in his eyes. The pain would last for ever. His love for her would never die. 'I took some time off to care for her, but she gave up in the end. All I want now is a reunion with her . . . to be at her side once more.'

'Oh Ian, I'm so sorry,' Cindy cried, and Tom held her as the policeman waved his hand.

'Come on, Cindy. I didn't come here to upset you. Besides, you know Lucy wouldn't want you to be like this.'

Cindy sniffed and tried to wipe the tears away. They continued to leak out silently.

'Then why did you come here?' Tom asked. He knew there was a reason, and braced himself to hear it.

Knox took hold of Cindy's hand. 'Do you remember those poison letters you've been sending Michael Brennan?'

Cindy nodded firmly, prepared to face the repercussions of her actions. She thought that the police would have said something about them before now if they were going to bother. Tom looked confused, but could immediately guess what kind of letters Knox meant.

'I thought they would get me into trouble a long time ago,' Cindy said.

'I know the warden at the prison,' Knox told her. 'When the first one arrived I instructed him to let it go through. I remembered how Lucy was, after she had been . . . assaulted.' Cindy nodded, grateful that he had deliberately not used the bad word.

'I guessed you were just trying to work some feelings and emotions out of your system.'

'I sent more than one letter, Ian,' Cindy confessed to him.

'I know how many you sent, Cindy,' Knox told her. 'Michael Brennan killed himself last night.'

11

The next two weeks were the best Cindy could remember in her whole life.

It was like falling in love all over again. Tom would return home from work bringing gifts and flowers. They planned a weekend away, just the two of them, in the Lake District before the heavy rain and winds of autumn arrived. Cindy was sure Jo wouldn't mind looking after Sarah and Richard for a few days. She had good maternal instincts, even though she would never admit it.

Cindy, I wasn't put on this planet to breed.

Tom surprised her twice, beautiful surprises, coming home early in the afternoon so that they could be together, make love freely, without the fear of childish interruption. They indulged each other in pleasures of the flesh like never before.

She hadn't seen Alan, never intended to see him again. She wondered how she could have been so foolish as to risk losing the only man who had ever loved her; a man she loved dearly in return.

Cindy thought about how close they had come to destroying their marriage, wrecking all they had. Did Tom realise it too? He must have had some kind of intuition, she thought. He knew that his drinking was not the only problem their relationship had suffered. Gracefully – if he did suspect anything – Tom never brought the subject up, and she was thankful that he never put her on the spot, under pressure.

They had the car resprayed – red, at the behest of the children. Cindy wanted a new one, now that *Little Researchers* was climbing back on to its feet, but they decided to wait a year.

She resolved never to tell Tom about Alan, and she hoped fervently that he would not hear it from anybody else.

Are you listening, Alan?

She had been nervous on the Wednesday, had imagined him

89

eagerly awaiting her arrival and remembered his anger the one time she had been late. How would he feel when she didn't arrive at all?

All through the morning and into the afternoon she had worked about the house, a bundle of nervous tension, waiting for his arrival. He never came, and into the evening she prayed he would not turn up at their home, knocking hard at the door, his angry jealousy for a woman he would never have again hitting boiling point.

Thankfully, he never showed.

They invited Ian Knox over to dinner twice, and it was obvious they were going to become close friends. He and Tom got along famously, finding a passion for old science-fiction and horror movies in common. *Quatermass* was a shared favourite, although Tom had a preference for the American classics of the forties and fifties.

If she gave them half a chance, the men would talk all night about invasions by body-snatchers, visitors from Mars and fictional planets, and 'things' from other worlds.

The second time over Ian had drunk a little too much beer. He left with a loud cry of, 'Watch the skies!'

Tom laughed good-heartedly, although the joke was lost on Cindy.

Ian told them he intended to retire in a year or so. He had some money saved up and he wanted to get away from England for a while.

Take a photograph of Lucy and lose myself in the world.

Ian seemed very sad and slow to smile.

After her reunion with Ian Knox Cindy had cried long and hard into the night for the death of Lucy. She wondered if there were any tears amongst them for Mike Brennan. He had killed Katie, but had always maintained that it was in self-defence, that her death had been an accident.

Cindy had blocked out the night it had happened so well that merely thinking of Brennan did not bring forth any memories, except mournful feelings for her sister and raw hatred for the dead man. If she wanted moving pictures, she would have to concentrate hard . . . but she did not.

Had she been responsible for Brennan's suicide?

A part of her was glad that he was gone. But the humanity of her soul was sickened and horrified by the letters an animal deep within her had written, encouraging him to take his own life.

She felt no salvation or joy. She was not happy that he was dead.

She had caused the loss of life, killed him as he had killed Katie.

She didn't know if she could carry that on her conscience, with her until she died, part of her heart and soul guilty. She felt remorse and wished for all the letters back.

She hoped that in time her mind would work out all her confused feelings.

A week later Cindy found herself in the unlikely situation of placing a wreath of flowers on the gravestone of her sister's killer.

'I'm sorry,' she whispered. 'I really am.'

Katie was still gone. The death of Mike Brennan had not brought her back.

Tom was too much in love with Cindy to even begin to suspect her of infidelity. He closed his eyes to the possibility that there might have been a time when she didn't love him.

But he wasn't stupid, and knew that he had been travelling a rocky road of depression and drunkenness which would only spiral down into a dead halt in the ground.

He had been lucky not to lose her.

The morning Tom poured all the bottles and cans away, the sun burning bright, rekindling hope in their marriage, they had made love as though it was their first time together. First with unbridled passion, and then carefully touching each other, slowly and softly.

He sensed Cindy had been having doubts about their life together, but in that moment they had both cast their worries aside and welcomed each other back. They had found a fresh hunger for each other, almost a greed.

In their newfound bliss, neither of them noticed the man who regularly watched and followed them.

If Cindy had spotted him she might have recognised him as the owner of the bookstore, the man whom Jo liked. And if they looked very closely, they might have seen him talking to himself... *like Dr Sam Beckett*, Sarah would have said, *from* Quantum Leap.

But nobody ever noticed him

And he continued to watch unobtrusively.

12

The first time they went out together they saw the latest Harrison Ford movie. It was the same night that Detective Inspector Ian Knox went to the Curtis household for dinner.

He paid for the tickets and bought sweets and popcorn, ice cream and drinks.

'You trying to fatten me up like a chicken?' she joked.

'No. I thought you might like it,' he stammered nervously.

'I do,' she told him.

Halfway through the movie their fingers touched and before the end they were holding hands softly. When they left the cinema their grip was tight and sure, with the unbreakable confidence of two people who have found each other.

Later, in the park, as she fretted about being mugged, they danced under the moonlight. She thought it was unbelievably corny, yet so romantic, as they were captured by the music of the night. Under a canopy of stars she kissed him for the first time.

Then he drove her home. She asked him in for coffee but he refused, saying he would phone her the next day.

He did.

That first date had come about when Jo had finally plucked up her courage, walked into the bookstore and asked him out. It was that simple. He had said yes.

Three days after the movie they had gone out for a meal at The Bradbury Lodge. He had shown her the delights of a duck dish which was exclusive to the pub, and she loved every morsel of it.

It was early days, but Jo believed she was falling in love with Joel. He was so pleasant and charming, and his affable exterior created the ideal foil for her flirtatious behaviour.

He was a perfect gentleman, treating her like a lady and not the fuck machine she knew she could be. She longed to sleep with him.

That night she drove him home. He asked her in. She accepted.

Downstairs they played strip Monopoly, laughing and joking. It was titillating, and they teased each other with their hands, each removing the clothes of the other when they landed on the opposition's property.

As he unhooked her bra she reached down towards his shorts. He pulled away suddenly.

'Let's wait until next time,' he whispered.

She asked him to come back to her place, hoping . . . But he kissed her at the door, biting the bottom of her earlobe softly.

'Next time,' he murmured.

'Next time we're going to screw all night long,' she promised.

Eleven days later, they went on their final date. It was important for Joel to be driving because he wanted to be in control the whole evening. He stopped by her home just before seven on a Tuesday.

They went to The Bradbury Lodge and once more Jo devoured the unique duck dish. Unlike their first visit here, the pub was not busy and there had been no need to make reservations. There would be no record of their visit. It made him happy that she so obviously enjoyed the meal. It was to be her last.

Joel had not intended to kill her so soon. The next day he would invade the Curtises' home, and that too was going to happen quicker than he would have liked. But the door in his mind was opening, although he dared not look inside yet, and his headaches were becoming worse and more frequent.

Over dinner Jo started to ask questions about why he had been outside her friend's home the night she'd eaten at Geoff Pritchard's. She sounded almost suspicious of him, and he decided she had to die.

Besides, as she could not wait to be with him, he could no longer suppress the desire to be enveloped by her dead flesh, feel her dead caress.

'I wasn't watching them, I was watching you,' Joel said quickly, trying to charm his way out of the situation. She was sceptical at his answer, not entirely convinced. He let a twinkle slip into his eyes and took her hand in his. 'Come on. Let's get out of here.'

They reached his house twenty minutes later, and once she was inside he knew everything was going to be OK. He secretly locked the doors of the house after showing her into the living room, and deposited the keys in a drawer.

He listened to his mother and father above the din of the television in their room, and then realised that they were beaming their voices to him on the psychic waves because they didn't want Jo to hear.

'He's brought her,' he heard his mother whisper eagerly, waking his drowsing father.

'What? She's here?' he queried. 'But . . . Oh dear. I look such a mess.'

Joel returned to the living room. Jo had undressed, and was standing naked in the centre of the room.

'Did you say something?' she asked.

Joel shook his head slowly and then walked across the room.

'Come to me,' she whispered, and held out her hand, closed her eyes. Waited for him to touch her.

Joel didn't even see her. He tugged her roughly across the room.

'What?' she gasped, as she staggered in his tight hold, her eyes springing open.

'Come on. You have to meet my parents,' he explained, and was already dragging her up the stairs.

'Hey,' she giggled. 'I know I wished for you to do something spontaneous, but . . . are you out of your mind?' This had to be some kind of sick joke. He was just taking her up to his room, that was all.

'He's bringing her up,' Joel's mother observed.

'What did you just say?' Jo asked, and stubbed her toe on the final step. 'Ouch – that hurt. This isn't funny! Let go of my hand.'

She tried to grab at the banister, but her hand flailed in the air. They were at the top of the stairs and moving swiftly down a hallway. She had wanted her voice to sound strong and authoritative as it normally was. Unfortunately her tone betrayed her for the first time in her life. I'm not afraid, she told herself. I am not afraid. *You should be*, another part of her mind whispered, and she shuddered in his cold grip.

'I want to get dressed.' Better, she thought, as they stopped before a door. Just tell him what's going to happen – take charge of the situation and show him who is in control.

'Don't be such a prude. They're half-blind anyway,' Joel told her.

They were half-blind? He was fucking blind. He hadn't even checked out her body once. She could be wearing a straitjacket or a suit of armour and he still wouldn't have noticed.

95

Suddenly Jo was very frightened. Nobody knew she was here, or who she had been dating. Not even Cindy, who was only aware that she had been attracted to the bookstore owner.

She was alone.

She tried to pull free of his hand, but his grip was vice-tight. Her stomach curled into a knot. She had to get out of here.

'This had better be a joke!' she said angrily, her voice trembling.

Joel opened the door and pushed her into the darkness beyond.

The first thing Jo was aware of was the stench – the over-whelming scent of air-freshener, and some other, more fetid odour. It took a few seconds for her eyes to adjust, but she quickly saw that there was nobody in the room. A television was playing quietly to itself, but the images depicted on the screen were a night-time scene and didn't help her vision.

Joel came into the room behind her and shut the door. He was sorting through a drawer for something. She couldn't see what he was doing, but then she caught a glimpse of a handkerchief as he stuffed it into his pocket.

Jo approached him, touched his arms. If she could manoeuvre him away from the door she might just be able to make a break for it.

'I think I'm falling in love with you,' she whispered softly, and felt between his legs. There was no erection.

'I'm sorry if I annoyed you, Jo,' he apologised, not even responding to her kisses, the last seduction of her life failing. 'Please, just say hello to my parents and then you can go.'

Those final three words signified something more foreboding to Jo than any of his strange behaviour. *You can go* . . . I'm trap-ped here, she thought in cold terror. He's holding me a prisoner and won't let me leave until I've played his creepy game.

'Hello. My, you're a fine darling to behold,' a woman said in a high-pitched voice, although something didn't sound quite right.

Jo turned, certain there was nobody in the room.

'Hi, babe,' a man said.

And this time she recognised the disguised voice of Joel. She faced him as he clicked on the light.

'What the fuck is going on here?' she asked, wishing she was dressed now that he could see her.

'Well, answer them,' he said softly, and motioned towards the bed.

In the darkness she had been certain that there was nobody there. As she was turning, she thought about the time she'd lost her courage to ask him out at the door of his store, and now wished she'd trusted her instincts, or had listened to Cindy.

She looked down at the bed, and nothing could have prepared her for what she saw.

Her first reaction was crazy . . . *so that's what all the air-freshener is for.* She tried to scream, but suddenly he clamped the handkerchief over her mouth, gagging her. It was wet with a fluid. She struggled, kicked back and tried to wriggle free, but he lifted her off the ground and held her still . . . Stronger than he looked or had ever let on.

The raw scent of ether burned her mouth and nose as she kicked feebly now, to no avail. Her eyes were wide with terror. They moved quickly left and right with panic, and then slowly left again before rolling upwards.

Jo's last thoughts were of that horrible stench. It brought back memories of biology class when they had been forced to dissect poor little frogs. She'd made a stand and refused to pick up a scalpel as she watched them being put to sleep.

'I'll love you when you're gone,' she heard Joel whisper from far away, and her final plea as she succumbed to darkness was untainted insanity.

Please don't let me be the frog . . .

13

The next morning, Alan sat before the console, slowly panning the cameras along each aisle of the warehouse. He left one of them permanently focused on the main doors, through which forklifts trundled in and out.

There was no sign of Cindy. She was not coming, he decided.

It was the third Wednesday in a row that he hadn't seen her. Who did she think she was, the little cow, using him like that? The sad thing was, if she came waltzing through those doors right now, lips red, clothes tight, he knew he would do anything to sleep with her again.

Cindy was special. She was the first. He had obviously dated other women, slept with several of them, but Cindy was the only woman he'd ever loved like this. She was not only beautiful; she knew how to use her sexuality and that made her powerful and strong.

He turned another camera, hopefully checking the floor.

This rejection hurt him.

She deserved better than her prat of a husband, and he believed he was the man who could give it to her. He had often thought about paying Tom a surprise visit, and breaking a few bones perhaps.

Blow the situation wide open in his prattish, four-eyed face . . . But that would hurt Cindy, he thought.

Damn her. After the way she'd treated him, she deserved everything she had coming!

'Come on, baby,' he whispered, staring alternately at the clock on the wall and the bank of monitors. 'Be here. Don't play hard to get.'

He decided that if she didn't show within ten or fifteen minutes, when his shift ended, he would go down to the gym and pump some weights, exorcise some angry testosterone, cast out some of the energy and pressure that was building within his system. He felt as if he was going to explode.

Then he would sleep. All afternoon and into the evening.

Alan smiled as he shrugged on his jacket.

Later, when he was certain that everybody would be home – the bitch and her wimp husband, the snotnose kids – he would pay them a visit and put all his cards on the table. Wreck their marriage. If she would not give happiness to him – then she would have nobody.

His anger had turned to hatred, and that hatred into something far more lethal. A loathing that could hurt innocent people.

14

Joel woke that morning sweating and hot with anticipation. He was alone in his bed, and for a second wished for the dead companionship of Jo. He had taken her home in the middle of the night after loving her, careful not to leave any fluids in or on her cold, dead flesh.

He quickly dressed, thinking of the coming day and night. He was like a child on Christmas Eve.

He went into his parents' room and kissed them lightly goodbye, and promised he would be back the following morning.

'But why do you have to go?' his mother asked.

'Business,' he told her, although it was no business she would ever understand. Only his father knew, because he had taught Joel everything.

'Good boy,' his father whispered. 'I'm proud of you, son. Perhaps I'll join you later.'

Joel nodded and left them in the company of Richard and Judy. They far preferred *This Morning* to *Anne and Nick* on BBC1. Those two came over so fake.

By eleven, Joel was heading down to London to set up his alibi.

Unbeknownst to Joel Phillips, the body of Jo Myers had already been discovered. Her mother had popped around for breakfast that morning, and found the bloody mess in her room. The body had been stabbed and so extensively mutilated, that at first she had not even recognised her own daughter.

The drive down to London took nearly three and a half hours, with one stop off for a bite to eat. He had eaten quickly without tasting the food because he couldn't wait to get into the city, start the ball rolling.

His single worry was that he was rushing things too much. It had only been a matter of weeks since he had murdered the Napier family, and before Jo Myers there had been two other women – the one buried under his mother's dead rosebushes, and a schoolgirl whose body he had cremated – over the past year.

As well as the Napiers, there had been three other families in the past four years.

It was time to move on. He could continue his killing elsewhere, and would always be able to find new women to love, but he sensed his time in Bradbury was nearing an end.

The Curtis family would be his last victims here.

He wished fervently that Cindy Curtis would learn about the death of Jo before he reached their home tonight, but knew that was impossible. Jo's death was much like the torture of the Napiers' dog. Their grief and shock would have been the first tear in the fabric of their perfect relationship. He craved their suffering, wanted to see them wallow in their painful loss.

Joel smiled. He would be able to tell the Curtis family himself during the long night hours before his bloody farewell.

He wondered what they would be doing today, glorious sunlight warming their soft skins. He yearned to be with them on their final day, but was satisfied that he would be the only witness to their last hours.

Their happiness would soon be a memory. He envisioned them holding hands in a winter bauble, which he was shaking gently. Snow began to drift about the tiny, close figures. It settled on their clothes . . . *The perfect family.*

His rage was building and he gripped the steering wheel tighter as he neared London.

He intended to shatter that bauble, smash it into a million pieces and destroy all their happiness. Turn them in on themselves like wild animals and make them hate each other before it was over.

Only then would he kill them, as the sun of a new day was born.

At one point in his journey he noticed that a police car was cruising in the next lane over. He eased down deliberately on the accelerator, just enough to get pulled over and be issued with a ticket.

Yes, Officer. I'm sorry. Heading down to London for an important meeting. Running a little late.

All part of his alibi.

Tonight, when their home was secure and he was loose in it, listening to their screams of pain, their cries for freedom, their pitiful begging . . . begging for the night to end, the warm sun to rise and with it the freedom of the light, he would only give them cold death . . .

Despite all his precautions somehow his father always managed to be with him and have a hand in the killing.

The door inched open and the column of white light that emanated from it drove a spike of pain through his mind.

I don't want to look inside. I mustn't see what is happening.

From behind the door he could hear the voice of his mother, and he turned the sound of the radio up. She was pleading with him. *Help me, Joel . . . help me!*

'No!' Joel screamed, and the voice faded as the door shut once more.

That was one of the reasons he always called up his disturbed days as Dr Joel Phillips, PhD, MD, MRCPath, forensic pathologist. It was his only defence against the violent childhood memories which had forced him to hate the families. They had to be punished, had to die.

The press of Bradbury and now the national papers were calling him the Initial Killer. He carved the initials and the tiny heart into his victims to rationalise their deaths, give them wicked meaning.

When he left Bradbury, he would once more change his appearance, his attitudes and his name. He would leave his parents behind. Their prying minds were a burden to his sanity. Their malevolent presence would always rule his actions because he would never forget the pain they had given him, and the many beautiful memories since he had reunited them.

It had been perfect recently, the past couple of years – a short while in a lifetime of pain and confusion. It was all he had ever wanted. For so long there had been something very wrong in his family, and he had put it right. He would always have the comfort of that knowledge.

No matter what they made him do.

15

Once in London, Joel found a hotel in Bayswater that was not too cheap, but not too expensive either. He went to his room and unpacked his overnight bag, carefully unfolding a suit and hanging it in the ample closet space. He undressed, deliberately roughly folding his trousers and shirt and throwing them over the back of a chair.

He climbed into the bed and pulled the sheets right out, then rolled over a few times, really messing it up. Then he pulled the sheets back on one side as he got out.

The bed looked as though it had been well slept in.

He smiled to himself and checked his watch. It was nearly two. He was on schedule and making good time.

He showered, letting ice-cold water run off his body, followed by steaming hot. Cold, hot . . . ice and fire . . . After half an hour he turned off the spray and dried himself.

He dressed in jeans and a shirt, a pair of running shoes. All of which were entirely uncharacteristic of him.

Then he phoned his parents, although he knew he didn't have to. He could send them a message on the psychic waves he'd discovered, surf it in. After he left them behind, he wondered how long it would take them to find him. Would they even discover his new location – or would they prefer to die in their comfortable home?

Nobody answered the fourth ring – as he knew they wouldn't – and the machine clicked on. He waited for the beep, as his own voice instructed.

'You both keep out of this,' he warned them, as he always did.

His mother would obey. But his father would be curious, and already he could hear him laughing.

'Stay away,' Joel threatened in a harsh whisper, and put the receiver down.

He went out for a pizza in Queensway so that he was seen by a few more people, just to establish his presence in London. He made a couple of crude suggestions to a waitress, and heard her call him an ignorant bastard under her breath. That was good. If nosy policemen came asking questions and showing his photograph, she'd remember him, all right.

Finally, before heading back up-country to Bradbury, he sought one last piece of evidence to make his alibi air-tight.

He found a prostitute, not too good-looking but not quite as ugly as a pig, and propositioned her. She guided him into a dark side alley where he handed her two hundred pounds.

'What's that for?' she asked, her hips big and square. 'I'm not into anything kinky. Suckey-fuckey will cost you fifty. You want anything else then we can negotiate. For example, if you want to wear a—'

'I didn't ask for the menu,' Joel snapped, and she shut up quickly. 'My name is Joel Phillips. Anybody comes asking questions, showing my picture, you'll say we spent the night together.'

'You're giving me money just to say that shit?' she asked.

Joel could feel his confidence growing as the night approached. He told the woman the name of the hotel. 'Remember – all night,' he instructed her. 'And I was a good lay. You'd better get that part right.'

By seven-thirty, he was back in Bradbury. Normally he would wait until ten or eleven before entering a house, but it was too much of a strain sitting in the lane, his palms sweating.

There were several reasons why he took control of the homes late at night. People were tired, sometimes in bed, as were their children. It was easier to take charge. It gave the neighbours a chance to get cosy and snug, their curtains drawn tight for the night.

But as he sat in the quiet, wooded lane, Joel had only his father for company. *How did you know I was back?* Joel mused.

'Go now,' his father told him.

'It's not yet time.'

'Go on, boy,' he urged.

Thoughts of the coming night were flooding Joel's mind. He was drowning in the righteousness and justice of what he was going to do. He realised he was dealing with his problems the same way his father had . . . striking out and hurting them, before they had a chance to hurt him.

106

He tried to envision his father as a young man, knowing he was walking on thin ice that was already about to crack as the door in his mind began to open. The pain was intense, but he looked into the light and saw . . . *his father, an angry young man, a knife in his hand, his grip tight.*

Before he lost control, Joel quickly slammed shut the door in his mind. His father's grip had been white-knuckled on the wooden handle of the blade. He'd intended to hurt somebody with it.

'Do me proud tonight,' his father whispered, trying to coax his way out from the room in his son's mind which was locked once more.

Joel smiled, glad that his father was happy. He lamented his missing mother, wished she could share in their joy. But he knew that once he had killed the family she would be returned to him.

He already missed her and wanted her back.

He put the hatchback in gear and pulled away from the trees. He carefully monitored his speed as he left the country lane. The last thing he wanted was to be pulled over now.

He cut a course through the streets of the town, and then drove over the bridge at the railway station. He was close, his heart beating fast. The father sometimes walked here in the mornings. He was so close now.

He reached their street, checked his rearview mirror and indicated. He turned down the road and stopped outside the Curtis home.

He pulled on a pair of surgical gloves and looked at his watch.

Ten past eight.

It was too early, but he could not stop. He was climbing from the car, locking the door, moving to the back of the vehicle and opening the boot. He lifted the Nike bag out and unzipped it, quickly rifling through the contents and making a final inventory.

Scalpels. Knives. Handcuffs. Rope. Ether.

The last item was an automatic pistol which he removed. He slammed a magazine in and shoved it into the front of his jeans. When he had lived in London he had been a registered member of a gun club. After fulfilling the requirements of the law he had procured a firearm.

The gun was always only a precaution, and he never intended to use it. Yet, when he was a child, it was never his number one ambition, right up there with becoming an astronaut or a professional football player, to become a serial killer, so who knew what would happen through this dark night?

As he walked up the front path, the door in his mind began to open and once more he dared to look in. *There was a boy, small and angelic, and he was watching*... What was he watching? Joel rang the bell, and his foot began to tap nervously. What could the child see? He inched the door of his mind open further, praying he still had control. *His father on top of his mother, making love.* Even with their psychic powers, they had never known he used to watch their sex games. *As he ties her with silk ribbons, tortures her with pleasure*... *and then he sees the knife in his hand, the fear in his mother's eyes and*—-

'Yes?'

He looked up. It was Mrs Curtis. She was holding the door open. No chain. It was so wide, like an invitation.

'Can I help you?' she asked.

Joel could hear music from inside, and it beckoned him in, as the boy in his mind stepped into the light of the room, into all the dark desires and secrets of his past.

The pain was overwhelming and engulfed him as his hand thrust out and gripped her throat. With the other hand he reached down, pulled the gun out and pushed it into her ribs.

'In the house, in the house!' he commanded and forced her back.

Joel kicked the door shut behind him, and choked her scream into a dying, pathetic mewl.

PART THREE

Until Dawn . . .

1

Tom looked up from the book he was reading as he heard Cindy let out a quiet gasp.

'Cindy?' he called, standing and suddenly tense. 'Cindy, you OK?'

Tom relaxed as his wife returned to the room, but then he noticed her expression. She was red in the face, and tears began to spill from her fearful eyes. There was a red mark around her neck.

'What's—?' he began, reaching for her.

Tom stared over her shoulder as a stranger walked into the room.

'Good evening, ladies and gentlemen, boys and girls,' the stranger said.

'Who are you? What are you—?'

'My name is Dr Joel Phillips, and I'm your guest for the night. Please, nobody move.'

Phillips pointed the revolver at them as they held each other, and put his bag down.

Sarah suddenly screamed and Richard looked back from the television.

'Silence that child,' Phillips told them, only to have Richard join her, creating a chorus of fear.

Tom glared at the man as Cindy fell to the floor and held her daughter and son together.

'Hush, sweethearts,' she whispered, not able to stop her own tears. They stopped screaming, but continued to cry. 'The man's just playing a game. Don't worry.'

'This is not a game, Cindy,' Joel told her.

2

Tom sighed deeply as he remembered, and wiped the last of his tears away with his free hand.

That was the moment he should have moved, he reflected now. The man – Joel Phillips – was distracted, watching the children and Cindy. He hadn't got complete control yet, and those early moments were surely vulnerable ones for him.

Control was a weapon. And now he had that control, had brutally forced his will upon them.

Tom tried to extricate his right hand from the handcuff that bound it tightly to the radiator piping, to which the second loop was attached. The pipe ran along the bottom of the wall. He tried to squeeze his hand out of the hoop, but it was impossible.

He hated the radiator piping. They had installed the cheap, old-fashioned central heating system for the coming winter months, when he would be working up here in the cold. He'd told Cindy that they couldn't afford it, but she'd insisted. *I don't want you catching pneumonia up there.*

Tom grunted with effort as he grabbed the pipe tightly in both hands and pulled as hard as he could. It lifted slightly off the wall, barely moved.

Whoever heard of a bloody radiator in a loft, anyway?

Cindy, you're nuts, he'd said to his wife. *Don't you know that heat rises?*

Tom shook his head and sent the memories away as he focused on the piping once more. With all his strength he pulled at it, without result. His left hand slipped and he fell back a step, collapsing in a heap. He looked around in the darkness to which his eyes had become accustomed. The loft had once been his den, a source of comfort and male pride.

Now it was his prison.

'Think, Tom,' he whispered to himself, peering into the grey darkness. There had to be something here that could help him.

But instead of planning an escape from the situation, his defeated mind was content to question his lack of action which had left him captured here and his wife and children alone with a dangerous stranger downstairs.

Why didn't you do something? Now you're up here, alone and naked. Trapped.

Shut up, he told his mind.

You did nothing then. There's nothing you can do now.

'Shut up!' he said sharply to himself, and turned back to the piping. He could beat that pipe: he had to. He pulled at it as hard as he could, felt his strength draining away as it came off the wall less than an inch. 'Come on,' he strained through gritted teeth, summoning every ounce of energy into his hands.

But it was useless. There was no way he was going to break the piping free of the wall, or fracture the handcuffs binding him there. He let go and the piping moved back into position. He sat down, his back to the wall. He couldn't face the pipe; it had become an antagonist, the enemy preventing him from protecting his family.

But you could have done that already, if only you had reacted. What's he doing now? What's the intruder doing to them?

That was Tom's greatest fear. He had no knowledge of what was happening. He hoped they were still together, prayed to a God he had never believed existed that they were unhurt.

He's killing them.

No.

It's your fault.

'No,' he whispered weakly. 'There was nothing I could do.'

Joel Phillips had taken advantage of their sudden confusion and horror. He'd grabbed hold of Cindy and pulled her away from Sarah and Richard, put the gun to her head, pushed it hard against her temple.

Tom began to cry harshly now, bitter tears of anger as he remembered.

He had been helpless . . . as he was now.

Phillips had made him tie Sarah's wrists together with a length of woven, nylon-fibre climbing rope.

The gun was on Cindy and he had to obey. Tom had been an unwilling accomplice.

'Rope,' the intruder had rambled, but Tom was not listening. 'A thousand threads all spun together to create the strongest rope in the world. Nobody is going anywhere. Now the ankles.'

Tom had hated what he was doing, searched for a way out. Anything . . . But Cindy was weeping, the violator of the sanctity of their home holding her tight, pushing the gun on to her head.

'Do it,' he'd commanded.

Tom had tried to tie the rope loosely so that it wouldn't hurt Sarah, and – if she was ever given the opportunity – she might be able to slip her hands and feet free. But the man had forced him to pull the rope tight, and then tighter still until Sarah was crying from the pain.

'It hurts, Daddy.'

'I know. I'm sorry, Sarah,' he'd said, compassionately touching her arm. 'Be a brave girl.'

'Now the boy,' Phillips had ordered.

And he'd weakly complied, tying Richard in a similar manner.

Tom hated Joel Phillips; for threatening Cindy, for making him hurt his children . . . but he also loathed himself for not fighting back.

In the loft now he closed his eyes, and could still see them, lying on the carpet, on their sides, small vulnerable faces wet with tears.

He prayed that they were not hurt . . . that they were still alive.

Then Phillips – using the threat of violence to Cindy as a weapon once more – had ordered him to gag the children with a strip of industrial tape from the roll that was in his Nike sports bag. Tom had followed the orders, biting two pieces off, all the time listening to Cindy's quiet pleading and sobbing.

'Please, please, don't hurt my children. Not my sweet babies. *Please.*'

That was when you should have done something, when you could have made a difference, his mind was kind enough to inform him.

He had reached into the man's bag for the tape, and found his hand amongst an array of blades, two pairs of handcuffs, more rope . . . But so many knives and scalpels sent him numb with shock. *They were already dead*, he thought at that moment. *Only their beating hearts and fearful minds and lost souls were yet to realise it.* For half a second his hand had gripped one of the knives.

Why hadn't he removed one of the blades? Made a stand?

Because Phillips had a gun.

You could have surprised him.

Bullets are a whole lot faster than any hand, he thought, trying to rationalise his fear . . . his suffering cowardice. Besides, I don't even know if I could kill a man.

Threatening your wife and children, you . . . should have cut his fucking heart out! he cried silently.

'Jesus . . .' he sobbed, bending his head so that he could hold it in both hands. He wished desperately that he'd had the courage to fight the man, and for once his relentless mind was kind. *He would have killed you, Cindy and the children*, it intoned. The intruder who had shattered the peace and love of their home would have murdered them all.

After gagging the children he had looked at Phillips, stared into his eyes. He had searched for traces of humility, but found nothing except the dead stare of an empty soul.

'Don't try to stare me down, Tom,' Joel told him.

He knows our names. First Cindy, and now myself, Tom had thought, and his expression of surprise had given his notion away.

'I know who you are. And I know you can't win,' Joel concluded.

That statement of fact was enough for Tom. There was no conjecture or uncertainty. No doubt. It was a given that they must accept. They were lambs ready for the slaughter of a madman.

'Don't hurt the children then,' Tom had begged, his voice a high-pitched crack as he watched his son and daughter writhe and cry on the carpet.

'Please, let them go free!' Cindy added, sensing hope for Richard and Sarah.

'This is not a negotiation,' Phillips said harshly, and released Cindy from his grip, pushing her across the room.

Tom caught her and held her, saw fresh tears of anger as she began to struggle violently. His hold was of comfort, but then he found himself restraining her, preventing her from doing anything foolish. Hatred burned in her eyes, an anger he knew words would not be able to control if she ever got out of his grasp. She would attack the man.

A bullet could still her emotion though, halt her pounding heart. If Cindy got free Tom knew she would charge at Phillips, blind to any consequences or the gun in his hand.

She would be shot. Killed. Dead and gone for ever.

She struggled valiantly, then after a few minutes began to calm down.

Tom wept now as he realised that a lot of her emotion had been directed at himself. She had screamed at him, calling him names and swearing as her fists pounded on to his chest. She had been angry at him, disappointed at his failure to defend them.

His thoughts kept coming back to the same point. It was as if he was trapped in a loop, destined for ever to blame himself for what was happening. Why didn't you do anything? *Why?*

He had no satisfactory response.

'It'll be OK,' he had whispered, trying to soothe her as she collapsed in his arms, willing to be held gently. 'We're going to make it through this. We're all going to be OK.'

The expression on Joel Phillips' face had been enough to tell Tom that it wasn't true. They were all going to die . . . and if that was the case, he thought now, surely it was better to have died fighting than handcuffed up here, defenceless?

That's absolutely right, Tom. So why—?

Yes, I know. Why didn't I do something to make things better? To put the bad things right?

Because if I had, I would be dead now. We all would be.

How do you know they're not already? They could be bleeding, suffering under his hand. They—

Because I have hope. It's all I have, and I can't let go of that.

Strangely, he remembered the beggar he had seen recently in Manchester, sitting outside Burger King. He thought about the damp card the man had been holding out front, bearing rough black writing.

NEVER DEPRIVE A PERSON OF HOPE BECAUSE IT MIGHT BE THE ONLY POSSESSION HE OR SHE HAS

He saw himself pitying the youngster who had fallen upon bad times, digging into his pocket and dropping change into a ripped, polystyrene cup.

Hope was all he had. *They are alive* – Cindy, Sarah and Richard. He had to believe that, could never lose his faith in it.

Then his mind cast back into the living room, earlier that night.

Phillips had removed a pair of handcuffs from the bag and thrown them into the middle of the floor.

'Handcuff Cindy to the radiator piping over there,' he ordered Tom, motioning with his hand.

Tom had followed the instructions obediently.

You're weak. Physically and mentally.

Damn this unknown voice in his mind, throwing doubt and blame on to him. Even if I'd had the courage to attack Phillips, we would all have been shot. I couldn't have overpowered him quickly enough.

But you could have wrestled the gun from him. At the least you would have been doing something, instead of enduring this mental torture.

The horrible waiting. The separation from his family was intolerable. His fear for what the stranger might be doing . . .

At least you would have fought him, died protecting all you love and cherish.

Tom screamed with rage and pulled violently at the handcuffs, only succeeding in rubbing the skin on his wrist raw and drawing forth a fine smear of blood.

Phillips never checked Cindy's handcuffs, Tom thought. He could have simply left the hoop on the piping loose, out of sight. Cindy could have covered his deception with her body. She would have been free now.

But by then fear had already conquered his system and ruled him, run a course through his whole body like the blood in his veins. He had locked the hoop, clicked it shut – and saw Cindy pull harshly at her wrist and look at him bitterly.

It's not my fault, he'd wanted to tell her, but instead looked away, standing to face Phillips.

'Take off your clothes,' Phillips had said, brandishing the gun in his direction.

'What?'

'You heard me, Tom. The next time you feign ignorance, pretend not to hear me, or ask any questions, I'll kill the boy. Don't doubt me,' Joel told him, and moved the weapon from Tom to Richard whose eyes went wide with panic as he breathed heavily through his nose. The sobs and screams of the children were continually muffled by the gags. The gun remained trained on Richard. 'Now, remove your clothes.'

'OK, OK,' Tom said, quickly holding up his hands in a gesture of supplication. 'Just don't hurt the boy.'

Tom had undressed slowly, thinking all the time that he had to do something, and all the time doing nothing. As each second passed he knew that their chances of escape and survival were proving slimmer and slimmer.

Yet he had continued to react numbly. First, his shirt, then his jeans. His socks. He'd hesitated before removing his Hong Kong Phooey shorts. He saw the man's finger tighten on the trigger of the gun, his eyes narrow.

He quickly pulled the shorts down and stepped out of them.

He'd glanced at the curtains, wished that they were not pulled so forlornly across the window, that a passing stranger could look in and witness his forced, indecent exposure . . . the horror that had entered their home.

'Up the stairs,' Phillips directed.

Tom moved instantly, walking at a funeral pace from the room. He looked over his shoulder, saw the children and Cindy's fearful expression. *Love you*, he mouthed . . . and then they were gone from view.

Phillips marched Tom along the landing of the first floor, and then up the narrow stairs which led into the loft. Up into this solitary confinement.

The man had quickly handcuffed Tom to the piping, and once more he was ashamed that he didn't resist or offer a struggle. There must have been an opportunity then, if only for a second. But he had missed it.

Joel Phillips had stood back and stared down at him. The intruder had smiled and laughed, and then – shaking his head – switched off the desk-lamp that provided the only light.

'Soon,' he whispered, and left, shutting the door at the top of the stairs.

You could have done something. There were chances.

Tom screamed in the dark and pulled against his constraints, tendons and veins standing out in his neck and arms.

'Come on!'

He struggled on, even though the piping barely moved. He was determined to get free. He must.

3

His face, Cindy thought. *We've all seen his face.*

Joel Phillips wasn't wearing a balaclava, or any kind of mask. Not even a stocking to disguise his features. He didn't care about them seeing him, being able to recognise him. They even knew his name, unless that was an alias.

He didn't intend for there to be an opportunity to identify him later. He was not there merely to rob them, or hurt them. He was going to kill them. None of them were ever going to leave the house again, except in a bodybag, carried by a stranger.

Joel Phillips was the Initial Killer. Or some sadistic copycat. Either way it left the Curtis family in a no-win situation.

He was even going to kill the children. *God, no.*

How could this be happening to them? Especially now, when everything seemed to be coming together so well.

Sarah and Richard were crying and Cindy did her best to console them from where she was sitting.

'Hush, children,' she soothed, trying to stem their tears. 'Don't worry. We're going to be OK.'

Their crying continued unabated, despite her soft words. How could they believe something she didn't have faith in herself? But she couldn't convey the hard truth to them – that they were all going to die, so she had to lie.

Damn Tom.

Cindy couldn't believe how submissive her husband had been, obeying the stranger's every word. When he had closed the handcuff shut about the radiator piping and she heard it *click*, locking her in place, she had hated him and looked at him with tempestuous eyes. How could he do such a thing?

She pulled the hoop ineffectually now.

Sarah began to cry again.

'Please . . . Sarah, Richard. It's going to be all right.'

No, Tom had done nothing to keep them alive, she thought –

121

but with a gun at her own head, and aimed at Richard, what could he do? How could he have fought back? She accepted that his compliance had been for their protection.

There had been no way for Tom to fight back. She knew that if their roles were reversed, her behaviour would have been similar.

They only had one way to act . . . without hope.

'Hush, sweethearts.'

All that counted was that they were still alive, she thought, as her own tears ceased momentarily, her make-up streaked by rivers of sorrow.

We're not dead yet.

She was sure that Tom was in the den. She had monitored the sounds as her husband was forced up the stairs and along the hallway above. If they had entered one of the bedrooms or the bathroom she would have heard them.

Tom was probably handcuffed the same way she was.

Or dead.

There were too many questions and not enough answers. Too much uncertainty and worry. It was a weapon of great mental use, she acknowledged. Phillips had isolated Tom, made sure there was no way of communicating with him. It had created massive insecurity.

Forcing Tom to remove all his clothes had surely made him feel more vulnerable, too.

'Please don't cry, children,' she sniffed. But why should they be able to stop when she couldn't even prevent her own tears?

Phillips was breaking them down. Jesus. How was anybody supposed to survive a situation like this? She pulled weakly at the old radiator piping, but it was of no use. Not only physically, but mentally. The only comfort she had – the only thing that was keeping her sane as she tugged pathetically at the handcuffs – was that she could see her babies trussed before her . . . *and they were alive.*

She heard the man moving about upstairs, tracked him from their bedroom into Sarah's and then Richard's.

What if he took Tom up to the den and . . . *Tom's already dead* . . . killed him? What if Tom was gone, and they had to fight this thing alone? She could no longer hear her husband's screaming. What if—?

No. That's how he wants you to think and behave. It's his weapon, remember?

She listened, sensing that the man was now in the bathroom upstairs. She looked around frantically. There had to be something she could do! But she couldn't see anything she could use to aid her. The heavy ornaments were out of reach, and for half a second she saw within her mind a strong image of herself smashing a bronze horse into the side of his head.

By now, the children had stopped crying. They were staring at their mother, pleading mutely for her to do something.

'Don't worry,' she told them confidently. 'Somebody will hear this.'

Then she began to scream and scream as loudly as she could, the sound ripping out of her lungs. It seemed useless and pathetic, but it was all she could do.

Somebody in their road must surely hear!

Cindy heard his pounding footsteps as he left the bathroom and ran along the hallway above. She tensed, but managed to lift her voice an extra few decibels as be began to stomp down the stairs. *Elephant feet*, she called her children when they descended so noisily.

She continued to bawl as Phillips came into the room.

She was unaware of the anguish she was causing Tom as he struggled against the pipe, certain that Phillips was inflicting some sadistic pain on her . . . much as his own screams of anger and frustration had tormented Cindy .

Phillips ran across the room and raised the handgun. Before Cindy had a chance to flinch or dodge, he bludgeoned the side of her head with the pistol. Holding the short barrel, be brought it down hard with a dull thud, silencing her instantly.

Cindy's head lolled forward and she felt warm blood on her face. *Don't faint; you can't faint, can't leave your children alone.* She fought to remain conscious, the voice a powerful light in her mind which kept the encroaching darkness at bay.

She saw him grab the bag from the table and quickly remove the industrial tape with which Sarah and Richard had been muted.

Cindy lifted her head and began to scream again. Somebody had to hear her.

'You bastard!' she exploded, and disregarded the eyes of her babies which went wide because they had never heard her utter the bad word before. 'You bastard!' she screeched as he approached, ignoring the pain as blood trickled down the side of her head. He reached down to hold her head still, but she leaned away and swiped at him with her free hand, smiling slightly as her nails scratched his cheek, bringing forth a fine line of blood. 'Get your hands off me! You hurt my children and you'll—'

But then the tape was across her mouth, and her rage could only continue within. She still tried to claw him, but he moved back easily, out of her reach.

'You're quite a fighter, Cindy,' Phillips observed, reaching up to touch his face where she had torn the skin. 'More than Tom. I like that.'

Cindy watched with fear as he moved to Sarah and sat beside her. She wrenched at the handcuffs and screamed silently, the tape effectively gagging her. He began to stroke her little girl's hair.

No . . . don't hurt her. No!

Sarah tried to squirm away, but Phillips held her firmly in place with his other hand.

'Be still,' he murmured. 'I'm not going to hurt you yet.'

Sarah's eyes were closed tight. Phillips looked up and smiled at Cindy, whose eyes were wide with fear for her children, yet burning with anger and hatred.

'You don't like me, do you?' he asked rhetorically, and then picked Sarah up and carried her out of the room.

Cindy listened to him go up the stairs, and again tried to track his movements along the hallway. She was sure he had gone into Sarah's room.

She looked around once more, searching the room quickly. The telephone was out of reach, but it was on the table next to Richard. There had to be some way he could punch a number in. She peeled the gag away with her free hand so that it was dangling from the side of her mouth.

'Richard,' she hissed, and the boy opened his eyes and looked at her. He was trembling. 'Richard, be strong. I need you to reach the telephone. It's behind you.'

Richard nodded and sniffed before rolling over. He could knock the phone off the table, and then it would be easy to punch a number in with his nose.

He was edging towards the table when Phillips returned and picked Richard up.

Cindy's heart sank.

Then Phillips began to stroke the boy's hair, touch him softly on the cheek.

'You're sweet,' Joel said. He had no intention of abusing the child, but it was fun to watch the mother fume, shaking her head back and forth violently. He replaced the gag and her cries of anguish were choked. Her eyes pleaded with him not to touch her son, or her daughter.

He wondered what she would say if he removed the gag now. Would she beg and plead for their safety, or would she insult him, unable to keep her rage in check?

Joel laughed. The night was only just beginning and already his options were wonderful. He carried the boy out of the room and up the stairs.

Cindy listened, and this time she was certain he had gone into her son's room.

Please be safe, my children, she prayed. *Please don't be taken from me.*

4

Joel gently laid Richard on his bed and leaned close to him. The
boy tried to cower away.

'Get some rest,' Joel advised him. 'Before the night begins.'

Richard tried to speak, but the words were muffled grunts as
he struggled behind the gag.

'Try to sleep,' the man told him again.

Joel left the room and paused at the flight of stairs which led
up to the den. There was no noise coming from the room where
he had imprisoned the father. That made him suspicious, and he
wondered if Tom was planning some kind of escape, if – perhaps
– he was stronger and more resourceful than his first futilities
had led Joel to believe.

Does your mind think dark deeds of me?

He contemplated going up to check on the father.

The single disadvantage of isolating family members was that
it was hard – impossible even – to keep an accurate watch on
everybody. He grinned. You can watch some of the people all of
the time, and all of the people some of the time. But you can
never watch *all* of the people *all* of the time. He laughed out loud
at this thought.

Tom struck him as being passive. He had submitted easily,
and Joel decided that he would not be up to anything subversive
– or if he were, he wouldn't be getting very far.

'I'll check on you later,' he promised, and then looked in on
Sarah.

'Go to sleep, little girl,' he murmured caressingly, almost like a
parent checking on a child of his own. His parents had never
done that for him. He had always been neglected as they played
the disgusting games he'd spied on, hidden . . . *his mother domi-
nating his father, tying him down with silk ribbons as she teased
him, and then his father would do the same as the roles were
reversed and he was watching, fascinated, eyes wide, wondering*

what it would be like to be tied and touched ... to play their games ... he had secretly yearned for it ... and then one night he had watched as his father tied his mother and ... 'No, please,' Joel whispered.

The pain was so intense he felt as if his mind was bleeding from a thousand wounds. He clutched his head in both hands.

'Please don't hurt her,' Joel begged.

He was a little boy once more. He had entered the room in his disturbed psyche again when he'd entered the Curtis house, and knew he would not find an exit until he had killed the family and left. And before he could do that he had to make them pay for his own suffering.

'Don't kill her ...'

He blinked, and suddenly the vision was gone, but he sensed that his father was here in the house with him, however impossible that might be.

'Father?'

There was no answer; he had expected none.

Perhaps they somehow possessed him with their psychic powers, made him do their bidding. He wanted to go back to the time when he was a small, curious boy, wondering what all the noises were coming from his parents' room, so that he would understand more, but for now he dared not look through the eyes of his childhood.

Even if his parents were in control, the game was still his.

'Sleep well,' he told Sarah.

He walked out of the room and along the hallway to the stairs, unaware that the snoring sounds Sarah was making were faked.

He wondered if the children remembered him from Alton Towers. Or if they recognised him from the times he'd waited for them just beyond the school gates, watching. He'd been careful then; had to be. There were always a lot of parents and teachers around, and a stranger looking longingly after the children as they ran from the playground would surely have been noticed. For all the watching weeks he'd been so very careful, and now he had his treasured prize.

5

Joel walked back into the living room and saw Cindy reaching across the floor. She was stretching as far as she could to grasp the telephone on the table beside the couch. But it was an impossible feat; she was not even halfway to it and could extend no more.

Joel smiled approvingly and watched silently in the doorway.

When she noticed his presence she jerked back and slumped down, hoping that he had not seen.

He walked in and sat down on the floor, only feet away, so close she could touch him if she desired. But instead she cowered away, and Joel grinned mirthlessly. The first time a victim had done that he'd found it funny, the second time it was less amusing, and now it didn't impress him at all. It was like an old, stale joke.

He studied her and marvelled at how much emotion a person's eyes could communicate.

When she'd opened the front door and he'd grabbed her throat there had been shock, and then at the sight of the gun her eyes had gone wide with fear.

He knew the expression of fear the best. It was something he thrived on, fed off. He would become familiar with it once more before sunrise.

There had been sadness as he threatened her husband and children, and of course tears, accompanied by a pleading look which cried: *Take me, do anything, but spare my children. Let them live.*

There had always been hatred, burning bright and eternal.

When he had returned just now her eyes had been scheming, narrow with deceit and sly intentions. Completing a circle, as he shifted forward slightly, they were wide with fear again.

'You have nice eyes,' Joel told her. Blue like a perfect ocean, a cloudless sky. He reached out to touch her but she squirmed away, along the wall until she ran out of pipe as it entered the radiator. 'And where do you think you're going?'

He stood and grabbed the waistband of her skirt, dragged her back along the carpet. She struggled uselessly, trying to get a hold on anything but failing miserably. Her cries were muffled by the replaced gag. He sat before her again.

'My patience is short, Cindy. Please don't test it. Don't worry,' he told her, and held her cheek gently where it was cut.

Just a little lower, Cindy thought. A little closer to my mouth and I'll bite your fucking fingers off.

'I'm not going to hurt you. Well . . . not yet, anyway. It's far too early,' Joel said vigilantly. It had been a mistake to come so prematurely. 'You might have guests, or unexpected visitors knocking on your door. Until darkness falls, you'll be safe. Until dawn . . .'

Joel smiled as she appeared to visibly relax a little bit. Her cheek was no longer trembling under his hand and she seemed less tense.

'We need to have a little question and answer session, you and I,' he said, and laughed. 'Well, I do. For now you can simply nod your head. Yes and no. Do you understand?'

Cindy didn't respond, and Phillips looked away. His grip tightened on her cheek, pinching the skin viciously, and when he looked back she could see that he was annoyed.

'I tried not to be violent when I was taking over the house. I didn't want to hurt anybody too soon. We have all night for that. I needed to generate fear and confusion.' He paused, sighing slightly. She was riveted by his every word and he relinquished his grip. 'Unfortunately, from my experiences I have learned that shocking brutality works best for that. But listen carefully, Cindy. Heed these words. Tom is in the loft and the children are in their rooms sleeping. I need you down here, dressed – alive – just in case somebody comes calling who might be suspicious if you don't answer the door. So I need you here. But the children . . . I have no use for them.'

Cindy began to shake her head frantically.

'I will not hesitate to kill them if you attempt anything stupid or disobey me. It will be a waste of their final hours. Perhaps,' he continued, standing and retrieving the gun from his bag, 'I'll simply kneecap little Sarah.'

Cindy recoiled slightly, her eyes wide again, running a gauntlet of emotions. She was breathing heavily through her nose. He

130

put the gun on the couch and sat before her again.

'The last family had a teenage daughter. She had a bad night. Painful. Even Anadin couldn't relieve the headache I gave her,' he laughed. 'Do you understand?'

Cindy nodded solemnly.

'OK. You're a fast learner – and this isn't too difficult, is it?' he said patiently.

A quick shake of her head, without hesitation.

No. Damn easy, in fact. Nods and shakes – no problem at all; just don't hurt my children.

The voice in her mind was strong and solid. Almost convinced that her children would survive the night. She didn't know where it came from, this voice, yet Cindy was sure she'd heard it years before, a long time ago.

The man was talking again; she concentrated, hoping she hadn't missed anything important.

'. . . disconnected the telephone extension in your bedroom, and the one in the kitchen,' he informed her, and shuffled to the phone on the table. He traced the wire to the wall and pulled it from the socket. He smiled at the dismay on her face. 'You like to talk, do you? That's three. Is that all the telephones?'

Yes.

'Now – are you expecting anybody tonight?'

Could she lie? Give him a quick nod of her head, and when he removed the gag, tell him somebody *was* coming, would be arriving later. Would that buy them some time? She could tell him that Ian Knox – a policeman – was visiting tonight (even though he was not). Would that make Phillips leave? Or kill them sooner?

Tom, what should I do? What are you doing?

Tom isn't here, baby. You're on your own.

'Now don't lie to me, Cindy. Remember the children upstairs. Think about their health before you answer. You have nice eyes, but they betray you far too often. You just weighed the odds, tried to decide whether lying would a wise choice. Let me tell you – it isn't. Don't make that mistake. You can die easy, or you can die hard.'

Cindy suddenly struggled against the pipe, and felt her heart skip a beat as it lifted from the wall slightly . . . but then nothing more.

And what are you going to do if you get free from the pipe?

A dejected shake of her head.

131

No. There would be no visitors tonight. Nobody she knew of anyway.

How would Phillips react if somebody showed up out of the blue, completely unexpectedly? That would make her a liar, and he would be very annoyed.

Maybe she could negotiate something – *to the best of my knowledge there will be no other guests tonight, but if there are I accept no responsibility for their presence and—*

'Do you love your husband?'

You bastard, she thought, and couldn't hold back her choked sob.

You know everything, don't you? You've been following us. Stalking us . . . just like you did all the others. Just like Tom said.

'Do you love Tom?' Joel repeated calmly, his eyes filling with slow boiling anger.

He stood and picked up the gun. He was going to go up to Sarah's room.

She began to nod frantically, grunting, but still he left and went up the stairs. She listened as he entered the room, and began to cry. The gag effectively killed her screams.

No! Don't hurt her! I answered you . . . please don't do it . . . please . . .

And then even her screams died.

She began to sob, had no control over her wild tears. In those seconds she gave up, felt her mind collapsing on itself – heard her sanity shatter under its weight.

It was over. She had failed. Phillips was going to kill Sarah . . . or hurt her beyond imagination.

This wasn't about buying time, Cindy wept. Or survival. Or escape.

It was about death.

She heard him moving about upstairs, but didn't bother tracking him this time. How could he do it? How could he simply walk up there and kill a small, innocent child?

Please don't let her be gone, she cried.

Then Phillips returned, the gun held at his side.

No shots . . . Hope surged in Cindy, a wave of suppressed joy lifting her head to look at him. She hadn't heard any shots.

But there was a betraying, wispy trail of smoke ascending from the barrel of the gun.

'The silencer is a remarkable invention,' Phillips said smoothly. 'I had my doubts when I first used one, but they even make a cannon like this sound like a sweet whisper in the dark. A deadly kiss in the night.'

Cindy pulled violently at the handcuffs and the radiator pipe. In her mind she could see Sarah on her bed, still tied, trying to cry out in agony. The gag swallowed her daughter's voice, and tears were running down her gorgeous, soft cheeks . . . *no, please, please no* . . . and then she saw her little girl's leg, a bloody mess at the knee, white bone painted red and exposed to the room. *Oh God, no!*

Then she saw Sarah dead. A neat, tiny bullet-hole in her forehead, blood soaking into a white pillow from a messy exit wound. *No, no . . . no!*

Phillips was suddenly at her side and she flinched away. He lifted the gun and placed the barrel against her wet cheek. It was warm on her skin.

Cindy lunged forward, surprising herself, and tried to claw his face, his throat, anything she could touch with her free hand.

You bastard, she tried to spit through the gag. *You bastard!*

Phillips caught her arm easily in a tight grip, held it steady, and tossed the gun on to the couch.

'I told you,' he said harshly. 'There are two ways to die.'

He moved away and produced another pair of handcuffs from the bag. Cindy struggled, but it took him only a few seconds to close a hoop about her free wrist and then fasten it to the radiator piping behind her back.

'You know, when you shoot a person, it's like a rush. The anticipation as you pull the trigger, the tension, the fear in the eyes of a sweet little girl . . . It floods your whole body.'

Cindy looked very afraid, Joel reflected. Her eyes were those of Sarah's the moment before he had pulled the trigger.

'It's like this great turn-on. Even better than sex. You should have seen her face . . . God, it was so beautiful.'

Cindy began to shake her head, tried to speak, repeating the muffled word *no* over and over.

'She was so confused. She recognised the gun as a weapon, but only as a fantasy object, something she had seen on the television. I placed it against her leg and . . . fed off her fear, her desire to be free. I was in control. The gun was on her knee and after one last look at her face as I savoured the moment, I squeezed the trigger, slowly.' He paused. 'This is just the beginning, Cindy.'

She was screaming again behind the gag. Her eyes were full of

133

anger and sorrow as he burst into laughter.

'You are beautiful, Cindy,' he told her.

'Yes, she is,' his father agreed. 'All those tears have ruined her make-up though.'

Joel didn't know how his father had got here, but he had opened the door in his mind and entered the past, was flooded by the blinding, painful light within and could see images from his childhood. *His father on top of his mother with a knife, and he was cutting her slightly as she groaned with pleasure, begged for more . . . His father looked to him, winked and smiled, and Joel nodded back, riveted to the spot, not knowing what to do now that he was discovered. He waited, as his mother writhed under his father's weight, tied by the silk ribbons . . . and then his father raised the knife above his head, glanced a final time at his son, and plunged it down into the body of the woman he loved. A geyser of blood splashed into his father's face and his mother began to scream, and the knife came down again. She noticed her son watching and begged for help even as the blade came down again and again, but all he could do was watch until his mother was dead and his father looked at him. Their eyes locked and then the man pulled the knife across his own wrists, causing deep, fatal wounds . . .*

Joel began to cry. He had no idea why his father had killed his mother and then taken his own life. He only knew that it had contributed to his turning into this monster.

Why couldn't they have been a normal family, like this one? Why did these strangers have so much?

He looked at Cindy, and suddenly she embodied all he had ever yearned for, all he had never had. He hated her for that, and lashed out with his fists several times, beating her.

Over and over.

6

Cindy could hear him in the kitchen. He was ripping the place apart in a violent rage, screaming *'Why?'* time and again, ranting. She listened as cutlery clattered to the tiled floor, plates smashed and bottles shattered, praying that she would hear the back door open and that – for some reason, any reason – he would leave them alone and alive. Simply walk out.

The bleeding from several small cuts on her face had stopped, but her skin was already beginning to swell and bruise from his pummelling.

'Not yet!' he cried, and she was sure he was talking to himself again. The man was insane. 'No, no. The family is mine. This is the last one. I might let you have the woman.'

There were still various bottles of drink in the cabinet opposite, which she and Tom had agreed to keep for when they had guests. If she could get the man to have a drink, he might become intoxicated, perhaps even negligent in his terrorism.

She could feel dried blood on her lips, and swallowed down saliva in her mouth. She ignored the pain, and prayed she would not pass out because then she would never be able to help her family survive this night.

Her only concern at the moment was for Sarah. It went beyond even that of escape . . . *survival, Cindy,* the calm voice in her mind corrected her. *You heard him and you believed him. Unless something goes wrong in his plans, he's the only person leaving the house alive.* Her daughter must be bleeding to death upstairs, if she had not already died from the shock and trauma of what had happened, or been killed by the vicious act.

She had to get help for Sarah.

The ranting and raving, the destruction in the kitchen, had stopped, and an ominous silence emanated from the next room. She heard a tap running and then the trickle of water ceased. What was he doing?

Phillips came into the room a second later. He had a couple of Paracetamol in one hand, and a large plastic beaker of water in the other. He swallowed the pills, taking a sip from the drink.

'Nice to see you've calmed down.' Joel said to Cindy, and bent to unlock one of the handcuffs at the pipe, leaving it open and dangling from her wrist. 'Here,' he said, offering her the beaker.

She wanted to take it and throw it in his face, wished it was an actual glass that she could shatter and cut him with instead of Richard's harmless Ren and Stimpy beaker. She could only hold it, and wait expectantly for him to remove the gag.

It was now close to eleven.

Nearly three hours had passed.

It was going to be a long night.

'Listen. You know what I'm capable of, what I can do. All that screaming earlier gave me a headache, woke my father. He's a bad man . . .' His voice faded away as he thought for a second and remembered what he had seen as a child. His father had killed his mother, and then taken his own life. But somehow the older man would murder this woman too, unless Joel took the lives of all the family first, and satisfied his own dark urges. 'I need to talk with you, get some real answers. I can only do so much with this yes and no rubbish. If I remove the gag, you have to promise me you won't scream. Do I have your word.'

Yes.

'Do you know what I will do if you scream?'

Another quick nod. *I've got a pretty good idea.*

'OK then. Here we go.'

Phillips reached forward and surprisingly gently , considering the savage way he had beaten her earlier, eased the tape off Cindy's mouth.

'Please, you have to call a doctor. Sarah needs—' Cindy began.

'You don't know what Sarah needs.'

'A doctor. Get her help. Please, you—' she stammered.

Phillips held up a hand to silence her. 'Take a drink.'

'But Sarah,' Cindy protested. 'You must—'

'Take a drink!'

Cindy sniffed. She hated the man and wished he was dead. She would feel none of the misguided remorse she had felt for Mike Brennan. She raised the beaker to her lips and gulped the water down, letting it wash about her mouth. She saved about an inch of the liquid in the bottom of the cup and by tilting it back managed to pour it over the sleeve of her blouse.

136

She lifted her arm and wiped her face, flinching slightly. She looked at the blouse. It was stained with blood.

'Sarah. She's in—'

'Sarah will be fine, until I decide otherwise. There was a first aid cabinet in the bathroom. I put a dressing on her wound,' he explained.

'But—' Cindy protested, only to be interrupted once more. Had he been up there long enough to do that? She hadn't heard him enter the bathroom, where the first-aid cabinet was.

'Now, you and I must talk. Do you love Tom?' he asked.

She decided not to answer. Damn him and his questions. His intention was to kill them all, anyway. She wouldn't tell him a single thing.

'I can put another gag on you,' Phillips told her. 'I didn't take the tape off so that you could sit there like a dummy. If you don't wish to join me in a civilised conversation I could cut out your tongue.'

Cindy gulped deeply, but still remained silent.

'Do you want me to go for Sarah's other leg?' Joel asked.

'No . . . please, have mercy on my children,' Cindy begged frantically.

'Then answer my questions!' he instructed angrily. 'Do you love your husband?'

'You know that I do,' she spat with equal anger. 'I've already told you once.'

'If you love him, why are you having an affair?'

'How—?'

'I've been watching you for a long time, Cindy. All of you. I like to watch. The anticipation fuels me.'

'Then you should know that I ended the affair weeks ago. *I love my husband*. More than anything else in the world.'

'Even more than your children?'

'You bastard,' she sobbed. 'Please, don't make me choose between them.'

'Not yet,' he told her. 'I always suspected the affair was over. You finished it the day we went to Alton Towers.'

We? Jesus Christ. How long had this man been following them?

'I went with my family to Alton Towers. Were you there too?'

What had Tom said that day? Something about killers who stalk their victims. *It thrills them to make contact with the people they intend to . . .* she swallowed deeply . . . *kill. Emotional and physical contact.*

'I rode the Haunted House with your children,' he informed

137

her, smiling gleefully at the memory.

Cindy was repulsed at the idea of this man being so close to her children, perhaps even talking to them, touching them protectively in the dark . . .

Suddenly she was certain that she knew this man. Recognition flickered across her face, and as she thought back over the past couple of months, trying to place him, she could see him watching her family on every street corner, lurking in shadows, queuing for rides behind them at Alton Towers . . . stalking them even in the safe harbour of daylight.

But it was more than that. She was suddenly sure that she had met this man, even spoken to him. But where, and when?

'I know you, don't I?' she enquired.

'We have met before now,' he told her.

Damn him, Cindy thought. He knew so much about them, even any flaws they might have; the problems in their lives. Everything. And they knew nothing.

Yes. But that could change, Cindy. It doesn't have to be that way.

Cindy recognised the voice this time. It belonged to Katie.

A long time ago when they were just teenagers, and Cindy was first learning about men, something nasty had happened. Mike Brennan had yearned for more than she was willing to give, pushed for more as he . . .

Cindy closed her eyes, blocking out the nightmare she had not experienced for years. Mike Brennan was dead. It was over for ever. But Cindy sensed that if she wanted Katie's help now, she would have to confront the images from her past before this night was over.

Katie was trying to help her, save her again as she had all those years ago.

Her big sister could talk her through this whole situation while she struggled to get her mind back together. She needed Katie.

Thanks, Big Sister. It's good to know you're here for me, Cindy thought.

Well, it isn't good to be here. I've had a lot of better times, so let's just get out of here as soon as possible?

OK, Cindy sniffed. Let's do the dirty.

She reached out with her free hand, slowly, so that he didn't think she was going to try to attack him again. But why not do that, she thought, if he gives me the opportunity?

Because of Sarah and Richard and Tom. They are vulnerable and not safe in the hands of this man.

She held his thigh softly, and then firmly felt the area of his groin, searching for signs of arousal. She hated every second of what she was doing, as her hand felt his growing erection.

'Way to go, baby,' Joel's father said, elated. 'Don't fight it, son. This feels good. Just let her do what she wants.'

Cindy had no idea what he was talking about. It was as if there was an unseen third person in the room observing their behaviour, and Phillips was talking to him.

Her hand hesitated. *I don't want to do this. I can't do this.*

Do it, Cindy. You must. It's the only way.

She began to slowly unzip his jeans, felt the teeth part. She reached in and scratched his stiff penis with her sharp nails.

Oh God, Tom, please forgive me.

Go on, Cindy, Katie told her. *Use your sexuality.*

'Are you married?' Cindy asked Phillips softly.

'No,' he responded calmly. 'But I had a girlfriend until this morning. We were only together one night. She was nice, but I broke up with her.'

Joel didn't feel anything she was doing, but his father was getting very excited by the hand-on action. He let him enjoy her pathetic tricks for a second longer, and then pulled away. His father would have been fooled by her pleasurable act, but he was not even distracted.

'Don't go, Joel,' Cindy pouted. 'I liked—'

He slapped her viciously, and then fastened his jeans.

'Jesus,' his father complained. 'You've got a lot to learn about how to treat a lady, son.'

'She's no lady, Father. She sleeps around, and I'm not on a date here!'

Shocked, Cindy left her hand on the carpet where it had fallen. He was insane, talking to himself like that.

She sighed. It had been working. Until he flipped out, and hit her again. He had been relaxing, giving into her sexual charm. She cringed inwardly at the thought of being with him . . . but if that was what it took to get out of here alive, get them all out . . .

What had gone wrong? What had made him so angry?

Her cheek was still stinging from his slap, and his hand had opened up one of the cuts. She felt fresh blood running down her face.

Cindy's strength had been building up. Hope, like a fading

candlelight in the darkness of her mind, had flared bright for a dizzying second. But now she was back at the beginning, suddenly weak once more, her small power and authority over him taken away, having gained nothing.

And then, for no particular reason, she turned away from his watchful stare and looked at the television screen.

His face was looking out at her.

Cindy performed a double-take, checking the man in the room and then looking back at the television. The volume was turned down so that she couldn't hear the words, and the report only lasted a few seconds before his picture disappeared and a new item came on.

When she turned back to the man she suddenly remembered where she had seen him before . . . who the girlfriend he had spoken of must be.

Her best friend. Jo Myers.

He was the owner of the little bookstore in town.

'What did you do to Jo?' Cindy asked in a panic, and then she screamed hysterically: *'What did you do?'*

7

Different policemen have different hobbies outside of the job.
But they all need something, one activity that helps them forget
all the badness in the world which they confront every single
day. Some have a favourite sport, even coach it at school level.
Some like to read, others to write. Some collect stamps. Bird-
watch. Cook and enjoy their own culinary delights.

Some simply savour the pleasure of spare time with their
girlfriend, family or wife.

And that had been Ian Knox's favourite pastime. Chatting
with Lucy until night fell, and then resting in each other's arms,
making love softly . . .

Now he painted.

He didn't like to paint, but it was all there was to do. His
friends often asked him out to get drunk, give his mind a chance
to forget the pain. But he did not want to forget, and he knew
that one day they would give up on him and stop asking. He
wanted to die with all the memories of Lucy burning bright.

He looked at the canvas before him. The picture was of a bleak
cityscape, towers touching the sky as a fire burned it to ashes.
He would call it *Bright Descendance*. He stroked more grey into
the doomed buildings.

Once he had enjoyed strolling with Lucy through forests and
fields and they had spent many hours making love out of doors,
with him drawing sketches of wildlife which he would later turn
into exotic pictures for her. Landscapes full of colour and life,
birds in flight, soaring in blue skies, wild creatures stalking
unseen prey and running in the wind.

Life.

There was no life in the picture he was working on now. No
vitality. The cityscape was burning. Everybody was going to die.

Knox stopped working on the piece and looked up at the wall
behind the canvas. It was covered with sketches and drawings of

Lucy. Some of the pictures had been done when she was alive, most after she had gone. He had found all the photographs he could of her and had done many pencil drawings until his heart had tired.

But no amount of pictures could bring her back.

He could no longer make a difference.

Knox thought about that for a second. There had to be something he could do.

The autopsy on Jo Myers had taken a while. Her body was so badly mutilated, it was almost as if her killer was trying to hide something, Knox had thought. It had revealed her stomach contents. Malone had identified some of the products in her digestive tracts, among them duck. He then informed Knox that the only place in town which served duck was The Bradbury Lodge, so unless she had eaten at home or somewhere outside of town, she had dined there the previous night.

That afternoon Knox had gone up to The Lodge. A young waiter – a college kid named Andy – remembered Jo and her male companion. Business had been slow that night.

Knox asked for a description of the man.

Andy was hazy, seemed more concerned with a blonde and her brunette friend at the far end of the bar.

'Son, I could really use this description if you can stop thinking with your cock for just half a second,' Knox told him, interrupting his fantasies about the two women. 'This is a murder investigation. The young woman in question was savagely and brutally killed. We need to find this man!'

'Sorry. Hey, I can do better than a description. I can give you a name if he made a reservation.' Andy turned the page of a heavy leatherbound book. 'No. Nothing.'

'Damn,' Knox muttered, disappointed. He had been hoping for an early break in the case.

Andy was back watching the two women, particularly the blonde who was wearing a short skirt. 'Do you think those legs go on forever?' he murmured.

Knox glanced over. 'I think they go on as high as her hips,' he told the kid drily. 'Get me a beer, Andy. I need a drink.'

Andy was lost in his dreamworld again and Knox clicked his fingers.

'Yeah,' the kid said. 'OK. I was just thinking – those two were in here a couple of weeks ago. I remember because one of them spilled a drink on some bloke, caused a bit of a commotion.'

'Is there a point to this, laddie, or are you going to get my drink?' Knox enquired.

'In a sec. I thought you people didn't drink on duty.' Knox looked at the young barman caustically and Andy continued: 'The woman, the one you're interested in – she was in that night, too, and I'm pretty sure she was with the same guy.' He quickly rifled through the pages and then turned the book so that it was facing Knox. Andy pointed. 'That's the bloke you're after.'

'Joel Phillips,' Knox read out, and jotted the name down in his notebook. He also recorded the date and the time they had eaten. 'Thanks, Andy. You're a star.'

'Yeah. I know. It's a shame *they* don't think so,' he joked, rather obviously indicating the women at the other end of the bar. The blonde smiled, and motioned for new drinks.

'Maybe they do,' Knox smiled. 'I'll be in touch.'

Ian lost himself in the beauty of Lucy as he retraced his steps through the other events of the day. *I miss you so much, my darling*.

They had run Phillips' name through the computer, Knox wondering where he had heard it before.

'He's a businessman: owns a bookshop in town called *Pages*,' Lewis had told him, sitting before the keyboard because he had faster fingers than Knox. 'You know, this sweetheart is just like a lady,' he said, talking of the computer. 'Treat her nice and she'll tell you anything.'

'I'm not surprised you don't have a girlfriend, Lewis.'

Carter Lewis was a good kid, a hotshot in the Department who was going to go a long way, perhaps even all the way to the top of the profession. It was just a shame that he talked as if he was trapped in an American buddy-buddy cop movie, Knox thought.

'Phillips had been living in London. Washed up on our shores a few years ago.'

'Got an address?' Knox asked, wondering why the name seemed vaguely familiar. 'Let's go and talk to this bloke, see what time he left the lady.'

'OK.' Lewis nodded, and tapped a couple of keys. 'Two, Bowden Drive. I know the area. I used to go out with a girl up there who could do—'

'Spare me the gory details, sonny,' Knox said, holding up his hand. Was the world full of randy young men? 'Come on. Let's get out there.'

Lewis looked at his watch. 'We might catch him at the shop.'

Pages was locked and shuttered, but neither Lewis nor Ian Knox found this unusual. A lot of the smaller shops shut early on a Wednesday, and if Phillips owned the business and didn't hire staff, he could come and go as he pleased, stay open whenever he wanted. They had visited his home address, but nobody was in.

'We'll try again later,' Knox told Lewis.

When they got no answer again in the early evening they had made an announcement to the media appealing for Phillips to come forward; he was not a suspect but they needed him to answer a few questions.

Now Knox looked from his wife to the burning city depicted in his painting. Phillips had not gone home for a reason, he thought. Knox bumped him up in his mind from wanted for questioning to suspected of murder. I should have forced an entry at Bowden Drive, he decided, suddenly sure that there was something inside that was pivotal to their investigation.

His stomach felt as though a giant fist was clenching all his muscles tight within. He still hadn't placed the name Joel Phillips, but that didn't seem important any more. They simply had to find this man.

Could there still be time for him to make a difference?

He remembered something Lucy had once said, laughing – she had such a wonderful, delightful laugh that could make him smile even on the darkest day – after he had driven for hours around the countryside without a map, lost, searching for a Bed & Breakfast he was certain he'd seen.

You have good instincts, Ian Knox. Here we are, driving around the middle of nowhere, searching for a building I believe is a figment of your imagination. But you'll find it eventually. It's those good instincts, Lucy had joked.

But when it came to police work, he *did* have good instincts. The best. And now a bad feeling gripped him and he felt sweat break out across his forehead. They should have checked Phillips' history.

He looked at Lucy a final time and then moved out of the room and into the kitchen where there was a Mickey Mouse telephone. He paused and glanced at a holiday brochure on the table. The magazine featured an interesting piece on the Grand Canyon. It was a year old. Knox turned away before he began to leaf through the pages, a sob escaping him as he remembered her dreams. *Now isn't the time*, he chastised himself, and quickly dialled Lewis' home number.

'Come on,' Knox fretted. 'Don't choose tonight to lose your cherry.'

The phone rang a third time. There was no way he would be able to fiddle with the computer; he would end up staying there all night. The phone rang and rang. 'Shite,' Knox groaned, about to hang up.

'Hello? Don't you know what time it is?' a voice grunted.

'Is that you, Lewis?'

The voice grumbled in the affirmative.

'You're supposed to use that line when somebody wakes you up in the middle of the night,' Knox informed him.

'You did wake me up,' Lewis complained.

Knox looked at the clock on the wall. It was a few minutes past eleven. 'Now I know why you don't have a girlfriend. Can you access the computer from there?'

'Yes. But it would be illegal.'

'All right,' Knox said patiently. '*Will* you access the computer from there?'

'I love a challenge. Just give me a second.'

The line went quiet and Knox heard a hushed whisper in the background.

'I have to go downstairs for a minute, Reggie.'

And then a female voice: 'Hurry back.'

A few minutes later Lewis came back on the line, 'OK, sir. I'm in.'

'Lewis, you sly fox,' Knox teased. 'You stallion.'

'What are we looking for, sir?' Lewis asked, wanting to get back upstairs to the warmth of Regina.

'Can you punch up the file on Joel Phillips? Get me some background?'

'Is that all? A schoolkid could manage that,' Lewis muttered, already hitting keys. 'Here we go. Born on—'

'Just anything relevant, all right? I don't care what birth sign he was born under.'

Silence for half a second as Lewis read down the screen.

'Holy shit,' Lewis whispered.

'What've you got? Talk to me, Lewis.'

'You are not going to believe this,' Lewis told his superior officer.

'I'm on the edge of my seat,' Knox assured him. 'What's the deal?'

'Nearly thirty years ago, before I was even a wicked twitch in my father's pants, there was a shocking murder with suicide here in Bradbury. Do you remember—?'

'Everybody on the force at the time remembers it, Lewis. That kind of thing didn't happen every other week, like it seems to these days. I was just a PC, in my first year on the job. I had my beat and my bicycle and very little to do with the investigation,' Knox told him. 'I'll tell you something though, laddie. Bradbury changed after that, after the discovery of that couple, and their poor kid, found sitting in the blood, staring at his parents' bodies. Catatonic, he was. Didn't speak for days. Bradbury was just a small town, back then – little more than a village community, not the sprawling mess we live in today. That kind of thing only happened down at the cinema or in the pages of a book,' Knox paused, 'not on our own doorsteps. No, Lewis, after the discovery of Mr and Mrs Luckins, people were a little less trusting. They began to lock their doors at night, weren't so friendly to strangers.'

'Do you remember the name of the child involved?' Lewis asked.

'I'm not sure,' Knox pondered. 'Roger, I think, or was it Richard? One of those "r" names. He wasn't around for too long. The media descended on Bradbury like a shoal of piranhas on a piece of meat. It was a frenzy – and the focus of it all was that poor kid. The whole experience must have traumatised him for life.' Knox couldn't work out what Lewis was driving at. 'The case was open and shut. DI Ramsey – the officer in charge of the investigation – and his superiors, decided it would benefit the child most if he disappeared. Only the police and immediate relatives were to have a record of his location. They found the young 'un a foster home and sealed the documents. I heard later that his new family had moved him down to London to escape the press. I don't know if that's true. There was a lot of talk, and some rumours went on for years after the investigation.'

'They did take him down to London,' Lewis confirmed, reading information from the screen. 'They brought him up, fed him, gave him a good education. He was a clever child – did well in his A-levels. He went on to medical school, later specialising in pathology, and was eventually taken on by our buddies at Scotland Yard. He took early retirement a couple of years ago, before moving back here, to his home town.'

'What was the name of the foster family?' Knox asked. This information had been sitting in the computer all along and they had failed to see it.

'Gareth and Kelly Phillips. The boy was named Roger Luckins before he became . . .

'Joel Phillips,' Knox finished. His voice became very quiet. 'What were the initials of his real parents?'

'You'd better hold on to your woolly socks, DI Knox, because this is going to blow them right across the room. G. L. and S. L.!' Lewis sighed. 'Christ, now it all falls into place.'

'I was just a PC,' Knox said unhappily. Should he have remembered the case, made some sort of connection?

'Is this my fault?' he asked Lewis uncertainly.

'Of course not, sir. There's no way you could have known.'

'Look – those initials aren't quite right. Maybe we're barking up the wrong tree. Can you pull up the Luckins woman's maiden name from there, Lewis?'

'Can do,' Lewis assured him, tapping at the keyboard or a few seconds.

Knox waited.

Where do I know your name from, Joel Phillips? I didn't know it all those years ago, so why is it familiar now? Knox suddenly began to doubt himself. He had been so washed up in his own sorrow . . . What if he could have solved this case earlier, before the deaths of so many families? If only he'd made the connection which now eluded him!

'I hear you, Lewis. Shelly Fay. G. L. and S. F.'

'We've got the bastard!' Lewis declared, jubilant.

'Not yet. I'll pick you up in five minutes,' Knox said steadily. 'I think we should go back to his house. He's killed Jo Myers instead of a pet.'

Knox put the receiver in its cradle, the name Joel Phillips still tormenting him. Had he met the man before? If so, where? When? Somehow, he knew the information was vital to their investigation.

8

He knows that a post mortem is not just about cutting people open and digging out their insides in any old order. It is a technical and precise science: a search for evidence and cause of death.

Before he even picks up a scalpel, an external examination may offer him many clues and evidence which could help to identify a killer or secure a conviction.

He begins with the head, shaves it to check for signs of bruising or lacerations not immediately visible.

The neck might hold bruising in the case of a victim who has been throttled, while strangling will leave an impression of the ligature in the skin . . .

When she was sedated, Phillips cut and slashed Jo Myers with the knife. After nine stab wounds, three to the abdomen and the rest to her legs and arms, she was still not dead. His next blow glanced off her cheek, shaving skin away. Her breathing was laboured, the light in her eyes flickering like that of a dying flame.

Bruising is indicative of a victim who has been beaten or held down. Ropemarks show if a person has been tied.

He looks at this victim's hands. He is a man of about twenty-five. His girlfriend is on the next slab, waiting to be cut open by a stranger. Joel looks at her. Saving the best for last, he thinks. The man has cuts across his palms. These are called self-defence cuts – when a person holds up his hands to prevent an assault by an assailant with a knife. The man died protecting his girlfriend.

Jo began to scream. The noise was loud – too loud – and Joel was afraid of it waking his parents or disturbing the neighbours. He brought the knife down, across her mouth, slitting her lips and tongue.

Scrapings under a victim's fingernails can often hold vital evidence, although that is not the case here.

Skin colour can also be helpful. Cyanosis – a deep blue

colouring of the face and lips – is a sign of asphyxiation or suffocation. Cyanide poisoning leaves a lilac tint to the skin, while carbon monoxide poisoning leaves the face a cherry pink. . .

Her face and body were red with blood, yet he was still cutting and slashing and stabbing. She was finally dead, but his work was far from over. For a while she'd blubbered, words not forming beyond her disabled lips and tongue, blood and slobber bubbling out, but now even that had stopped.

If the skin is very pale it may be a sign of internal bleeding or blood loss.

Vaginal damage is a positive sign of rape.

Jo looked so pretty, Joel thought. He wanted to be with her, awash in her blood as they lay together for a short while. But he knew he could not touch her now.

'Go on,' his father urged, reaching out.

But Joel stopped the hand. 'No. Next time is yours, Father. I'm moving on soon. You can have the next one.'

Joel studied the body for a while. In death, the glories of the flesh could be so beautiful. But, sadly, this time he must make her ugly. He intended for this body to be discovered, so he could not love her.

He began to carve into Jo Myers' body as if he was cutting a huge roast at a family Sunday dinner; chopped off all her toes and fingers.

The police must not associate the death of Jo Myers with the murders of the Initial Killer until long after he had safely left the region.

9

'Did you kill Jo?' Cindy demanded, already weeping.

'Yes,' Joel said calmly, but suddenly the pain was searing and he began to scream. 'No! Don't make me watch again!'

. . . his father lifting the knife, whirling it down as his mother begs and pleads frantically with him, but all he does is watch, paralysed, as his father murders her and . . .

'Don't show me again!' Joel bellowed, and ran from the room, clutching the small container of Paracetamol. She heard the tap running, and then it was twisted off.

When he came back, water was dribbling down from his lips, off his chin, and she knew that he'd swallowed more tablets. If he ate enough of those things, Cindy thought, they could make him drowsy. He might start making mistakes. If only she could get him drinking the alcohol now, it would have a quicker effect.

Joel began to breathe easily, and she knew the pain must be subsiding.

'Please don't cry,' he said softly to Cindy. 'Do you remember the day we met?'

The day that we met, Cindy thought. Oh Jesus, please help us. The guy was Looney-tunes, absolutely madder than the Hatter at his tea-party.

You've established that already, Cindy darling. Let's try and get off first base here. You were out with Alan and . . . Jo wanted me to check out the man who owned a small bookstore in the town centre.

Cindy remembered what she'd told Jo later. *He's a lot older than you, Jo. And a bit weird-looking, too.* Weird was only the beginning of it, she thought now. Oh God, Jo. Why didn't you listen to me? *Why?*

Cindy sniffed and closed her eyes, halting her tears. She resolved to do all she could to avenge the death of her best friend.

151

'I'll never forget that day,' she whispered now, and let her tongue play over her lips, let her eyes show a hunger for him, trying once more to seduce him. She needed information, anything. She prayed that she could use any knowledge she discovered to her advantage.

Jo was dead. The news had been a shock to her system, but now her mind was numb to the fact, had accepted it ... but meanwhile poor Sarah was upstairs, probably bleeding and in desperate need of medical attention.

'Why were you attracted to me?' Cindy asked.

Yes, why? And why the other families? Why did you fixate on me? On my family? Do tell.

'I think it was your perfume,' Joel's father told her, losing himself in her eyes. 'The scent of Coco.'

Cindy watched him beginning to slip, not aware of his alternate personalities, and offered a beguiling smile.

If only her hand wasn't still handcuffed to the radiator piping. The gun lay on the far side of the floor, near the couch and disconnected telephone. Cindy was certain she could beat him to it.

But could she actually use it, given the opportunity? Could she point it at the man, pull the trigger? Shoot him ... kill him?

You killed Mike Brennan.

No. He killed himself. I'm glad he's dead – he could be doing his nasty thing to other women. But I didn't take his life.

You were the catalyst ... But forget Mike Brennan for now. Think of Sarah.

Thanks for reminding me of that, Katie. Sometimes you can be a real pain in the neck, did you know that?

The images came quickly, unbidden and unwanted. Sarah, lying on the bed, writhing and bleeding. Crying for her mother.

Yes, Cindy thought grimly. If she was ever given the opportunity, she would have no qualms about killing this man. She'd grab the gun, aim it at his stone heart and pull the trigger. Watch him bleed and die.

She smiled sweetly at the thought, and realised he had moved closer. She could feel his bad breath on her face. Any closer and their lips would be touching, they would be kissing and – the thought was repulsive, but if she had to, she would welcome him.

Please, please forgive me, Tom.

Use it, Cindy. Your sexuality is a weapon. Use it to survive ... a chance for your family to live through this terrible night. Look at him ... watch him succumb to you.

152

'I like the scent, too,' she whispered softly, and moved to one side as naturally as possible, parting her legs slightly. But not too much. *Don't give him it all yet.* 'I could wear it now if you like.'

'Yes,' Joel's father responded immediately.

'Do you want me?' Cindy asked, opening her legs a little more.

That's good, Cindy. Give him something nice to look at, something sweet to distract him.

She tugged at the piping, wished there was an object within reach. She could bash him on the side of his head, but she dared not look around for a weapon now. She was in the middle of her performance and did not want to lose his horrible attention.

She moved her body closer and their lips touched. She slipped her tongue into his mouth, hating every second, all that she was doing.

If he slips his tongue inside, bite it off, Katie advised.

His tongue touched her mouth, wet her dry lips, and she wrapped her free hand about his waist.

'Come to me,' she breathed.

Rip it out and spit it in his face, her sister urged.

Cindy felt it on the front of her teeth. A little closer, she thought. A little deeper. She opened her mouth slightly and prepared to snap her teeth shut, like an inhumane animal trap. But his sadistic torture was inhumane . . .

But then he backed away slightly.

She pulled at the piping. 'I can't do anything for you like this,' she pouted sexily.

But Joel backed away completely and sat on the floor near the couch.

'My father was here just then. He likes you,' he informed her, and studied her.

Cindy managed a smile, and then crossed her legs. He was a confused son of a bitch, a crazy bastard. He might even be gay, but she doubted that. Jo usually had a reliable eye for such things.

But for now, whatever his problem and hang-ups, if it wasn't going to aid their dilemma and provide them with an advantage, she didn't want him looking at her or touching her.

Good call, Little Sister.

'He wants you,' Joel told her without emotion, and then walked over to the window. He opened the curtain a crack and looked out, shaking his head. 'I thought we had an understanding?'

Cindy guessed what had happened. They had a visitor. But that couldn't be, she panicked. She'd told him there would be nobody.

Joel quickly moved to the kitchen and returned with a wet J-cloth. He contemplated ignoring the caller, but the man walking up the driveway might have seen the curtain move, and the lights were on in parts of the house. It might be enough to make him suspicious. If Cindy had lied earlier he might even be expected.

He began to wipe the dry blood from her face when the doorbell rang. She flinched away, and then felt the gun pushed under her chin.

'Who is it?' Joel hissed.

'I don't know,' she stuttered. 'I told you we weren't—'

'You lied to me!' Phillips said harshly.

The doorbell rang again and then the visitor began to pound on the door.

'I know you're in there!' the man called from outside. 'I want to talk!'

Cindy sighed deeply. Of all the nights Alan had to show his face and cause trouble.

'Answer him!' Joel commanded quietly.

'Just a . . . just a minute!' Cindy shouted.

'Now, listen carefully. You look a mess, but do the best you can to get rid of him. If he enters the house, he dies,' Joel explained coldly. 'Do you understand?'

Cindy nodded. 'Yes,' she said weakly.

'Good.' Joel unlocked the second set of handcuffs before removing them both from her wrists. 'I'll be close, Cindy. I'll be listening. If you try to run or pass him some kind of stupid message, I'll kill you both and then Tom. And then the children . . . very slowly.'

10

Tom sat defeated, his back against the wall, drowning in dark uncertainty.

What was happening downstairs?

He had tried with all his strength to get free from the radiator piping, but could not. Even if he succeeded, he did not know what he would do next.

How long had he been up here? What time was it?

Cindy and the children had to be all right. They simply had to be. He was still holding on to a frayed thread of hope, that this was not the Initial Killer, but some kind of fraud, pretending to be him and getting thrills out of their fear. If they did exactly as he said, maybe they wouldn't die tonight.

He looked down at his cuffed wrist and tried to manoeuvre his hand out of the loop, but it wasn't going to happen. His wrist was rubbed red raw and bleeding from his struggles. He ignored the pain.

What if he did get free?

If he attacked the man and failed to overpower him ... Tom sighed. He wouldn't win a fight, he had no doubts of that. He had never been in a brawl before; not in a nightclub or a bar, not a street scuffle or even at school. Throughout his schooldays he'd kept his profile low and his grades high, avoiding trouble. And in university there had been different goals – to party as much as possible, dodge lectures, get drunk and stoned as often as possible without going crazy on a small grant ... and still manage to graduate.

So, without experience, having never thrown a real punch in his life, how could he hope to fight a man armed with a gun, whose only intention was to kill the whole Curtis family before dawn?

The best way you can. Fight hard and strong, and die knowing you did all you could to protect your family.

But he could not. If he failed to overpower Phillips, his own actions would undoubtedly kill them all.

But we're going to die, anyway. Make a stand!

He leaned against the wall and offered up a silent prayer to any gods who might be listening. He had never been faithful to any type of religion, never even considered it or cared for the Church, but now he wept as he searched for something to believe in.

He could not find confidence or spirit in his own actions, so he looked outside . . . past Cindy and the children, beyond the boundaries of their home. He needed to believe in a Higher Authority so that if they died tonight, there would be something for him to hold on to. A belief that they would still be together in the next life.

He cried and hated himself for all his omissions of protection. He passed what felt like hours, but were actually only minutes, time stretching in his dark solitude, thinking of all that someone braver and more imaginative would have done by now, and how little . . . *nothing; absolutely zilch* . . . he had accomplished.

Tom sobbed as he pictured Cindy in the living room, lying naked on the now bloody carpet as the man defiled her. He wept as he saw Richard and Sarah dead . . . and slowly, a violent rage began to fill him.

He had to get past this. Rise above his lack of confidence and strength. Get off this fucking pipe and fight for all he loved!

And suddenly he was pulling and wrenching, the metal hoops digging deep into his skin as he tried to render himself free. Fresh blood sprang up on his wrist as he heaved at the pipe with both hands, his feet braced against the wall.

But it would not break.

'Come on!' he screamed. All he wanted in these seconds was for Joel Phillips to be here, within reach, and he would vent all his fury on the man who deserved it. He'd rip his fucking head off! 'Come on!'

He was determined not to give up, but finally, exhausted, he let go of the pipe and it sank back to the wall.

It had all been to no avail.

There had to be something he could do, he thought desperately.

That was when he heard the doorbell.

Somebody was here! They were saved!

Tom began to work on the pipe again.

'Up here!' he yelled. 'Hurry!'

And then he felt the pipe shift a little more, hope beating in his heart.

11

Ian Knox and Carter Lewis arrived at Joel Phillips' home address just before twelve-fifteen.

'So who's the girl?' Knox asked, grinning as they walked up the front path of number two, Bowden Drive.

Knox had paint on his sweatshirt and Lewis was dressed in jeans and a shirt. The night was warm. Lewis paused as they reached the front door.

'Regina Lowe.'

Knox rang the bell. 'Regina Lowe? You're shagging Reggie Lowe from the office?'

'I like to think of it as a little more than *shagging*.' Lewis smiled tightly, thinking for a second. 'I might as well tell you now, sir. We're getting married next year, and I want you to be my best man.'

There was no answer and Knox knocked hard a few times.

'I don't know, Lewis,' he said eventually. 'I'm not into speeches and I don't think I'm going to be around much longer.' It was late in the game and he had one last thing to do before he was ready to die and join Lucy. He wanted to fly to the Grand Canyon. Sit on its edge and see if the magic actually worked, if it could wash his concerns away as he stared in awe of it. Just as Lucy always believed it would. 'Let me think about it.'

'All right. Fine by me,' Lewis said, sounding hurt.

'Sorry, Lewis. Of course I'll do it,' Knox said warmly and shook the younger man's hand. 'You know I will. Congratulations, lad. Now let's go to work. This blighter isn't home. I'll check round the back.'

He walked down the side of the building, through a gate which led into a small, overgrown garden. There were no flowers or plants or trees to brighten it up and the long grass was in desperate need of cutting and mowing. He clicked his torch on and panned it about the garden and then on to the back door.

159

He tried the handle, but the door was firmly locked.

I have to get in there, Knox thought. It was a powerful desire – call it Policeman's Intuition – but he was sure that if he searched the house he would find the key to the killings, and to the strange nagging in his mind that he knew Joel Phillips, or his name, from somewhere.

He heard Lewis' footfalls coming down the side of the house. 'Anything back here?' the younger detective called.

'Quiet, Lewis,' Knox cautioned. 'I don't want the whole street to know we're here. Get on the radio and see if you can obtain a warrant to enter and search the premises.'

'It's unlikely, sir. You know it.'

'Give it a shot anyway. Wake the Chief Inspector if you have to – I'll take the heat,' Knox told him. 'I'm about done on this beat, anyway,' he whispered under his breath as he watched Lewis move off.

He waited a few seconds, giving Lewis a chance to reach the car, and then dug out a small leather case from his back pocket. He unzipped it, to reveal a small set of lockpicks.

I never thought I'd have a use for you chaps again, he thought, and remembered a time long ago, before he had become a policeman, when his favourite hobby as a young tearaway was ripping off stereos and televisions. It was strange how someone's life could change. Once – many years ago – he had been well on the way to becoming a successful minor-league criminal, and now he was one of the best coppers in the Cheshire region.

He selected the correct lockpick, aware that time was short. Lewis was still at the car.

'You stick the lockpick in,' he sang in a whisper, and jiggled it until he was certain he had tumbled the simple locking mechanism. 'You take the lockpick out. You do the Hokey-Cokey, and you turn about.' He hummed quietly, performing a little jig and spinning once on the spot. 'That's what it's all about!'

He tried the door and was unsurprised when it opened.

'Maybe crime does pay,' he joked to himself, and slid into the premises, imagining Lewis and himself sitting on the porch waiting until dawn before they even got close to obtaining permission to legally enter the building.

The house was quiet and Knox sensed immediately that Phillips wasn't home. They had to find the man soon. He quickly walked through to the front door and unlocked the dropcatch just as Lewis came jogging up the path.

'What the hell are you doing in there – sir?' Lewis asked, astonished. Then he put on a bad Scottish accent, imitating their whisky-drinking, red-faced superior. 'No joy on the warrant. The boss said, "You're oot o' your fuckin' mind, wakin' me in the middle o' the night with what you've go'." '

Knox sighed. 'I've got a feeling about this place, laddie. Lucky for us the back door was open.'

Lewis smiled knowingly. 'This is still an illegal entry. We could get reprimanded for this.'

'Step inside before a neighbour notices us and calls the police,' Knox advised, gesturing with his thumb. 'We won't get in trouble if we suspect that somebody is in a life-endangering situation.'

'And do we suspect that?' Lewis queried.

'Yes. Oh yes. Somewhere, the night is only just beginning. Let's see what we can find.'

12

Alan didn't know what to say when the door opened and he saw the state of Cindy's face. She looked terrible. Blood trickled off her lip from a tiny split where she'd bitten herself. Her face was bruised and cut, and she had been crying. Her eyes were bloodshot and moist with fresh tears waiting to fall and Alan felt all his anger drain away, to be replaced by pity.

'Jesus . . . Did you tell him about us? Did the bastard hit you – is that what this is all about?' he demanded, pushing on the door slightly, but hesitating when she didn't stand aside to admit him.

'No,' she said, her voice a high-pitched crack in the night. 'Please, you must leave, Alan.'

He tried to look past her, over her shoulder and into the house. Everything seemed normal enough, but Cindy was definitely upset, afraid of something. She looked like a wounded animal, about to be devoured by a savage predator.

'What's happening here, Cindy?' he asked.

'Alan,' she whispered, looking around. Where was Phillips? She couldn't see him. 'Please . . . get help. Call the police.'

Unlike Tom, Alan was strong and used to fighting. The reason behind his impressive muscular structure was because a gang of lads had once beaten him and a friend up and robbed them of fifty pounds, when they were just scrawny kids out shopping with Christmas money. That day he'd vowed that nobody would ever hurt him or anybody he cared for again.

He often moonlighted as a bouncer at a nightclub in Manchester on his days off. Not because he needed the extra income, but because he liked to fight, especially in a position of authority where he had control. He wanted to prove himself, show the world what he had become. That nobody could touch him.

Now Cindy was in trouble, and she needed his help.

'Stand aside, Cindy,' he told her strongly, and pushed the door wide open.

'No, Alan!' she gasped. Phillips would be listening just behind the living-room door. Could she make a run for it? He would surely kill all her family.

If Alan had heeded her words, and turned on his heels, he might have made it out of the driveway alive, could even have contacted the police. But instead – he could hear somebody screaming upstairs: was the bastard hurting his own children, too? – he moved Cindy out of the way and stepped into the vestibule.

'Don't worry, Cindy. I'm here now,' Alan assured her, gently holding her arm. There was nothing he couldn't handle, and he was not afraid of her husband. 'Where is he?'

'Right here,' Phillips responded and stepped from the living room, the gun in his hand. His finger was already closing on the trigger and Cindy began to beg and cry.

'Please don't hurt him. He's done nothing. Nothing!'

Alan turned and saw the man approaching.

Fear was carved in Alan's granite features as he charged forward, letting go of Cindy, his decision to attack made in a split second. A grave mistake.

He might have made it out of the door if he'd tried. He could have ducked into the shadows of the garden and hidden. Got clean away . . . but then he took a chance on being quicker than the stranger. What if he could get to his hand before he squeezed the trigger?

He would save Cindy, and she would love him . . . for ever.

He loved her. That was all that counted, why he had selfishly come here . . . and made his fatal error.

Alan had only taken two steps when he heard a venomous spit, and saw a flash of light in the shallow darkness of the vestibule. As it dawned on him that the man had fired, he was already falling, his right leg buckling beneath him.

He hit the floor hard, grunting. He could see the jutting white bone of his knee, mashed by a bullet and coated with a thin film of blood.

The pain was intense.

Cindy began to scream again, and theirs was a chorus of fear reaching out into the street for help. Alan saw her, frozen, hands at her mouth in horror.

'Run,' he gasped. *Why don't you run?*

His other leg jolted, but somehow, Alan was ready for the agony this time. First the cold numbness, his leg dead for a sudden instant, and then a crescendo of pain, louder than their screams, searing hot and bright. And then the brightness engulfed him, as he was blinded by shock. It was a sedative that knocked him unconscious as he saw the man step over his body . . . *nothing he could do* . . . and bring the butt of the pistol down hard on the side of Cindy's head.

Then he shut the front door, and with it, the warm night was lost, neighbours taking a last, late walk with the dog, a car cruising by, the rustle of a cat in the undergrowth, staring at the moon with unthinking golden eyes.

All shut out as the door slammed. Imprisoning them in a nightmare where the bars were unbreakable . . . and the warden was called Death.

13

Knox and Lewis didn't risk putting lights on within the house for fear of alerting passers-by to their illegal intrusion, so it took them a little while using only torches, to efficiently search the ground floor.

They found nothing.

'Maybe we were wrong about this dude,' Lewis muttered.

Knox looked up the steep stairs. 'Let's check up there. If I'm wrong we'll get out of here pronto. You got any climbing equipment?' he asked sarcastically. 'Any crampons?'

'Here you go,' Lewis grinned, and handed Knox a small packet.

'Very funny, Lewis,' Knox hissed. 'You should have your own TV show. I said *crampons* – not *condoms*. Save those for Reggie.'

A few seconds later they reached the top of the stairs.

'I'm too old for this caper,' Knox groaned, out of breath.

'Yes, you are,' the younger man reassured him.

'Thanks. Just what I needed to hear,' Knox said and opened the first door carefully. A bathroom. They looked it over for a minute, but found nothing. And yet, the hairs on the back of his head were prickling uncomfortably.

'I mean it. You ever thought of retiring? You've got your pension. There's a lot to see in the world.'

'I know what I want to see in the world,' Knox said, trying to conceal the sadness in his voice by sounding flippant. 'But to leave the community in your not-so-capable hands? You must be joking.'

Knox opened a door and they walked into the main bedroom.

'Jesus,' Lewis gagged. The stale smell of air-freshener and that of old, dead flesh was overwhelming.

Knox knew that their search had ended. He found the light-switch and clicked off his torch.

'Oh God.' Lewis clamped a hand over his mouth.

'If you're going to puke,' Knox told him calmly as he walked to the bed, covering his mouth with a clean handkerchief as he breathed the putrid air, 'make sure you do it outside the house.'

Lewis didn't need telling twice; Knox heard him pounding down the stairs and out of the front door.

On top of the dirty bedclothes lay what looked like two mummified corpses. Their bones were wrapped in leathery flesh that was discoloured to a rotten yellow. Their mouths were agape, frozen until the end of time in rictus smiles, and from one a tiny fly buzzed out. Huge stitches in the bodies suggested that autopsies had been conducted upon these people.

Finally, the horrible stench of the dry bodies undergoing the slow process of rehydration, mingling with the stale air-freshener, overwhelmed Knox and he left the room, too, closing the door.

Who were they, this gruesome couple?

If Joel Phillips was the Initial Killer, Knox decided that the bodies might well be those of his parents, resurrected from their final resting place.

He shuddered, remembering now where he had heard the name Joel Phillips. Remembering now a night he had shared with a serial killer.

Since the death of Lucy, there had been many nights for Ian Knox when he couldn't sleep. He'd roll over, caught in a delightful dream in which he and Lucy were sharing the world between them, making love on every continent, drowning in each other's eyes for ever . . . and as he rolled, his arm would touch the vast emptiness of the bed and he would sit bolt upright, awake instantly, shuddering as the cold truth hit him hard.

During these nights, consciousness was a burden until the morning, when a new dawn grabbed him and tried to beat life into his slowly dying heart.

Once, early one morning when the dream had left him alone again, Knox had decided to go for a drive in an attempt to clear his head.

On his way through Bradbury, down Old Church Road, he noticed a red hatchback reversing out of the graveyard there. Curious about its presence near the abandoned burial-ground, he parked in front of the vehicle and got out to speak with the driver.

'Can I do something for you?' the driver said, quickly winding his window down. He was a mature man, with a cultured voice and air of authority.

Knox noticed the smudges on his face, could see a blanket covering lumpy tools and bundles in the back of the vehicle. Fleetingly, he wondered if the man had a shovel in his car.

No, you fool. The weather's all wrong for body-snatching. You need a storm, lightning and thunder. A howling wind.

He smiled at his own dismal attempt to amuse himself.

'Yes,' Knox replied courteously. 'I am a police officer. You can explain to me what you were doing in the old churchyard.'

The man paused and wiped his eyes, sniffed a little. Knox tried to see if the man had been crying, but couldn't make out any details.

'I've just moved back into town and was looking up my . . . my parents,' he explained in a low voice. 'They were buried here years ago. I haven't seen their graves since I was a child. I just wanted to talk . . . I don't know, it sounds so stupid, doesn't it?'

Knox gazed at the sad man before him. *It's not so stupid*, he thought, and wanted to tell the stranger of his own experiences, all the times he had sat talking to Lucy, her features a memory he carved into the marble rock of her headstone.

'It's not stupid,' Knox said aloud. 'Don't ever wish for that pain to go away. What's your name?'

'Joel Phillips. Yours?'

'Ian Knox. DI Ian Knox. Listen, friend. I understand your loss. Really I do.' He reached out and placed a compassionate hand on the man's arm. 'But it's late, and people live on this road. Creeping about like this will probably give them a scare. Why not come back during the day?'

'You're right, officer.'

'Call me Ian,' Knox interjected.

'You're right, Ian. I'm being silly. I'll call back in the morning,' Phillips said, winding up his window.

Knox tapped on the glass, and he unwound it a little.

'How did you get your car in there, anyway? I could understand you scaling the gate, but that place was locked up tight.'

'The chain was broke,' Phillips lied. 'I just drove in. Kids did it, I reckon.'

Knox nodded. Churches and their environs were always popular places to visit if you were young. Drugs, sex, rock and roll. All on their dead ancestors.

He moved his car and Phillips drove off. He then went to the

169

gate and inspected the chain. The break was smooth and even. It had been made by somebody with professional equipment, or access to the right kind of tool. He looked after the car of Joel Phillips as it faded into the night, suddenly wishing he'd asked to look under that blanket.

Now, taking deep breaths outside the chamber of horrors, Knox understood that Joel Phillips had dug up his parents that night. You could have stopped it then and there, he reproached himself, but you were taken in by his sob story and now he's on the loose killing families.

Yes, I could have ended this before it even started, Knox thought sadly. I could have followed up on Phillips the very next day, or had the chain inspected by forensics to see what – and who – had broken it.

It could be over now, he thought, and I could be at home, dreaming of Lucy in my arms, waking to find her still missing.

14

The sun was a golden coin casting warmth over them all and the front garden was beautiful. Many children she didn't know were playing endless games in the grass; some running, others throwing a ball, yet more enjoying a skipping game with a long rope. Amongst them she recognised Richard and Sarah playing tag. She smiled and waved at them, and they smiled back.

A shining new car pulled into the driveway and a man climbed out.

It was Tom.

She waved to him and he walked to the doorway, where she was watching the children enjoy themselves.

'Let's make love,' he whispered.

Suddenly thunder boomed and lightning crackled. Darkness claimed the land, giant, thick clouds casting a shadow over everything beneath them. The rain fell heavy and hard. Cold to the touch.

From the doorway she could see the plants and flowers begin to wither. And then the children ... *no, not the sweet children* ... stopped playing their games and collapsed to the ground, dying in the acid rain. She saw Richard and Sarah fall amongst them.

The sky laughed with the sound of booming thunder and she faced Tom.

He was a rotting corpse, his face eaten away by maggots that crawled across his face, out of his eye-sockets and toothless mouth.

'Let's make love,' he croaked again, holding out a hand of pale skin and visible bone.

They were all dying ... dead.

And Cindy shivered as she accepted her husband's hand, and joined their festering ranks.

Cindy woke suddenly, sitting bolt upright, gasping, her left eye flinching crazily as she opened it. Her eyelid had hurt when she first blinked, and she realised that it had been sealed shut with dry, crusted blood from his last blow.

It had all been a nightmare. The children and Tom were still alive, but they were all trapped here, and she was convinced that they would never see the shining light of day again.

She tried to reach up with her right hand, groaning, but it didn't move . . . *back in the handcuffs, Cindy* . . . and then with her left, which – to her surprise – she discovered was free. She wiped at her eye and then studied her stained sleeve. It was smeared with fresh blood. She could feel it, trickling down her cheek.

She saw Alan lying on the floor. He was gagged, but not hand-cuffed or hog-tied like the children. The carpet about his legs was soaking: he must have lost a lot of blood. She observed him grimly. There was no need to bind him – he wasn't going any-where in his condition.

Alan had provided her with a brief taste of freedom, the old flavour of the world she'd once known. Now it was a place she was sure she would never see again.

Cindy couldn't take her eyes off his knees, which were a bloody mass of mangled bone and tissue. She dry-heaved and coughed as she thought of those wounds on Sarah's small legs. How could an eleven-year-old girl have survived that?

Suddenly, Alan blinked several times and he was awake . . . and horribly aware of everything that had happened, all that had been done to him. She could see the pain etched on to his face, see how badly he needed to scream and let some of that agony out. She watched him reach up weakly and pull the gag from his mouth.

'Fuck!' he swore on a sob, and she realised then that he was just a kid, that he didn't know the difference between love and lust. She should never have used him. *I'm so sorry, Alan*, she thought. 'It hurts!' he gasped.

'Can you walk?' Cindy asked urgently.

'Not without a wheelchair,' he said, and managed a grim smile. 'Oh God. They never show this side of things on TV . . . or in films. The hero gets shot and in the next scene he's doing somer-saults.' Alan groaned, and coughed up some phlegm. Cindy saw blood in it as he drooled down his chin in long bootlaces.

Alan was in a worse state than he looked, which was pretty bad, Cindy reflected. She felt desperately sorry for him. If it wasn't for her callous rejection of him, he would never be here.

She was suddenly sure he was dying.

They all were.

Alan glanced around.

'He's not here,' Cindy whispered. 'I don't know where he is.' She prayed he was not with her children.

Alan tried to drag himself across the carpet, doing his best to lean on one side so that his wounds were not roughly pulled over the floor. He left a trail of blood behind him, like a snail leaving slime in its wake.

'Please don't move, Alan. Save your strength,' she advised.

'Have to,' he uttered to himself.

He ignored her and managed to get closer to Cindy after a few agonising minutes. She recoiled as blood from his wounds touched her legs. It felt cold. She wanted to pull away from him, but human compassion meant she could neither move nor show her disgust.

'Why didn't you go for help?' Cindy asked quietly. She reached out with her free arm and held his hand. His skin was clammy. He was trembling.

'I thought it was your husband. I couldn't leave you with him. I saw you needed . . . help. Couldn't leave you,' Alan struggled.

'Don't speak,' she told him, and held his arm gently. 'You need your energy.'

She looked at his wounds, but quickly averted her gaze. It was Sarah's legs she saw.

No. Don't think like that. You have to stay sane and get every-body out of here alive. It's up to you.

'No,' he groaned. 'You have to know. I came inside because . . .' He coughed, and more blood dribbled out of his mouth. She was sickened as it dripped on to her leg. 'Wanted to fight for you.' He gulped and swallowed deeply. 'Wanted to save . . . You have to know I love you, Cindy. I love you.'

'Hush,' she cried, tears streaming silently down her face.

Alan was going to die for her.

Perhaps he'd not realised that when he'd knocked on the door, or even as he was bolting across the entrance hall and the first bullet knocked him down. Alan was going to die, and it had to have meaning for him. She could give him that. A small lie would make his death a little easier.

She moved her hand to his mouth and placed a finger on his wet lips.

173

'Hush,' she repeated softly, subduing him as he tried to speak once more. 'I know you do, Alan. And I love you, my sweetheart, I'm so sorry we had to find out this way. I love you too, darling one.'

It was the most convincing lie she'd ever told. It had to be.

'How very, very touching,' Joel Phillips said as he walked into the room from the kitchen, softly applauding. 'I'm truly moved. A final, motionless, musicless, sweethearts' dance. For bringing your lover here for me, Cindy, I have a surprise for you.'

He walked through the room and up the stairs.

Cindy held her breath and prayed that he wasn't going to hurt anybody else. That her children were alive, that Tom was OK . . . and then he returned, holding Sarah's hand and she was walking . . . *walking*.

She looked unhurt. Wasn't bleeding. Had not been shot.

'Oh, Sarah!' Cindy wept. Phillips held her on the far side of the room. 'She's fine,' he told Cindy.

Cindy stared at her daughter, and they both managed to smile through their tears.

'Mother!' Sarah cried.

Sarah was alive!

Cindy felt as though she'd been breathing foul, poisoned air, and suddenly it was cleansed. She held out her free hand and Phillips let go of Sarah so that she could run over. Cindy wrapped her arm around her daughter, protected her from the watching man.

'I'm here, angel!' Cindy said, and cuddled her closer as Sarah glanced fearfully over her shoulder. 'Don't look at him, pumpkin. These are our few minutes. I'm here, so don't worry about him.'

Joel thought about killing the girl there and then. Shatter Cindy's promise. Instead he waited.

'Everything's going to be all right,' Cindy continued, trying to smile for her daughter. Her teeth were stained with blood. She saw Phillips grin and shake his head at her final statement, but she chose to ignore him.

She hugged Sarah closely, tightly. These were their few, scant seconds, and she would not waste them confronting Phillips.

'I love you, Sarah. Everything's going to be OK.'

And then the fresh air suddenly turned toxic again, as Phillips scooped Sarah into his arms and lifted her away. Their embrace was broken.

'No!' Cindy pleaded, reaching out as Sarah was carried from the room, back up the stairs. 'No, you bastard. Let her go! No . . .'

15

Joel came down after about ten minutes. Just enough time to tie up Sarah again, and check on Richard and Tom, Cindy calculated.

She was so relieved that Sarah was OK. The fact that her daughter was not bleeding to death upstairs was a worry less to contend with. It made thinking a little easier.

Joel walked over to them without speaking. Cindy and Alan were clinging to each other and when he separated them he was forced to drag Alan from her tight grasp. Alan closed his eyes and flinched, rammed his own fist into his mouth, determined not to scream as his legs rubbed across the carpet.

Joel left Alan in the centre of the floor and then moved to the table, where he'd dumped his bag. He rummaged through it, and when he brought out his hand, he did so slowly. First Cindy saw his wrist and then his fingers clamped tightly about a wooden handle. Then a blade emerged, gleaming in the light. It was long – about nine inches – and curved slightly towards the tip. One edge was serrated. The light playing off the blade cast beams on to the walls.

'No,' Cindy whimpered, and he silenced her with a severe glare.

'You all have to suffer,' he told them and walked over to Alan, crouched beside him and softly touched his cheeks with the knife, cut his nose slightly. Alan flinched away, his eyes fearfully following each motion of the blade. 'For what I never had . . . and you, my unfortunate friend, do not belong here.'

Cindy gasped as the man moved quickly down to Alan's legs and began to dig into one of the wounds with the knife. Alan screamed. The ferocious pain continued even after the man stopped his operation and stood, holding his bloody treasure. The bullet was small, less than a centimetre long without the casing, and Alan was amazed that something so tiny could cause so much agony.

Cindy turned away at the sight of the bloody bullet – Phillips holding it up and studying it in the light – and the awful suffering inflicted upon her former lover.

Look, Cindy! Katie ordered.

Cindy's head turned to face them, but she closed her eyes and could only hear Alan's laboured breathing, his horrible, feral noises. She wished for the sound to end.

Watch, Cindy. You must. It will make you strong.

No, she cried inside, shaking her head. No, I can't, I don't want to.

'What happened to the reconciliation?' Joel asked.

Cindy heard the voice from far away. It was not her Big Sister; the voice came from outside her head.

'You'd better talk to me, or you'll be sorry. Now: are you and Tom back together? Or, as poor Alan here seems to believe – is your affair in soaring, passionate flight?'

Answer him.

'Tom and I came back together,' Cindy said hastily. 'Something went wrong in our marriage. I don't know how or why, or what. But it's better now. I never told him about Alan.'

Cindy's eyes remained closed as Alan began to moan again, and she imagined Phillips digging at his other leg with the sharp blade.

'God, please don't,' Cindy begged, but Joel ignored her.

'What about you, boy?' Phillips asked.

He was greeted by silence as Alan stopped screaming once more, biting into his own arm, gritting his teeth and panting heavily.

Then she heard Alan groan, and was certain he had been kicked.

'Talk to him,' Cindy urged.

But the silence continued. Long and still.

'Do you really think there may be a place in Cindy's heart for you?' Phillips sniggered. 'Did you actually believe her when she said that she loved you?'

More laboured breathing, and Cindy wished she knew what was happening but was too afraid to open her eyes, didn't want to see the horror.

You have to look.

'No, please don't make me,' Cindy wept to her sister.

And then Alan began to howl like a wounded animal, a

terrible sound which pierced her heart.

Cindy opened her eyes suddenly, without control. It was as though her sister had reached into her mind and flicked a switch that said OPEN.

Phillips was leaning over her ex-lover, slowly carving flesh away from his arms, as though trimming slivers from a joint of meat.

'Answer him,' Cindy blubbed again, unable to avert her eyes as their jailer and torturer cut methodically, leaving strips of skin and meat and red flesh on the carpet.

'Fuck you!' Alan suddenly spat, and Cindy saw the knife dig a huge chunk out of his bicep. 'You fucking insane creep. You fucking poxy nutter.' Alan wept, wondering how long the pain would last, before he passed out and died. He wanted it to be over, but was reluctant to leave Cindy alone with this man.

Phillips suddenly stood. 'You all have to suffer. I never had any of this. They never gave me anything. My family were cold and—'

Joel stopped, cocked his head slightly. His ravings had woken his father from a deep slumber. He held his head again as it began to throb . . . *the knife entering her torso over and over again as he smiles and watches* . . .

'Is it time?' his father asked him, and Joel began to shake his head.

'Soon,' he promised, and realised he had to focus on Cindy and Alan before his father managed to get a grip on the knife and could slaughter the mother. 'This is interesting,' he whispered to them, as Cindy watched the crazed conversation with himself. 'Your friend – your true love, Mrs Coco, has a high tolerance for pain. He won't even answer simple questions. But there are more ways than one to hurt a person. The human body, all its biological functions, is just a shell – a giant, intricate mechanism. A house for the spirit. The soul. A person can be paralysed, not feel a thing . . . but he can still be hurt.'

Phillips left Alan writhing on the floor and crossed to Cindy. He handcuffed her free hand about the radiator pipe despite her valiant struggles.

'No,' she hissed.

'You know what I'm talking about, don't you, Cindy?'

She nodded.

'Like when I pretended to shoot Sarah,' he laughed. 'It's psychological, isn't it?'

'Yes,' she said immediately.

179

'Do you see how easy it is, Alan? Just the three of us sitting here having a conversation—'

'You bastard!' Alan spat.

Phillips rolled his eyes disapprovingly. 'I'm trying to be polite and civil. Why can't you say something nice for a change?'

Slowly his hand snaked up Cindy's skirt, softly touching her legs.

'No,' Cindy cried, her voice barely audible.

She felt his fingers hover above her knee, and then they began to gently massage her inner thigh.

'I can cure your insolence,' Phillips told the wounded man. 'No problem. And I won't need to lay finger on *you*.'

'Please don't do this,' Cindy said, choking on her sobs.

His hand lifted off her thigh and then his fingers found the silk softness of her panties. He pressed against them.

'Does this excite you?' he asked.

'No,' Cindy croaked, and tears began to fall from her eyes, 'Please not this. Anything, but not . . .'

'Leave her . . . alone, you pervert!' Alan managed, but Joel ignored him. The man was not a threat, and would be dead soon.

'And the salvation you felt when you saw Sarah, unhurt and alive. Walking and talking. Still breathing when you held her in your arms. Did that feel good?'

Cindy felt his hand move from her panties and rest on her leg again, and she breathed a silent sigh of relief. She could see Alan over his shoulder, moving slowly, as quietly as possible . . . *not very quiet*. Katie whispered. *Sounds like an elephant. A herd of elephants, in fact*. He was crawling towards them, and she didn't know what he would do once he got close.

Then Phillips' hand was suddenly back up her skirt. Only this time his touch was that of cold steel.

'Jesus . . . don't do this,' she sobbed, her voice faint with horror. *Please God, don't let this happen to me*, she implored.

And she knew that it was the blade being wiped on to her thigh, leaving smears of Alan's blood on her skin.

Alan was still coming across the floor, but what could he do? He would be a distraction at best. The man would kill him quickly, and her private violation would only be postponed.

She felt the top of the blade being pushed against her panties, sensed the material tear as though the blade was easing through melted butter. And then the tip was touching *her*, and she began to hyperventilate.

'Did it feel good when I brought Sarah down the stairs?' Joel repeated tersely.

'Yes,' Cindy babbled, scarcely knowing what she was talking about. All she knew was that blade probing her, touching her . . . cutting her as his hand moved sharply. 'Yes,' she wept.

Please let that answer be enough to appease him, she thought.

The pressure disappeared and the silk ripped as he pulled the knife free, began to stroke her legs with it.

'Joel,' his father said sternly. 'You said I could have this one because you are moving on. Don't hurt her there.'

'I'll do what I like,' Joel told him, and to make his point, dug the blade into Cindy's leg. Cindy yelped. 'She has to pay. They all have to pay.'

He's crazy, Cindy thought. What was he muttering on about? Why was the blade still on her leg?

Because he's out of his fucking mind!

'I brought you up better than this,' his father nagged him. 'You're a very sick puppy, son. You need to check on to a psychoward and seek professional help.'

Cindy felt the blade make another shallow cut, and the blood trickled around her leg and down to her knee.

'Shut up!' Joel suddenly screamed.

It's Alan! Katie explained. *He's hurting Alan, not you. He wants him to respond.*

'Answer him, Alan,' Cindy begged. 'Talk to him.'

She saw Phillips' eyes light up and knew that she was right.

'Alan, speak to the bastard for God's sake!' Cindy screeched, her anger ripping through the room.

Alan was close to them now, his hand outstretched and only inches away from Phillips. If only he had not been shot, cut up so badly . . . *Jesus, his blood was everywhere . . .* He might have overpowered the madman.

But now it was useless.

Tears fell silently from Alan's eyes. Now he was so close . . . and he could do nothing.

'Please,' Cindy sobbed, and felt the knife cut her leg again.

Alan looked up. From his position he could see where the knife was, saw faint traces of blood on her white, torn underwear. The blade was slicing into Cindy's leg. What the hell had he been thinking? Did he actually believe he could save Cindy from this monster . . . while he was bleeding and dying? He was useless to her!

'Dear God,' he cried suddenly. 'Don't hurt her, please. Kill me, but not Cindy.'

Phillips removed his hand from between her legs. He turned, knowing exactly how close Alan was.

'You're pathetic,' he chuckled, and pointed across the room.

They all looked, the crippled man twisting around awkwardly.

The pistol was on the couch. Cindy didn't know anything about guns, but it looked loaded. Alan began to weep, his hand flapping on to the carpet. He could have ended it. He could have killed the intruder.

'I knew you would come after me if you saw me hurting Cindy – without even looking for options,' Phillips sniggered. 'Even in your pitiful condition.'

He bent down and unbuttoned Alan's shirt, then strolled over to the couch and retrieved the gun. Cindy struggled against the pipe as he returned and pointed the weapon at Alan's chest, which was smeared with blood and sweat and tears.

'No!' she implored, stricken with horror. 'Please!'

'Any last requests?' Phillips asked in a businesslike tone, pulling back the hammer on the gun.

'I don't want to die,' Alan told him. 'I'm not ready. I can't die.'

'Everybody dies sometime,' Phillips told him.

Watch it.

'No,' Cindy sobbed, responding to the man's actions and Katie's order.

'Can't die yet,' Alan blubbered.

Phillips began to squeeze the trigger.

Don't look away. You have to see him die. Take his hatred, his loathing and make it your own. Take what strength he has left.

And Cindy watched, not even blinking as Alan let out a final cry, a defiant howl of rage. Then four bullets hit him in the chest. The holes in his skin were small and ragged, black with powder around the edges, only a little blood leaking out of them.

Then she noticed the growing stain on the carpet as blood surged from the exit wounds, creating a moat about his lifeless body.

16

'Do you really think he's out there tonight?' Lewis asked, gulping from a can of Coke. It was going to be a long night so he needed some caffeine inside him. He would have had a coffee, but he hated hot drinks.

'He's out there all right,' Knox said, sipping from a steaming cup of coffee. 'He's a nasty man who likes doing bad things. And I think he's hurting somebody even now.'

They had heard from Malone ten minutes ago. He'd identified the bodies as those of George Luckins and Shelley Fay Luckins, the mother and father of Joel Phillips. A police contingent was thoroughly searching the house now.

Presently Constable Jenkins – tall, with a moustache – returned from the Evidence Room holding the personal Filofax of Jo Myers which he had been sent to retrieve. He handed the book to Knox, who quickly opened it and flipped to the address section.

Knox was convinced that Phillips was going after somebody who knew Jo Myers – either as a friend or through her profession as a teacher. He prayed it was not a parent of a child because that might take until dawn to check, and that would be a daybreak too late. He already had a man waking the headmaster, seeking to obtain the addresses and telephone numbers of all the children at the Bradbury Junior and Mixed Infants Primary School.

'OK,' he said as Lewis wandered over, dropping the Coke can in the trash. 'Have a car despatched to any homes that don't answer. And Jenkins,' he said, noticing the long list of numbers they had to cover, 'pull up a chair. We could use a hand here.'

The telephone numbers were listed in no visible order. Had they been alphabetically assembled, Knox would have seen the name of his good friend Cindy Curtis somewhere in the first two pages. Instead, her name was near the back of the list.

17

Tom slumped against the wall in the den, shivering in the cold darkness, hugging his naked torso. He was sure that night had descended properly, now that the moon was riding full and high in the sky.

Counting time until dawn.

He shuddered again, but this time it was fear – deep within and drilling into his heart.

He looked woefully around, making out vague shadow images in the eternally dark blanket that enshrouded him, his eyes grown accustomed to the depth of morbidity swallowing him. Trapped here, he knew he would never experience the light of day again.

Earlier he had tried to switch the light on, but it was out of reach.

He had listened to the cries and screams from downstairs, and prayed that the children and Cindy were unhurt ... that they were still alive. He hoped that Richard and Sarah were both sleeping peacefully, unaware of what was happening in the living room.

Perhaps Cindy had escaped, he fantasised, listening to the dead silence, wondering how well he was interpreting the sounds he'd heard. Those screams and shouts of unbridled terror.

No, he mused, Cindy was still down there. Alone. In need of his help.

There had to be something he could do.

He could make out the desk, its shape looming out of the darkness like a ship emerging from a sea of mist. On top of it were the computer, modem, printer and disk-drive. Pencils, pens, a ruler and a notepad. A couple of books he was reading. The desk lamp, which provided the den with its only illumination.

There was no obvious weapon.

Tom stretched forward, reaching as high and far as he could – one side of his body still crouching because of his hand that was cuffed to the radiator piping.

His free hand touched the desk, and he began to feel along the top surface. He had to get hold of something . . . anything. Even a pencil would do; he could impale Phillips in the head with it, or gouge his eyes out when he came back up here.

He felt the metal bracelet dig into his wrist as he strained further, was aware of the old-fashioned piping marginally lifting away from the wall.

His hand clumsily knocked a paperback to the floor and he froze as its pages fluttered open.

Tom waited, counting a full minute on his ragged heartbeat, until he was confident that the man hadn't heard the noise. He resolved to be more careful, making as little sound as possible. The last thing he wanted was the intruder . . . *the killer of families* . . . to be up here before he was ready for him.

If I make a move, it's got to succeed, he thought, unplugging his mind. If he comes up here and I attack him, but I only injure him, then he's going to leave me shackled while he goes back downstairs and murders them. Butchers all my family.

Sarah, Richard, Cindy. They would all die.

Tom's fingers continued to search along the desk. Over the printer, touching lightly on the cables and wires which held all the appliances together. His hand rested on the modem, and he remembered what Mike had told him when they had installed the system.

The modem is basically a telephone for computers.

The handset was placed in the modem base. Phillips cannot have recognised its use, or else he would have ripped the whole system out.

There was no weapon here, but there might be the chance of sending a plea for help – a message in a bottle for the modern age.

Tom was not technically minded, but he had a basic idea of how the computer functioned.

Within reach was part of the keyboard, and the monitor. He smiled feverishly. The modem would be his bottle, which he could direct to a specific shore.

He didn't know how it would work exactly, but Mike was forever rambling on about something called Bulletin Boards, and all these great friends he had whom he'd never met but with whom he communicated via computers and modems. Mike had always tried to arouse Tom's interest in his hobby, and now Tom wished he'd listened.

If he had, he might be able to contact the police, or Mike at home, instead of only having the ability to send a note to the office. Thankfully, Mike had taught him how to *talk* to the office computer, although he'd scoffed at the notion at the time.

He grimaced as he strained for the power button on the monitor, and depressed it. It clicked quietly, and he smiled as the hard drive purred and automatically booted up.

The screen turned black for a second, and then cast a green glow into the room.

He entered the correct entrance code for the modem – making a mistake the first time because his typing skills were minimal – and then he quickly began to enter a short message, under constant threat of discovery.

Because part of the keyboard was out of reach, he hoped that what he was writing would make some kind of sense when it was transmitted to the office.

o :ml## c 11 polic

Tom paused, suddenly certain that he'd heard somebody moving on the landing below. He froze for a few seconds, his heart pounding, sure he could hear Phillips creaking up the stairs to the den.

Tom's finger hesitated over the keys. Should he grab the modem and send the message? But it made no sense, written like that. Mike wouldn't know why to call the police, only that the message had come from Tom's home. He might even believe that it was some kind of joke.

Tom listened carefully, but could hear nothing below.

Keep going, he thought, and began to type again. Nobody was moving around on the landing . . . he hoped.

o :ml##c 11# polic ##init 1 ##kill r##tom

Suddenly, losing all his courage, his imagination playing a thousand dangerous games as it cast sounds that didn't exist into his mind, he decided he could do no more than that. Phillips might come up at any second.

His fingers hovered over the modem. He hoped that Mike would decipher the message if he saw it.

Please let the procedure be correct, he prayed. Ever since Mike had shown him the system, he'd found no use for it.

He picked up the handset and punched in the office number before placing it back on to the modem base. It rang four times, and then the computer at *Little Researchers* acted as an answering machine and came to life.

Tom listened as the computer translated his English message into beeps and whistles as it was sent down the line.

He waited for several inexorable seconds as two words flashed in the top right corner of the screen.

SENDING MESSAGE

Then two more words appeared in their place and Tom grinned, breathing a sigh of relief.

MESSAGE COMPLETE

It was unlikely that Mike would be in the office this late, but for some reason he might check into the computer. Or, Tom prayed, he would go into the office early tomorrow and notice the MESSAGE WAITING scripture flashing when he accessed his terminal.

Tom touched the monitor, lightly rapping his knuckles on the glass screen. The tube sounded hollow. Could he shatter it? Use a shard of the glass as a weapon?

He picked up the desk lamp at the bottom of its adjustable neck, and rammed its base into the screen.

The glass smashed inwards with a *popping* and *fizzling* sound, and the monitor itself was knocked back a couple of inches. Thankfully there was a rim running around the edge at the back of the table, preventing it from falling off.

He carefully withdrew the lamp from the guts of the monitor. His hand was bleeding, and he could feel tiny splinters of glass under his skin which his hand had swallowed. Trembling with shock, he sat down at the wall again, licking his dry lips. He couldn't see properly because he was surrounded by complete darkness once more, the eerie glow from the screen banished by his act of destruction.

Breaking the monitor had made a loud sound, but he was sure that it had been drowned by the shouts and screams he could

188

suddenly hear drifting up from the living room.

What was happening down there?

There were three large shards of glass cutting into his hand, and he concentrated on them, trying to block out the horrible sounds from below. Two were in one of his fingers, and the longest – about an inch in length – poked out from another. He thought he could feel a fourth piece, but there was no additional blood. Then he realised it was a sliver of glass – a long, thin splinter – that was buried under his skin.

There was no way he would be able to get that out, as well as all the other tiny diamond pieces which he imagined glittering in his flesh.

He solemnly touched the largest piece.

I do not want to do this, he thought.

Just ignore the pain. Pretend you're Arnold Schwarzenegger in a movie or Bruce Willis picking glass from his feet in Die Hard. *This is special fake glass that doesn't hurt.*

But it did hurt and he closed his eyes to the pain as he eased all three pieces out with his shackled hand. He felt them slowly come free and as each fragment slipped out he sensed his skin opening slightly and heard a sickening sound, before the wound closed again.

Vomit rose in his throat but he swallowed it back down. It tasted vile.

He tried to think of something else as he performed the operation.

Who had been at the door?

They weren't expecting any visitors tonight. Perhaps a neighbour had called around unforeseen. Whoever it was, Tom was sure that they were dead or dying by now.

But would they be missed? Was there somebody this actual second, out in the world of the living, beyond these walls, concerned about their missing wife or husband, boyfriend or girlfriend?

Was that person calling the police?

No . . .

He had to believe that he was alone. There was nobody to call the police. No cavalry would come riding out of the sunrise to save the Curtis family. He had only himself to depend on. He was on his own.

They were secluded from reality – trapped in a nightmare that would only end with the rising sun.

Tom stood again as blood continued to run from his hand, and reached over to the monitor. He removed a piece of glass from the inside of it that was a couple of inches long and in the shape of a triangle. All its edges were rough and sharp.

He gripped it tightly.

This glass dagger would stab their assailant.

It would kill.

He deserves to die, Mike.

The memory came from nowhere, rising in his consciousness.

Deserves to die . . .

Don't get carried away and all over-optimistic, he counselled himself. Cindy could be dead . . . they all could be. This was just the first step.

He smiled grimly. The only way they were going to get out of the house alive was to fight back. There was no chance for them to talk their way out of the fatal situation. There would be no negotiations for their freedom. They were not hostages.

We're dead already as far as Phillips is concerned, Tom thought. *So we'll show him a fight he will never forget – if he lives to get out of the house.*

He put the dagger down near his feet and stood up searching along the desk once more with his fingers. They touched what he was looking for: the desk lamp. He grasped it tightly and lifted it carefully to the floor. He used his leg to steady it as he unscrewed the bulb with one slippery hand, turning and twisting until it came free. Gulping with relief, he placed the lamp, with the bulb under the table.

Now the man would have no light when he came up here. It might make him suspicious and extra-cautious, but Tom needed every advantage he could create.

Tom sat back and slipped the triangle of glass under his leg. He looked at the door. Light was shining in through the cracks, and he could hear somebody on the landing below.

Leave the children alone, Tom thought. Come up and see what I have for you.

He could hear heavy breathing; it sounded as if the man was dragging something heavy up the attic stairs.

Then the door opened and a shallow column of light washed into the room.

Tom prepared to lunge.

18

While her father struggled to find a weapon in the darkness of the den and her mother watched Alan die; while Detectives Ian Knox and Carter Lewis continued to phone all of Jo Myers' contacts; while Richard slept, dreaming that when he woke the horror would be over – itself a bad nightmare having passed in the night – Sarah stared longingly out of the window from her bed, where she was trussed and bound and gagged.

She knew it wouldn't be much longer before she was free. She would climb out of the window and run to find help, save her parents and brother . . . who was dumb, sure enough, but that didn't mean he wasn't worth saving.

She would dance under the full moon, the orb which had looked in on her for hours now, the baleful eye of the night torturing her with its freedom.

She let the tears continue to fall silently and turned back to the thin ropes with which she was tied.

Not long now . . .

David Copperfield was her favourite magician, although her parents called him an illusionist. As well as being funny and entertaining, he always used great rock music in his shows and her mother said he was 'a real heart-throb'. Sarah thought so, too. A resident of Hunk City.

She continued to attempt to pull her slender wrists through the hoops of the twisted nylon rope, flinching as it burned and rubbed her skin raw.

To distract her from the pain and the awful, frightening sounds below, Sarah thought about her favourite hobby.

Another thrilling act was that of Penn and Teller. She loved their simple gore-fests, which the two young men presented with a twist of sardonic humour. When she was bored or feeling down, nothing cheered her more than grossing her friends out with a disgusting trick she'd learned from them. That was a further

191

reason why she liked Penn and Teller; they didn't mind giving away some of the secrets of their mystical trade. Richard, needless to say, was dead scared of them.

The most famous British magician was Paul Daniels. He didn't rate too highly on Sarah's list of favourites – her wish-list of magicians who she would allow to make her disappear; in fact, he was close to the bottom, if he registered at all.

But at least he was a mildly amusing family entertainer.

She put her dislike of Paul Daniels down to the fact that she had grown up, to her meagre eleven years, on a diet of American shows and personalities. So Paul Daniels shouldn't be singled out, but . . .

Once, a few years ago, the British magician had performed a Hallowe'en trick which had supposedly gone wrong. Hundreds, nay thousands, of concerned viewers had phoned in to see if he was OK, and even more to complain that the show was an obvious hoax and in bad taste.

Of course, Daniels was fine – but Sarah, even at a tender age, had hoped fervently that he had been splattered all over the screen for real.

No such luck!

As well as her current, living favourites, she also revered Houdini, the greatest escapologist who had ever lived. Last month she had watched a TV documentary about the great man which her mother had recorded on video for her. While it praised the man as a genius, it also showed how he performed some of his stunts – the training and practice necessary.

When Houdini was a young man starting out in his unusual chosen profession, a volunteer had tied him with a thick rope. As this was being done, Houdini had tensed all his muscles, made them as big and hard as possible, so that when he relaxed he would have a little – not much, just enough to make a difference – room to move.

So, after Sarah had seen her mother alive and the bad man had walked her back up the stairs to her room, she had been brave and let him come close without kicking, screaming or struggling. As he'd tied her wrists together, and then her ankles, she'd concentrated greatly, her brow furrowing into a tiny frown. She'd made tiny muscles, not even knowing if she was doing it right . . . but smiled when he left, because when she relaxed, the rope loosened slightly.

There was less room in her ankles, but she believed the freedom in her wrists was enough to get her small hands out.

Sarah cried as she worked at the ties that bound her. Not only because of the pain and the blood, but because her mother was alive – her father and Richard too, she hoped – and if she didn't get out of the rope and find help they would all look like the stranger in the living room.

Be strong, Sarah, her mind intoned. It was using the voice of Bart Simpson. *You can do this. He can eat your shorts when you get out of here.*

Sarah grinned for a second at the thought.

Gross! This is bloodier than an Itchy & Scratchy episode, man. We gotta get outta here.

Her wrists were bleeding badly but she continued to wriggle them against the rope in an effort to ease her hands free. She thought about the mysterious full moon and the empty park beneath it, the tree and the grass. Earlier she had seen a fox as it trotted silently across the field – she had watched it, mesmerised for minutes.

Suddenly, with one final mighty tug, her left hand slipped out of the rope.

Ay carumba!

She grinned through her tears and remembered the fox, running with only the moon for company. Soon she would join it, and run free.

She froze as the light outside her door came on, shallow beams creeping between the cracks. She eased her hand back into the loop, giving it plenty of room so that it would be easy to slip out again.

She didn't know why the man was here, except to hurt them. But she knew that he was working off his own crazy logic and agenda, and that his circuits had somehow become mangled up.

Crazier than Krusty the Clown . . .

She was certain that if he caught her trying to escape, he would kill them all.

Sarah didn't want to die.

She stifled her tears when she saw his shadow under the door. She didn't want him to check up on her now . . . *please, don't look in . . .* She had to be silent, but even that might make him suspicious.

Sarah focused on the shadow as the man passed the room. It sounded as if something was shuffling along the floor, and she could tell that he was dragging an object. She thought about the man in the centre of the living room, and then her mother, and was glad she had not removed the gag yet because it choked her shocked cry.

But what if the man outside the door was her father, and he had overpowered the stranger? Shouldn't she let him know that she was OK?

Sarah smiled and pulled her hand out, excitedly removing the gag, sucking in her breath as it peeled off her skin. Her father must have somehow got free and killed the stranger, or knocked him unconscious. He was putting the man up in the den.

She was about to call out: '*Dad, come quickly, I'm in here!*' when she realised that if her father had overpowered their captor, he wouldn't be creeping about the house. Or would he?

Her heart hammering with nerves, she remained silent for a long minute, listening to the man slowly climb the stairs, and then the den door creaking open.

Yes, it must be her father. He was putting the man upstairs where they would hold him a prisoner until the police arrived.

There was another pause, during which she could hear nothing but her own breathing.

She began to kick impatiently at the knots binding her ankles together.

Then the stranger said one of the words she and Richard were not allowed to use, and she jerked to attention. 'You stupid shit!'

'What's wrong! Can't you see in the dark?'

That was the voice of her father. He must have been in the den all along. She had nearly beckoned the bad man into her room, jeopardised all her progress.

'I'll be back,' the man warned her father, and Sarah heard him clumping back down the stairs.

She put the gag back on, frighteningly aware that it was not sticking to her very well and if he looked in – if he put the light on – he would see it dangling off her mouth.

He was on the landing, approaching her room and she was fumbling to get her hand back into the hoop.

Oh please . . .

19

Joel had never felt such anger as that which was boiling inside him now.

What the fuck did Curtis think he was doing? Did he think it was going to help, reaching over and unscrewing the light bulb? It was merely an inconvenience, but one for which he would make Cindy pay dearly.

A little entertainment for Father before the main event.

'Do you mean it?' his father asked as Joel thundered down the stairs.

'I promised you her, didn't I? I'm moving on after tonight. You can take the bitch,' Joel grunted.

Before dragging Alan's corpse from the room, Phillips had uncuffed one of Cindy's wrists – unlocking the hoop at the radiator, leaving the metal bracelet dangling from her hand. She was rubbing blood from her eyes when he stormed into the living room.

None of the other families had dared to fight back. They had spent the end of their lives trying to bargain for survival, ready to sacrifice each other if only they could go free. That was how it should be – their love for each other broken down. Eradicated.

Cindy could see that he was angry. She had half a second to wonder what was wrong – and then he was across the room in a flash, his fist coming down hard on her jaw, a ring on his finger tearing the skin open.

She bucked with pain and tried to jerk away, but he stopped her with a vicious kick to her ribs.

'Is this how you hit her?' he demanded, Joel's interrogation of his father making no sense to Cindy. 'Is this how you beat her?'

'What?' she gasped, her breathing laboured.

Again his fist came down, even harder this time. Luckily the blow glanced off the side of her head as she ducked.

She fell back and tried to crawl away, on all fours along the side of the wall – her movement severely restricted by the shackled hand – like a mouse scurrying from a cat . . . or a cat from a snarling dog.

Phillips kicked her again, halting her progress. This time, the force knocked her up against the wall, actually lifting her off the floor for a second.

'Is this what you used to do?' he grunted angrily.

Cindy coughed, and realised he was talking to himself again. She spat thick blood.

'Yes, yes!' his father cried excitedly. 'But it was often more personal than this.'

. . . and he watches, his eyes wide as his father gently cuts his mother, drawing forth fine lines of blood from her. He knows now that this is part of a game they play, a love-making ritual. They both gain pleasure from the pain . . .

Joel knew that the sado-masochistic games enjoyed by both of his parents had evolved into something slightly darker within himself. He found pleasure in the dead, loved the touch of their cold skin on his own, enveloping him.

. . . his mother is naked, kissing his father, licking him all over as he teases her with the blade and she begs for more, more . . .

Before Cindy could recover from a third kick his hands were on her, groping, clawing frantically at her blouse, ripping it open, sending the buttons flying. Then he pulled the knife from the back of his jeans and slid the blade under the front of her bra. The knife cut easily through the lace and silk, and the cups of her bra parted.

All the time she was struggling, trying to squirm away . . . weeping.

Then the cold blade of the knife was hard against her skin, under the nipple of one breast. Each time she moved, even as her stomach heaved, he applied more pressure. She could feel fresh blood there, and knew that if she struggled much more he would remove one of her nipples with surgical inaccuracy and without anaesthetic.

'This is how you like to be touched, isn't it?' his father demanded.

Yes, his mother whispers, wrapping her legs about him as her son watches, scared and mesmerised at the same time; addicted to what he sees in the room each night. His father slides the knife down her stomach, digging slightly at her belly button and his mother wears an expression of pleasurable anguish . . .

'Is this how you like it?' Phillips demanded angrily.

Cindy continued to sob as the knife prodded at her belly button, not hearing the words.

Cindy, talk to the guy, Katie instructed.

'By the hands of a stranger?' he enquired, slicing into her skin. 'Is that what you enjoy?'

Speak to him!

'No!' Cindy screamed. 'No, please – no!'

Phillips dropped the knife behind his body and his father leaned forward to kiss her.

Reach behind him, Katie ordered. *Embrace him with your free hand, and reach down for the knife. Then stick it into his evil back!*

'No, no, no,' Cindy wept, over and over again.

She couldn't move, not even when his hand snaked up her skirt and into her blood-stained panties. His hand rested on her pubic hair for a second that lasted an eternity, and then his finger slipped into her and she closed her eyes.

Blocking this out will not work. Cindy, move your hand. You can end this now! Finish it! Katie commanded sternly. *Cut his rotten heart out!*

She tried to squirm away, but he grabbed the knife and placed it against her throat. Too late.

'Don't make me use the blade!' Joel's father whispered savagely.

And Cindy froze.

As the Initial Killer flipped between two equally insane personalities, she realised that the comforting voice of Katie was no longer within her. Her heart and soul suddenly felt cold, the heat of her older sister having abandoned her. Cindy had given in to him; failed her sister as she had so long ago . . . when she had gone out with an older man named Mike Brennan who had—

'Oh God no!' she cried. 'Not now. Don't make me remember it now.'

Her sobs were heaving and she felt her sanity collapse like a house of cards as he violated her . . . *and Mike Brennan began to rip at her clothes in the cold rain which slashed into her face as* . . . She clamped down on the scene from her past. Then she'd had Katie to save her.

Here she had nobody.

Katie was dead. No amount of voices inside her head could help her or make a difference. Katie could not return from beyond the grave to save her.

She wondered when Phillips would remove his hand and the

real rape begin, followed by her death . . . her only release from all this terror. The final, killing blow she would welcome with open arms, grasp it tight and never let go as it took her into the next world . . . a better place.

Joel looked at the clock on the video recorder. It was nearly three in the morning.

It would have to end soon. The games had been fun, but he was running out of time. He had promised his father this woman so he would want some time to fool around and play with her, and he still had to torture Tom yet, let him know about Cindy's affair. And the children.

Then he would finish it. Leave everything behind and start over.

He removed his hand.

'Not long, sweetie,' Joel's father whispered, and licked the sweet moisture from his fingers.

Cindy's eyes were closed tight, and her body was trembling as it began to convulse. She didn't try to move or struggle as he peeled off her blouse and bra, left them tangled at her handcuffed wrist. He forced the skirt down her legs, unfastening the zip when he could reach it. He dragged it from under her feet and finally removed her underwear.

She was naked.

Her body continued to quake, and she didn't seem to care that she was exposed to him. Her eyes were vacant, bathing in blood.

Joel looked at her for a short while, lost in his own fantasies, wondering how it would feel to have her soon-dead limbs wrapped about him as he entered her. He didn't know if he would have time to entertain himself.

He stood and went into the kitchen. He was sure he'd seen a torch in here somewhere. He rummaged through the mess and found it, half-hidden under a pan. Then he returned to Cindy, clicking it on to test the batteries.

He shone it on her face, directly into her eyes.

Her pupils did not dilate. She was in shock. He had finally broken her spirit.

20

Detective Inspector Ian Knox rubbed sleep from his eyes as he began to punch in another number.

So far they'd had no luck – only sleepy voices complaining about being disturbed in the middle of the night.

The odds were, the number they were trying to contact would have had the telephone disconnected by now, pulled from their sockets in the wall.

'Come on,' he fretted as the phone continued to ring. 'Pick it up.'

Lewis put his phone down and sighed. 'How many people did this girl know, anyway!' he complained, and looked at his next designated number.

So far they had got two numbers without a reply. A car had already reported from the first – everything was all clear and checked out. The parents were away with the younger kid. His elder brother had his girlfriend around, and they were humping the night away. The telephone hadn't disturbed them.

The police were still waiting to hear from the vehicle despatched to the second.

'Thanks for your help,' Knox said into the phone, and put the receiver down. 'This is going to take all night,' he complained to Lewis, who was apologising profusely to an annoyed old man.

Suddenly a woman poked her head in the door. She was out of breath, and had to pause for a second before speaking. Her name was Razanne Sayle and she had run up from Despatch.

'I would have used the phone,' she said, 'but all the extensions on this floor seem to be permanently engaged and you guys are not answering your beepers.'

'Uh-oh,' Knox responded, patting his pocket. 'Must have left mine at home.'

'Me too,' Lewis concurred. 'What have you got, Raz?'

She squinted at him. Everybody knew she hated the

shortened version of her name, or any other variation. 'What was the second address you wanted checking out?'

Lewis ran a finger down his list. 'Twenty-one Ringley Street. Out in the suburbs, somewhere. Why? What have you got, Razzmatazz?'

'Wouldn't you like to know?' she said, and turned directly to Knox.

'Well?' he said impatiently.

'We just got a call from twenty-three Ringley. A woman says she can hear all kinds of noises coming from next door. She's afraid to go and look herself because her husband is away on business,' Officer Sayle informed them.

'That's our scumbag,' Lewis told her. 'Advise the neighbour to stay put until we arrive, and have the second car go to her house.'

'I want Miner and Gould out of bed. And armed units from the city,' Knox said. 'Alert the Chief Constable of our situation.'

Special Officers Miner and Gould were the only registered police marksmen in Bradbury. They were permitted to carry small firearms sealed and locked away in their vehicles. Procedures were strict. They could not even remove the guns without special permission. They had to sign for the revolvers at the beginning and end of each shift when they checked the weapons out, then returned them. All ammunition was also closely monitored. In special situations they could be issued with Remmington rifles.

'That's going to take time,' Sayle said.

'I want them at that address twenty minutes ago,' Knox said shortly when he reached the door. 'The roads will be dead at this hour. Lewis, you're with me.'

Lewis was right behind him, and then, as an afterthought, he dashed back for the Filofax.

'Move it, Lewis!' Knox bellowed as he gunned the engine of his car to life.

21

In the funnel of shallow light that emanated into the den from the narrow stairwell and the landing below, Tom studied his weapon.

Cindy began to scream again. It was a horrible, hysterical sound and he gripped the glass tightly, felt it cutting his own palm as he opened his mind to his darkest and most grotesque visions of what the man was doing . . . how he was torturing her.

He wanted to kill the man; was suddenly sure that he could do so without hesitation.

Then he heard Phillips heading slowly and heavily back up the stairs, along the landing and up to the den. He slid the triangle of glass under his leg once more.

Phillips struggled as he dragged a body into the room. He shone a torch into Tom's eyes, causing him to squint.

'I've brought you a little company,' Phillips said amicably.

A perfect moment for Tom to strike would have been as Phillips was bringing the body into the den, but the bastard was out of reach. He lifted his hand to block the light.

'Who is it?' Tom asked as he studied the body in the pale light.

He didn't recognise the man, but knew that the stranger was dead. Most of the flesh on his arms had been carved away, and there were gory wounds in both of his knees.

The poor kid was dead, all right.

The man pulled the body closer, and left it resting next to Tom. This would have been another ideal opportunity to lash out with the glass, but the light was again shining directly into his face, dazzling him, and he was suddenly afraid.

Cold, wet flesh touched his legs and Tom shivered, but did not move away for fear of revealing his hidden weapon. He wondered if he'd had his chance – and missed it.

The man stepped back and held the torch down.

'Did you know Cindy was having an affair?' Joel asked.

Tom smiled slightly. It wasn't true, of course. He had finally got a handle on what the man was doing. He was messing with their minds. Divide and conquer. He separates us, Tom thought, tortures us, plays psychological games and makes us weak. We are alone, and unable to refute the lies he tells us. He breaks down our defences and tries to make us hate each other before we wish we were dead.

And then he obliges us, leaving us at the sunrise of a new dawn, before the next family.

But why? What are his motives? What keeps him insane, has made him this way?

'That's not true,' Tom responded evenly.

'This is the man,' Joel told his captive, trying to elicit anger from him. He pointed at the dead body. 'He's the one.'

'No. You're lying,' Tom said, fighting to remain calm. The intruder was close, but not yet within striking distance. 'That's just some poor guy who stumbled upon what you are doing. Think about it. Somebody could be out looking for him. He could have told them where he was going. They might have called the police.'

The fist was unexpected and caught him hard in the face. Tom felt his nose explode and was sure it was broken. If only he'd reacted sooner, he could have slipped the glass splinter from under his leg and rammed it deep into this bastard's throat.

'Is Cindy all right?' Tom asked, not really expecting to get the truth.

'She's dead,' Phillips told him, smiling serenely.

No.

Tom struggled against the pipe, and veins bulged in his throat and arm.

It's not true. It can't be. Don't believe him.

'You want to hurt me, don't you?' Phillips asked.

'What about the children?'

'You're all dead,' Joel sneered. 'You're just too stupid to realise it yet.'

Blood leaked from Tom's nostrils and he wiped it away with the back of his hand. The man had retreated to a safe distance once more.

'Why are you doing this?' Tom asked. 'Why did you kill him?'

Joel grinned. 'I saw the books when I first brought you up here. I wondered if you would try to analyse me, get into my head.'

'Why do you kill the families?'

'Because I can. Sometimes bad things happen to good people.'

'What happened to you? Was it your mother? Your father?' Tom persisted, sensing the man was uncomfortable with his line of questioning. Perhaps it was even causing him emotional pain. There had to be something going on in his mind – he couldn't have just been born that way, a malignant cancer of pure evil growing and maturing inside until it reigned over him.

'I could cut out your tongue. Then you won't be able to ask so many questions.'

Again the cocksure response, Tom thought, as though he is evading the questions.

'Why us?'

'I have to kill you all. Break up the love I could never have or be a part of. They used to punish me for things I never did, and I saw them . . . do things, unspeakable acts of sadistic desire and passion as they explored the boundaries of pleasure and pain. They used to let me watch . . . I have to smash the bond of love you all share.'

Phillips moved closer to Tom . . . *a little closer; come to me . . .* and reached out to him.

Tom reacted swiftly. He pulled the glass out – cutting his own leg in the process – and lunged forward, slashing the air with his weapon. All in one smooth motion.

The glass from the monitor ripped Phillips' cheek and he let out a yelp of surprise. He staggered back, lost his balance and fell over.

Tom quickly began to advance down the pipe, but Phillips was already on his feet and stumbling to the door of the den. He held his cheek and then looked at the splash of blood in his palm.

Tom jumped up as high as the handcuffs would allow, and waved the glass in front of himself. He stretched as far as he could, almost caught the man's arms, but Phillips backed down the first couple of stairs.

'Come on!' Tom screamed with rage. 'Come on, you bloody psychopath! Let's do it. Here and now!'

Joel stared at him. He reached up and touched the wound again. They had never fought back until now. The gash was deep; it hurt. He began to cry.

'Let me take care of this,' his father said. 'Think they can just hurt my boy like this? They have no idea. Let me help you, son.'

Doubt filled Tom's mind. He had to get the man to fight. He

couldn't let him leave now. He would surely go down and kill Cindy and the children, before returning.

He waved the glass again.

'Let's party,' Tom invited.

'It's time,' Joel's father said, and walked down, out of the den.

22

Knox looked across the street at the still house. There were no lights on inside it, no obvious movement. The streetlamp nearest to Knox had been smashed by vandals, so he knew that he and Lewis had probably not been seen by the man within.

He grabbed the radio. 'How long before the city boys get here?'

Static crackled. 'Their ETA is less than twenty minutes. There was a holdup on the motorway – something about a bus and—'

'We can't wait that long,' Knox told Razanne Sayle at Despatch. 'Get their arses moving.'

A local unit pulled up and two uniformed officers climbed out.

Knox pointed to one of them. 'You're with me out here. Jenkins – you go and have a quick chat with the lady at twenty-three.'

'Yes, sir,' Jenkins said, and ran to the house.

A third car arrived, skidding to an abrupt halt, close to Knox's feet.

Gould and Miner got out and quickly moved to the back of the car.

'Sure you boys passed your driving test?' Knox asked sarkily, with a smile.

The two marksmen briskly checked their equipment and loads, and then marched over to him.

'Where do you want us?' Miner asked.

In their dark, protective clothing they would be invisible in the night. Miner seemed without personality, but the truth was he didn't believe he had time to joke in his work. Their job was damage protection, but it sometimes led to people getting hurt, sometimes even killed. That's what they were trained to do. It could be a grim occupation, carrying grave responsibility.

'Miner – you take the back of the house,' Knox commanded, and Miner was already creeping down a neighbour's yard. Knox believed the rifleman would know best about where to hide, to give himself the best cover and the optimum shot. 'Gould, you've

205

got the front. I want you where you can see the door and the front window.'

'Hey, this is just like Burger King,' Gould offered, as he crouched behind a fence and activated the laser-sight on his weapon. 'You want it, you got it.'

He touched the sensitive trigger gently, and a narrow red beam cut a path to the centre of the door.

Knox leaned into the car and picked up the radio unit. 'Where are these city shooters, then?'

'They're still not off the motorway,' Sayle told him. 'ETA about fifteen minutes.'

'Sir,' Lewis said urgently, lowering the infra-red scanner he had been using to see through the front wall of the house. 'I've got movement on the ground floor.'

'I can't wait any longer,' Knox muttered. He pulled the hand radio off his belt. 'You ready, Miner?'

'Yessir,' the marksman said, activating his own laser-sight and training it on the back door.

'We have to go now. He could be killing people in there,' Knox said, and pushed a button on the car radio so that it would operate as a megaphone.

23

Cindy strained as far as she could, but couldn't quite reach the ornamental poker in the fireplace. The tips of her fingers brushed against it, but... suddenly it toppled from its stand and fell over noisily.

There was no way she could even get close to it now.

Then Tom began to scream, and she sensed that he was trying something, attempting to valiantly fight back.

That's the only way we're going to get out of here, she thought. By fighting fire with fire.

Suddenly Phillips blustered into the room. She saw his cut cheek immediately and sorrow filled her heart as she realised what must have happened.

Tom had failed; he'd cut the man's cheek – a fair-sized piece of flesh was hanging off – instead of his throat.

Cindy smiled as he stopped before her. The wound was deeper than she had thought. It was a jagged, awkward cut that left a chunk of red flesh dangling from a thread of skin. It probably needed stitches and was bleeding profusely.

'Are the children—?' she began.

'They're dead. You're all dead,' he said tonelessly, and reached behind her, unlocking the handcuff at the radiator pipe.

'Not the children.' Cindy began to cry.

He picked her up, the tangled clothes falling away from her arms, easily warding off her futile blows. She saw the gun on the table and reached out for it. Her hand brushed lightly against the weapon – she felt the patterned texture of the grip – but she couldn't quite get her hand round it . . . and then they were out of the room and going upstairs.

'No,' she wept. 'Not Richard and Sarah.'

It would soon be over, she thought. She would soon be dead, together with her children. And then Tom. All together. The perfect family . . .

207

* * *

Cindy dressed for him at his command after he had removed the dangling handcuffs from her wrists. He stood before the closed bedroom door, guarding her carefully. They were clothes she only wore for Tom – and a long, long time ago, for a lover named Alan. He was dead now . . . as they all would be soon. It was easy to comply.

She had given up, her spirit and soul finally defeated.

Joel's father watched her closely, looking for any deception or rebellion, even though he knew there would be none.

She was broken, her sanity scattered about the house in a million pieces. He smiled. She looked lovely as she fastened the basque and stockings. He would take her as his son had promised, and then leave them all for Joel to dispose of.

He felt his cheek, causing a painful, tingling sensation to pass through his face.

Tom had to suffer for that; he had to hurt. Joel would find new limits of pain and push him up against them.

Cindy was putting on make-up now.

She would do anything for him, and after their love-making she would welcome death. It would be a release for her.

The make-up looked terrible. Her tears were a constant flow from a bottomless well, ruining each pastel shade as she applied it.

But even that, mixed with her own cuts and forming bruises, soft shades of yellow and blue, could not hide her beauty.

She stood and smiled, an unhappy grimace.

He saw why as her hand wrapped around a bottle of perfume. She allowed the scent to wash over her pale body, and then placed it back on the dresser. He recognised the aroma before he saw the label.

Coco.

24

'He's moving upstairs,' Lewis informed Knox, as he tracked the man on to the first floor with the infra-red scanner.

'What's going on in there?' Knox asked rheotorically.

'God knows. I've lost the bugger,' Lewis whispered, lowering the scanner again.

'What's he doing?' Knox worried. Suddenly they heard a window shatter at the back of the house, and gunfire as Miner opened up.

'Holy Shit!' Knox exclaimed. 'Check on the family,' he ordered Lewis, and bolted down the side of the house.

He could see Miner jumping down from a tree, swinging his weapon around in the dark and bringing it up.

'Police Officer!' Knox called, before Miner discharged his weapon again and put a hole in his gut.

'He jumped through the fucking top window and went over that fence!' Miner gestured, disappointed that his shots had only kicked dirt up at the man's heels. 'He must have spotted us!'

They both ran for the fence.

Constable Jenkins hoped he'd be quick enough when he came out of number twenty-three. He saw Lewis moving for the door of the house, Gould walking parallel on the far side of the drive, offering him coverage.

'Detective Lewis!' Jenkins called, and vaulted over the low dividing fence.

'Stay down! Get on the ground!' Lewis hissed, as Gould aimed his weapon until he made out the uniform and then pointed it at the door again.

'We screwed up,' Jenkins said urgently. 'Mrs Watlins just told me these guys are all on holiday. This isn't the Initial Killer – unless he sidelines in boosting stereos.'

'Jesus,' Lewis sighed. 'We got the wrong fucking house.'

25

The hope that Tom was clinging to in the den of his home in the form of a computer message in a bottle – became a real possibility of rescue when, after a long night celebrating, Mike Littler and Danielle Watkins decided to return to the office of *Little Researchers* in the hours just before dawn.

Mike wanted to show her the contract that was now signed and sealed, the sheaf of papers that was casting a lifeline to his business. Danielle had always told Mike that when the company got back on its feet they would get married, and tonight – during a romantic dinner – he had presented her with a diamond ring that glinted sharply in the candlelight.

The feelings of amour their conversation had created were now turning more sexual and the office was a lot closer than either of their homes.

They entered, and as Mike began to rummage in the safe, Danielle went into the main office, undressed, and perched expectantly on his desk, wearing only the new ring that signified their engagement and future marital happiness.

That was when she noticed the message on the screen, blinking for attention.

MESSAGE WAITING

Danielle reached over after contemplating the screen for a moment. She wanted nothing to distract Mike. The business was obviously on his mind, and he might want to investigate this surprising piece of computer mail.

She could hear his footsteps approaching. Quickly, she jumped off the desk, found the socket for the computer, watched the scripture blink one final time and then deliberately switched off the machine.

The message disappeared and she sat on the desk again, smiling invitingly as Mike walked in.

The contract dropped to the floor and the love they then made left Tom Curtis truly alone in his torment.

26

Sarah listened to the screams. She had to get out of here, get them help.

She sat upright as her second wrist came free, and began pulling at the knots on her ankles.

One foot was almost free when she heard the bad man walking past her room. She froze for a second, but continued when she heard him enter her parents' room and close the door.

A few minutes later she had extricated herself from the cords. It was a magic moment, but one that filled her with uncertainty.

She wanted to be with her mother and father, Richard too, and know that they were all OK. But at the same time, fear demanded that she get out of the house – a place which had become a dark prison, a graveyard and a place to die.

She couldn't fight the bad man on her own. She had to get help.

She sobbed as she silently eased the window open, and strangely, thought about school. It was stupid, but in four or five hours she would be sitting in the classroom. She hoped that she and Richard could have the day off.

As she climbed down on to the roof outside her window, she looked at the shed five feet below. Her mother thought the escape route which she often used in the summer was dangerous, and had forbidden her to climb there, but Sarah believed her parents would understand tonight, especially since it was not wet and slippy.

Carefully, she leapt on to the shed. It would do no good for her to fall and break her leg now. The roof trembled and vibrated upon her impact.

She moved stealthily to the edge of the shed roof. The fence was the same height and a few feet away; beyond that lay the short grass of the park. It was a leap she had made often, but now she paused and looked back up at the house. Sarah

213

wondered if she would ever be brave enough to go back inside that building.

The light in her parents' bedroom was on. What was he doing in there?

'Mum!' she cried, and then turned her back, jumping before she could have a second thought.

She tumbled over when she hit the ground, and rolled as Richard had taught her so that she didn't hurt herself. She quickly climbed to her feet.

She was out.

She was the fox, running in the park.

Under the moon.

Free in the night.

She ran as fast as she could, falling twice.

Unfortunately, the first house she came to was that of Roger Barlow, Bradbury's resident vampire. She paused before the high gate. Even if he wasn't a vampire . . . *he was* . . . he was an old, slow man. And if he was a vampire, he would still be out, circling high in the night sky in bat-mode, searching for blood.

She suddenly remembered that a teacher at her school, Mr Pritchard, lived two houses down, and she sprinted as speedily as her legs would carry her to his back gate.

She pushed it open, careful of the tight hinge which made it slam behind her.

Out of breath and panting, she ran to the door. She rang the bell and began to knock and bang until a light came on.

'Hurry!' she cried out. 'Please hurry!'

Then she saw someone behind the frosted glass in the door and heard a male voice grumble, 'This had better be good.'

27

'Bloody hell,' Knox cursed as he jumped from the top of the fence, his radio slipping from his belt and shattering on the street.

He looked down the road, saw the man pounding the pavement twenty feet away. Knox took off after him as Miner looked over the top of the fence.

The man rounded a corner and Knox looked back when he reached the junction in the road. Miner was barely halfway to him – he was a slow bastard.

Knox was sweating heavily as he continued after the man; his breathing was laboured and a stitch was developing in his side.

Come on – old ladies with Zimmer frames move faster than this, he chastised himself, pushing unknown energy out of his tired body. Don't let Chummy get away now.

He glanced over his shoulder. Miner was just rounding the corner.

A milk float was trundling slowly up ahead, just starting out on its early-morning rounds. Knox slowed cautiously. The man had disappeared behind the vehicle while he'd been looking back for Miner.

He caught up with the float, nodded to the milkman.

'Where'd he go?'

The man pointed down an alley on the other side of the street.

Jogging alongside the slow float, Knox stared at the milkman for a second. Something wasn't quite right, but he couldn't put a finger on it.

He heard Miner call his name and looked back in time to see the marksman take a stance and point the rifle at him. Miner waved urgently, motioning for him to get down.

The killer must be close, Knox thought.

He turned back to the milkman, saw beads of sweat trickling down his dark cheeks beneath the cap pulled low over his eyes.

Knox spotted a crumpled, unconscious body lying in the dark well of the vehicle, near the pedals.

The bastard had almost got away with it!

Suddenly the driver lunged for him, and Knox staggered back as Miner fired one shot.

It was enough to put the driver down.

Knox looked at the wounded body, and rolled it over.

'Fuckin' pigs,' the man groaned, and Knox saw his face as Miner ran to them. 'Can't shoot me for ripping off stereos.'

'Who are you?' Knox said angrily.

They had made a big mistake. This was not Joel Phillips.

Lewis moodily picked up his radio as the call came through. This whole scene was a shambles. Not only had they got it wrong in a giant way, but now he had lost contact with Knox and was left with the mess in his lap.

'A guy called Geoffrey Pritchard just phoned us,' Officer Sayle informed him. 'He said a little girl – one of the children at the school where he teaches – is at his house. She's upset, says that a man has been hurting her family all night. He can't get anything else out of her.'

'Tell him to stay put,' Lewis said urgently. 'That's our man. You got a name and address?'

'Yeah. The little girl is called Sarah Curtis and she lives at fifteen, Weaverdale Street.'

Lewis quickly leafed through Jo's personal Filofax, scanning the names until he found Curtis in the listings.

'Jesus, that's on the far side of town. Try and get in touch with Knox will you, Raz – and get all units to that house. Gould – you're in my car. Let's go!'

28

'Not again, not again,' Cindy mumbled as her trembling fingers unzipped the front of his jeans. His hands were groping her, frantically feeling her all over as though he had not been with a woman for years. His wet tongue was on her neck and then he was kissing her.

She closed her eyes as she held his erect penis and tried not to feel anything. She slowly welcomed him, drawing him inside.

This is rape!

Big Sister Katie had returned after her sabbatical, but Cindy buried the voice in her mind, did all she could to ignore it.

She no longer wanted to fight. She simply wanted it to be over.

She gripped his naked buttocks and clenched them tight, her nails digging into his skin and scratching him.

You don't want this! Katie screamed.

She was steadily finding the rhythm, the beat, as she welcomed him, grinding and pumping with her pelvis.

You don't want this! Please remember, Cindy . . .

He groaned and she kissed him on the lips, silencing him.

Remember!

She didn't say no, or cry for him to stop. She held him tight and refused to struggle . . . as she once had . . . the rain slashing into her face, Mike Brennan's body weight holding her down.

That's right. Think about it.

She remembered – for the first time since the nightmares had ceased – being thrown to the hard, wet ground, large hands, strong and powerful and commanding, spreading her legs apart . . . *now* . . . one hand ripping her panties down, the other unzipping his trousers . . . suddenly realising what was about to happen . . . *get* off *me* . . . slapping him, long nails ripping skin off his cheek . . . *You little bitch. Prickteaser . . .* his fist coming down hard.

She closed her eyes to the memory. Please don't make me look, she begged Katie.

You have to. This is rape. This is the same.

Their hips moved and swayed as Joel's father pushed harder and harder.

She could no longer block the images out as the nightmare from her past became a reality in her present.

Vicious hands ripping at her blouse, a stupid grin as he leered at her breasts, seeing she wasn't wearing a bra. The rain cold on her skin . . . helpless . . . his tongue on her breasts, his teeth softly biting her nipples. She pushed her legs up. . . . *get off me* . . . but he forces them down.

Help me, Katie, Cindy begged silently as the memories choked her. Please help!

You're almost through it, Katie encouraged.

And then a bottle coming down suddenly, smashing against the side of his head. A familiar voice as his weight shifted off her . . . *get up! Get away from Cindy!* . . . Big Sister, helping her pull her clothes on as Brennan suddenly lashes out, drunken, thwarted and enraged, a piece of broken glass in his hand. And then the glass is in Katie's throat. Blood gurgles as she collapses, shocked. An ambulance is coming . . . *got to get her to a hospital* . . .

Cindy sobbed silently at the awful memories.

Katie had saved her then, and it had cost her own dear life. And now she was here again, trying to help and bring Cindy back home safely.

Sweat poured off them, the sex angry.

I don't want this, Cindy thought. I want him off me. I don't want to die.

Then use this as a weapon, Little Sister. Don't let all this agony be for nothing.

That was the breakthrough. As one hand clutched his bottom, the other found the pocket of his jeans, which she had pulled down to his knees.

Dear God, please forgive me, Tom.

She felt around in his pocket, carefully digging to the bottom. Her fingers touched warm metal.

The key! She had found the key to the handcuffs.

Her hand closed about it, and suddenly she was aware of everything. All the pain and the horror she was going through . . . and all her prayers as she released her hand from his jeans.

She would never be so repentant as in the seconds following this disgusting, vile act.   .

She moaned, covered her actions as she placed the key on the floor, just under the bed. Then she rolled violently so that she was on top of him, in control. She pinned his hands to the bed, held his wrists down.

She saw him struggle and smiled weakly.

If only she had the knife.

She kissed him a final time, and then stopped. No more hip movement. No more kissing. No more holding or touching. Nothing.

You made it, Cindy. You survived.

She let go of his hand and rolled off, lying beside him.

She had looked into the abyss, let it stare back at her, had been swallowed by it . . . and then she had clawed her way back out again. She had come back alive . . . *alive* . . . and with a glinting piece of warm metal that she named Hope.

29

Cindy snatched up the key from under the bed as soon as Phillips shut the door, struggling to control the urge to vomit in disgust at what she had done. She hated the fact that his fluids were inside her; she felt unclean.

But she had to move quickly, get the children and Tom free before the killer returned. She climbed off the bed and padded silently to the door. Putting her ear against it, she listened, heard footfalls fading down the stairs.

She eased the door open. It creaked loudly in the silence. She could not see him, and prayed he had not heard it. She didn't know why he had left the bedroom, only that he could return at any second. Time was short, speed of the essence.

Don't hesitate – move now!

If she was caught running about the house it wouldn't make any difference, Cindy decided as she pattered quickly up the stairs to the den. Phillips was going to kill them all now, anyway, and she would prefer to spend her final minutes with Tom, fighting for their freedom, than lying in wait for his deadly return.

She entered the den, and looked about the room, her eyes adjusting to the shallow darkness.

She spotted Alan on the floor. Dead.

Get going, Cindy, or you'll all be joining him!

And there, in the corner, digging through all the junk as best he could with one hand shackled to the radiator pipe, was Tom. She ran to him, her heart skipping joyful beats at the sight of him, breathing and alive.

'My love,' she gasped.

He whipped round nervously, a toy water pistol gripped tight in his trembling hand. He was aiming the useless weapon at her.

'Cindy?' he whispered.

Tom had been sure that the dead man next to him wasn't truly dead.

There had been a sound from the body not unlike wind breaking and Tom knew that the corpse was alive. *Undead.* He sensed its weight shifting as it moved towards him, dragging itself along the floor . . . closer and closer.

Tom had scuttled down the wall as fast as he could, certain that he could feel bloody hands touching his naked back, cold nails scratching him.

He had reached the junk pile of old furniture, games and clothes and had been searching for some kind of weapon with which to fight off the grisly corpses . . . when he'd heard the voice of his wife.

'Cindy?' he whispered, the gun falling from limp fingers.

'Tom, I love you,' Cindy cried as she fell to his crouching position and uncuffed his wrist. For a frightening moment as she fumbled with the key, she was convinced that it was not going to fit the lock.

'Oh Cindy,' Tom wept, hugging her, holding her tight and wishing he never had to let go. 'I missed you. I'm sorry I didn't fight him, I missed you so much. The children – are they—?'

Cindy eased out of his grip and held his shoulders, looked deep into his eyes. 'I don't know. There's no time,' she whispered frantically. 'I'm sorry for everything.'

'No, I—'

'No interruptions, Tom. Listen to me. The affair was a terrible mistake. I'll never be sorry enough, and I want to beg your forgiveness for all I've done. You have to understand one thing. I love you, Tom. Do you hear me? *I love you.* I always have, despite everything . . . and always will.'

She hugged him, tears flooding her face.

'I love you, too. With all my heart. Where is he? Is that bastard still here?'

'I have to go back to our bedroom and wait for him there. When he's in the room with me, sneak down from the den, find the children and get out of here.'

'No, I'll never leave—'

'It's the only way,' Cindy sobbed. 'Get out of the house and call the police. I'll be OK. You'll return with help in time. I'll be alive when you come back for me. I promise.'

'I can't leave you with him,' Tom protested.

'I can distract him, Tom. You have to save the children! I'll be here when you return. *I promise.*' She kissed him on the lips. 'I love you.'

'I love you, too. Please don't go . . .'

But she was already gone, scampering across the den floor, out of sight before he had the chance to react and hold her back. He couldn't leave her here.

Save the children.

It was an horrific choice to make. He finally knew that Cindy was alive, and now she wanted him to leave her with this psychopath while he fled with the children. There had to be another way.

He couldn't leave her behind.

The silence of the den surrounded him, filling his heart. All he was left with was the scent of Coco adrift in the room, and the memories of their marriage.

'No!' he bellowed. *'No.'*

30

Cindy ran as quietly as she could down the narrow stairs from the den, and paused at the bottom, looking around the wall.

Phillips was not on the landing yet, but she could hear him whistling as he came up.

She raced across the landing and pulled open the bedroom door. His whistling was louder and her heart missed a beat as she slipped into the room. She quickly shut the door, praying he had not seen or heard her, then lay down on top of the bed again and tried to control her breathing, to hide the deceit in her eyes... *you have nice eyes, but they betray you far too often...* and to hide her joy. Tom would save the children. Surely her own life was worth that, and perhaps he would return in time to save her as well.

But what if their jailer had noticed the key was missing from his pocket? She shuddered in terror.

The door opened and the man stood there grinning.

Did he know that she'd left the room?

In his hand he held a knife. The wooden handle was short, the sharp blade long and bloody.

Cindy nearly swooned. She should have stayed in the den with Tom, tried to escape with him. But if Phillips had come up the stairs with the gun, they would both be dead by now, the children, too. Defenceless, Richard and Sarah would have been the first to die.

Instead, she would be going first into the next world. She prayed that there would be warmth there, and a bright light after all the pain. A beautiful, safe place, where she could wait for Tom and the children to join her in a blissful reunion. It would be years from now, after they had led full, eventful lives. But they would be together again one day.

She understood now that Tom was never going to return in time.

31

Carter Lewis spoke into the car radio as he guided the vehicle through the quiet night streets of Bradbury.

'This is Lewis,' he said. 'I want the city units redirecting to fifteen, Weaverdale. You understand that, Sayle?'

'Copy that,' the static-shrouded voice came back. 'Fifteen, Weaverdale Street.'

'Look out!' Gould suddenly shouted, reaching over and jerking the wheel.

Lewis looked up in time to see a drunk stumbling out into the street, and then the speeding car was bouncing up the kerb.

'Oh Jesus,' Lewis groaned, trying to keep control of the vehicle, but it came to a sudden halt as it encountered a lamp post. His head hit the wheel as his neck jerked forward.

Cursing, Gould caught himself just before he hit the dashboard. He should have fastened the seat belt.

Lewis lifted his head, unaware of the bad gash just beneath his hairline. He twisted the key in the ignition. The engine whined and failed to come to life.

'Come on,' he told it. 'Start!'

Gould picked up the radio. 'Officer Sayle,' he sighed, 'be advised we are now on foot. ETA at fifteen, Weaverdale approximately five minutes.'

Lewis tried the motor again, pumping gas, flooding the engine. He blinked as blood trickled into his eyes. They had to get the car going – the people at fifteen, Weaverdale might not have five minutes.

'Come on,' Gould said, jumping out of the car. 'We're wasting time here.'

32

Tom slipped out of the den and tiptoed down the attic stairs. For some crazy reason, the water pistol was still in his hand.

He peered around the wall into their bedroom. The door was open and he could see Phillips leaning over Cindy, who was lying on top of the bed. The man was doing something to her wrists, and when he moved back Tom could see that he had tied them to the bedhead with some kind of ribbon.

'She used to like this,' Joel's father whispered, and began to cut her slightly with the knife.

Cindy cried out in terror as he fondled her breast with one hand, while cutting her stomach with the knife held in the other.

Tom moved forward and boldly pointed the gun.

'Get away from her!' he shouted, fear governing his voice.

The man looked back, and rolled off Cindy who fell silent, unconscious. *Was she dead?*

Phillips smiled as he walked towards the door of the room.

Tom's hands trembled and sweat poured off his naked body. Could the man see that the gun wasn't real? *Did he have the real gun in the bedroom?* If he did, it would bring a quick and painful end to Tom's bluff.

Tom could see that the blade was covered in dripping blood. Tears streamed down his face, blurring his vision.

'Drop the knife!' he commanded.

The man stopped, just inside the bedroom, the knife held in a tight, white-knuckle grip.

'Kill them all,' Joel's father told him, 'and then get out of here.'

The man took a slow step forward, and light from the bedroom glinted off the red blade.

If Tom could see that kind of detail, he knew that Phillips must be aware of the clear plastic sheen of the gun he was holding, the chamber with its ammunition of water. A crazy bluff.

229

Phillips walked closer.

'Time to die,' he whispered and raised the knife above his shoulder.

Tom managed a slight grin.

'Toy gun, arsehole!' he laughed, and suddenly discharged it at the man, spraying water in his eyes.

Phillips' smile disappeared as he realised he had been tricked. Blinking the water away, he screamed with rage and ran at Tom.

They hit each other hard, grappling as Tom struggled to keep the knife away from his body. Phillips was stronger, and Tom soon found himself being pushed back.

The blade was close to his face, and he could feel its cold, wet touch on his cheek, the tip digging in him.

Tom suddenly let go of Phillips, relinquishing his grip and stepping aside.

The knife glanced off his cheek as Phillips fell forward, losing his balance. He turned, staggering backwards towards the stairs.

Tom punched Phillips in the face as hard as he could, felt his nose break under his knuckles, and then moved forward, taking advantage of his surprise tactic. He ran at the man who still hadn't regained his balance, and caught him full in the torso.

Together they tumbled down the stairs in a tangle of limbs, a lethal blade suddenly free between them as it came loose of Phillips' grip.

Tom fell on to the knife and it buried itself deep into his shoulder as they continued down. He screamed, but then his head hit the banister hard at the bottom of the stairs and he was spun into oblivion.

33

Tom!

The voice was faint, calling him out of the darkness and back into the light of the living.

'Tom!'

This time the voice was louder, stronger, bringing with it a white-hot pain in his shoulder. His eyes blinked open groggily and he saw Cindy crouching above him, tears washing her face.

'Cindy,' he gasped. 'You're alive!'

She kissed him quickly, and as their tongues touched, before he could think or protest, she pulled the knife from his arm and dropped it to the carpet. He swallowed his scream and groaned as she helped him to his feet. He tried to walk, but his ankle must have been twisted in the fall because it gave way under the slightest pressure.

He leaned heavily on his wife.

'Come on,' she whispered. 'We're not out of this yet.'

'Where is he?' Tom asked as they moved off the stairs.

'Down here somewhere. Richard is safe upstairs. I've untied him and told him to escape over the shed roof. I don't know where Sarah is. I managed to wriggle out of the knots. My wrists hurt like hell.'

They were moving towards the front door when they heard footsteps pacing around in the living room, and a clicking sound which Tom correctly identified as a fresh clip being loaded into the gun.

The real gun.

'Ssh,' he mouthed urgently, motioning with his arm. They had to make it to the back door.

'I hope Richard is outside,' Cindy gasped. He hadn't wanted to leave his mother and father alone with the bad man.

They stumbled down the narrow hallway, bodies bustling together as Tom leaned on her. Freedom was getting closer and closer.

'Nobody move!'

The voice was strong and commanding. They both stopped and turned.

'Did you really think you had a chance?' Phillips asked them, his other cheek cut from the fall down the stairs.

Every second lasted an eternity as they stared at each other down the hallway. Time stretched to Infinity.

The gun moved slightly so that it was pointing at Cindy. Her body was bloody, bruised and swollen. She was aching all over, and so tired. She was glad that they were near the end.

The night was over . . . daylight would soon arrive, the sun's rays fighting through the frosted glass in the front door.

Tom's muscles tensed and he stood on his own, forcing his ankle to take the pain. He took half a step forward, but Cindy stopped him.

The gun moved back to Tom. Phillips was selecting a target, deciding who would die first.

Tom's hand found Cindy's as blood poured from his wounded shoulder, and he held it tight. A secret message passed through their strong touch. Their fingers tingled, their love for each other unbreakable. Even after they were gone, they would be together . . . bonded by this feeling.

The gun was aimed at Cindy again.

The man's eyes narrowed and Tom saw his finger closing on the trigger. The hammer fell back, and at the last possible moment, before Cindy could stop him, he dived in front of her.

An explosion of sound – a dark hymn – bounced off the walls of the narrow hallway.

The bullet hit Tom high in the chest, and he staggered back on to Cindy. As he hit the ground, Cindy fell with him, bracing his fall as best she could.

She quickly clutched the wound with both hands, trying to stop the loss of blood . . . but there was so much. Hurriedly, she ripped off her stocking and applied it to the ragged hole in his chest.

At first, Tom felt numb. But after a second the pain was as though the sun had reached out to touch him – bright and hot and burning inside, flaring out from the bloody point of impact.

His breathing was laboured.

'Don't die!' Cindy wept, watching the hesitant rise and fall of his stomach, his blood all over her hands as she struggled to keep him alive. 'Hang on, please. You can't leave me now!'

She looked up as the Initial Killer walked towards her.

'You bastard!' she sobbed brokenheartedly. 'Tom, please . . .'

Suddenly Phillips turned around, and she looked up from her dying husband to see a figure through the frosted glass of the front door, rushing forward.

Phillips began to approach the door as it burst open.

34

When Knox and Miner returned to Ringley Street, their wounded suspect in tow and an ambulance on its way, they were informed about the vacationing family.

'Oh, that's all we need!' Knox exploded. How could they have got it so wrong? 'Jenkins, where's that little sod Lewis?'

'He took Gould and headed for a new address,' Jenkins informed him.

'What address?' Knox asked, a bad feeling enveloping him. He suddenly felt very sick.

'A guy called Pritchard phoned in from—' Jenkins began to explain.

'What *address*?' Knox bellowed, grabbing the lapels of the constable's shirt.

'Easy, sir,' Miner said, pulling Knox back.

'Fifteen, Weaverdale Stre—'

'Jesus,' Knox said, shocked. The bastard was going to kill Cindy and Tom Curtis, their great kids. He ran to his car, digging into his pocket for the keys. 'Miner – come on! I only hope we're not too late.'

35

'God in Heaven!' Gould gasped as he opened the front door.

'Don't shoot!' Lewis screamed. The killer was walking towards them, aiming a pistol.

Gould was bringing his own weapon up, held in one hand; with the other he was pushing Lewis back. His body armour might still protect him from a shot at such close range if he was lucky, but Lewis might as well be naked to any gunfire.

Gould's gun was halfway up, resting on his hip. He was about to squeeze the trigger, the killer less than ten feet away and still approaching, but Lewis was struggling forward, distracting him.

They were both aware of the young couple in the hallway, watching and bleeding.

Cindy and Tom saw the action in a horrible slow motion. Guns were raised, but Phillips fired first. The impact knocked the armed police officer back, and in falling, he pushed Lewis into the garden.

Gould grunted as another bullet hit him in the chest. This one knocked him to the ground, and the rifle fell from his grasp.

Lewis reached for it, and Gould saw the detective's hand explode in a hail of blood and fragmented bone.

Lewis began to scream and ran down the driveway, cradling his disabled hand. He reached the car and flung the door open, leaning in for the radio.

'Sayle, are you there?' he moaned. 'We need a—'

Phillips aimed patiently across the garden and into the street. He pulled the trigger and Lewis died instantly.

'No,' Cindy sobbed as she watched, holding Tom. 'Dear God, let this all end.'

Phillips looked back and pointed the gun into the house.

Gould groaned, getting a hold of his rifle. His black body armour was decorated by white, metal explosions where it had

237

stopped speeding bullets. His ribs were going to be well bruised, if not fractured. It hurt like hell.

He couldn't let this bastard kill the couple. Shakily, he lifted his weapon, but it was loose in his grasp. He nearly dropped it, but then got a firm grip. By now, though, the man was already standing above him, ignoring the occupants of the home.

Joel calmly fired several shots into the police officer's chest, three of the bullets penetrating the armour. Gould died, dropping the gun for the final time.

Phillips looked back at Tom and Cindy as he heard sirens in the early morning air. More police were coming. He had to get out now, get far away from here.

They were paying him no attention. Cindy was weeping over her husband's body and Joel wondered if Tom was dead. He hoped so. He had not killed them, but he was leaving the Curtis family in a lot of pain, tormented by experiences they would never be able to forget.

Panic began to edge into his thoughts. He had to get away from this place. He had to leave Bradbury far behind.

He ran down the driveway and into the street. His car was parked across the road.

Suddenly the woman began to scream, and he hesitated. Confused, he looked around, then realised that it wasn't a human scream he'd heard, but the brakes of a car squealing.

The car hit him full on, its horn blaring, the handgun flying out of his hand as he bounced up on to the bonnet, his head smashing against the windscreen.

The car screeched to a halt and he rolled off the front, hearing – and feeling – a loud crack as his arm broke beneath his back when he skidded along the ground.

Joel groaned and lifted his head, searching for the gun.

All he could see was a dark, avenging angel silhouetted against the slowly rising sun. She was carrying the rifle of the dead police officer and was coming for him.

36

Cindy let go of Tom, laid him gently on the floor as she watched Phillips stand above the cop and kill him.

End this horror, Cindy. Stop him from destroying any more families.

She stood and walked in a catatonic state to the door. She watched the man flee across the garden and out of the drive; was not aware of picking up the rifle. She focused solely on Phillips as she saw the car hit him, the gun fly from his hand. He landed badly, awkwardly, and she was certain his arm had been broken from the way it was twisted.

She reached the street and started towards him.

'Jesus! You all right, mate?' the driver exclaimed as he climbed from the car, not noticing Cindy until he was halfway to Phillips.

Cindy looked into the police car as she walked by. The cop's head and hand were ripped apart – as Reggie Lowe's sanity would soon be, driven open by a savage spike of grief.

She walked closer and as the driver of the car bent down to see what injuries he'd inflicted, she aimed the gun.

'Get away from him!' she said harshly.

The driver looked up. 'This man needs— Oh my God! What are you doing with that?'

'Move aside!' Cindy commanded. The man ran in the opposite direction, heading for the nearest house. 'And phone for an ambulance. A man is dying over there.'

When he hesitated, she lifted the rifle and fired above her head. The sound echoed in the still morning, silencing the song of a thousand waking birds as they took alarmed flight. The recoil was unexpected, jolting her shoulder.

The man began knocking desperately on the nearest door.

Cindy looked down at Phillips.

She aimed the gun at his head, swallowed deeply as her finger applied pressure to the trigger.

'No,' he groaned. 'Please.'

Cindy lifted the weapon away from him and wiped her sweating, bloody brow. She didn't know if she could kill this man, even after all he had done to them. She pushed the barrel of the weapon harshly into his face.

She closed her eyes as her finger found the trigger once more and siren-song filled the street.

He has to die.

She felt her finger closing on the trigger, held her free hand in front of her face so that his blood and brains would not splash on to her.

He must die!

She could hear car doors slamming around her, heavy feet stomping across the street. And amongst it all a familiar voice.

'Cindy,' Knox said firmly. 'Put the gun down. This isn't the way.'

She opened her eyes and turned her head.

'Ian,' she sobbed. 'He hurt my babies. And Tom. I have to do this.'

'No. Lower the weapon. If you shoot him, you'll lose your family.'

'I've got a clear shot,' somebody said.

'Nobody fires until I give the order,' Knox instructed.

Kill him, Cindy, whispered her sister from beyond the grave. *You killed Mike Brennan. Now kill this man.*

I didn't kill Brennan, Cindy thought. He took his own life.

The gun felt heavy in her hand and her arm was aching. She was tired. All she wanted to do was to be with Tom, asleep in his arms.

Her body was trembling as she dropped the gun and began to walk away.

Joel's head throbbed and he felt sure it was going to explode as a thousand hot needles penetrated his brain. He was a little boy one last time, watching his parents' pleasure . . . *and then he sees the knife . . . he watches his mother's murder, and then his father takes his own life . . .* Joel knows what he must do, but does not have the courage to kill himself.

There is only one solution.

'Cindy!'

Tom was in the doorway, leaning on the frame. She could see the horror on his face and turned.

Phillips had stood up in a flash and was approaching swiftly, his action a blur as he pulled a short, hidden knife from his waist. He attacked her with it in the same sweeping motion, the blade less than an inch from her face, coming down at her eye, when ... his arm tore off under the force of several shots converging on the same ligaments, gore painting her face as his body convulsed and jerked like a marionette, the sound of gunfire a rippling, malevolent drum solo.

Cindy closed her eyes and keened in horror as the Initial Killer was ripped apart.

She ran to Tom and was grateful that a paramedic was already administering first aid to his horrific wounds. He was unconscious again.

'Tom,' she sobbed.

Another ambulanceman looked up. 'He's going to be OK. You'd better sit down so I can check you over. Then we'll get you both off to hospital.'

Cindy was about to comply as officers milled around her. 'Find the children,' she whispered, and looked up as Knox came walking across the street, emerging from the blinding daylight. It was dull in the hallway and the light outside made her squint.

He had one arm around Sarah, and was holding Richard's hand with the other. Both the children were unharmed.

Cindy staggered out, and Knox let go of them.

They ran to her.

Epilogue

The media did their job over the next few days, glorifying the crime, the violence and personal tragedy selling newspapers, gross images winning TV viewers. The Curtis family became tragic celebrities, who shunned the limelight – heroes to a nation depressed by increasing violent criminal activity.

Cindy – after more than a year of internal debate – finally sold the rights to their story to a book publisher, an agent creating a bidding war which left them enough money to relax about finances for a good while. She worked closely with the author – as did all the family, after extensive counselling to help them relive the nightmare and come through their crisis. The film rights for the book were sold for a considerable sum. It was negotiated into the contract that Cindy and Tom would be consultants on the project.

This was a dream come true for Tom, who had always wanted to experience life behind the scenes of a movie.

Once filming was complete, Tom gave his share of *Little Researchers* to Mike Littler, his old schoolfriend, and promised to write as soon as the Curtis family was settled on the west coast of America.

In a new career, Tom began to read screenplays, intending to set up his own production team with the same studio that had financed *Until Dawn*. He found a good horror yarn called *Home-Town*, and hired a director to create his vision.

It was on the eve of *HomeTown*'s successful release that Ian Knox came to visit their new home for the first time.

Knox had quit the force, dropping all prefixes to his name, and was living off a healthy pension plan. After eating a hearty welcome meal he told them to pack a couple of bags.

'I've got something wonderful to show you,' he promised.

Over the next few days they drove out to the Grand Canyon, and found a place on its rim.

'This is a great spot,' Knox sighed as they joined him on the edge of the plateau. They sat down, feet dangling below.

He had visited the Canyon once before, and it was medicinal to his aching heart. He was swallowed by its immense beauty, the vastness of untouched nature that shimmered because his eyes could not encompass it all.

He came to this place when he missed his wife too much, and believed he could no longer live without her. It was expensive therapy. But it worked.

'Lucy was right,' he said, his voice tinged with sadness. He only wished she had lived to know it. Forgetting problems and worries was easy here, a place of tonic to quench his thirst for happiness.

They all linked hands and watched as hikers started down trails and strangers enjoyed the company of strangers.

'This place is wonderful,' Cindy said, and began to cry silently. 'You still miss her, don't you?'

Knox smiled gently. He was slimmer, and the expression on his face less anxious than she remembered it. His skin had a healthy tan too – a testament to the time he now spent travelling.

'I'll always miss her,' he told Cindy softly. 'But the pain is easier now.'

Cindy managed a smile of her own. Ian was right: all their pain was easier now.

'What else have you got planned for us, Ian?' Tom asked as he shared their awe. Even Richard and Sarah were sitting still.

'Lots of different things,' Ian laughed. 'I thought we'd start with a paddle in the Colorado. It's a long walk down, so we'd better take our picnic with us.'

Cindy smiled, her heart lifting on a cooling breeze as they all stood, still holding hands.

Life would go on for ever, despite the dead.

Time healed all wounds.